Chevalier

The Welsh Guard Mysteries

CHEVALIER

by

SARAH WOODBURY

To Peter and Jolie

A Brief Guide to Welsh Pronunciation

Names derived from languages other than English aren't always easy to pronounce for English speakers, and Welsh is no exception. As far as I am concerned, please feel free to pronounce the names and places in this book however you like. I want you to be happy!

That said, some people really want to know the 'right' way to pronounce a word, and for them, I have included the pronunciation guide for Welsh sounds below.

Enjoy!

a an 'ah' sound, as in 'car' (Catrin)
ae an 'eye' sound (Caernarfon)
ai an 'eye' sound (Dai)
c a hard 'c' sound (Catrin)
ch a non-English sound as in Scottish 'ch' in 'loch' (Fychan)
d as in 'David' (Dafydd)
dd a buzzy 'th' sound, as in 'there' (Dafydd; Gwynedd)
e an 'eh' sound as in 'bet' (Medwyn)
f a 'v' sound as in 'of' (Caernarfon)
ff as in 'off' (Gruffydd)
g a hard 'g' sound, as in 'gas' (Gruffydd)
i an 'ee' sound (Catrin)
l as in 'lamp' (Hywel)
ll a breathy /sh/ sound that does not occur in English (Llywelyn)
o a short 'o' sound as in 'cot' (Conwy)
rh a breathy mix between 'r' and 'rh' that does not occur in English (Rhys)
th a softer sound than for 'dd,' as in 'thick' (Arthur)
u a short 'ih' sound (Gruffydd) or (Tudur), or a long 'ee' sound if at the end of the word (Cymru—pronounced 'kumree')
w as a consonant, it's an English 'w' (Llywelyn); or as an 'oo' sound as in 'book' (Bwlch)
y when it is located in any syllable before the last one, it is an 'uh' sound (Hywel). At the end of a word it can be 'ih' as in 'Llywelyn' or 'Gruffydd', or 'ee' as in 'Rhys' or 'Cymry'.

Cast of Characters

Catrin – lady-in-waiting
Rhys – quaestor; knight
Simon Boydell – captain of the King's Guard
Edward – King of England
Eleanor– Queen of England
Edmund – Prince of England, Edward's younger brother
Margaret—lady-in-waiting
Robert—Catrin's deceased husband
Justin—Catrin's son
William de Valence—Earl of Pembroke
Henry de Lacy – Earl of Lincoln, Lord of Denbigh
Richard de Burgh – Earl of Ulster
Gilbert de Clare – Earl of Gloucester
John of Brittany – heir to the Earldom of Richmond
Humphrey de Bohun – Earl of Hereford

1

Nefyn

26 July 1284

Day One

Rhys

I will praise the sovereign, supreme king of the land,
Who hath extended his dominion over the shore of the world.
I shall not deserve much
from the ruler of what has been written.
Three score stood on the wall,
Difficult was it to hear the words of the sentinel.
A sword bright and gleaming to him was raised.
Before the door of the gate of hell a lamp was burning
And when we went with Arthur, thrice enough men to fill
Prydein,
Except seven, none returned from Caer Fedwyd.

T he contestant in the bardic competition was singing from a poem by Taliesin, one of the greatest bards Wales had ever produced, about a raid on the Otherworld by Arthur. Though Rhys had only ever heard the ballad in Welsh, the bard, who was Welsh himself, was singing in French, having apparently translated and rearranged some of the verses for the benefit of his new audience.

As he and Catrin moved closer, Rhys had a moment's pang, asking himself how any self-respecting Welsh bard could bear to sing at the king's tournament—but then he had to follow his internal question with a mocking laugh because he himself wasn't merely singing in the king's tournament: he was protecting the king.

The first bard was joined in the second verse by another man, twice his age and possibly his father, who within moments of opening his mouth proved to have one the most beautiful voices Rhys had ever heard. Catrin shivered beside him to hear it, and even the English spectators stopped their socializing to listen.

The song came to an end, there was a moment of respectful silence, and then the people around them cheered, patting their chests rhythmically with one hand, stamping their feet, or clapping their hands together to show their approval.

Catrin gave Rhys a wide smile and hooked her arm through his. "Isn't this fun?"

Even as he acknowledged, somewhat grudgingly, that it was, she nudged him, drawing his attention to the outlandishly dressed court jester juggling four balls at once. He wore a overlarge hat, which kept falling past his eyes, and a bright green tunic covered with leaves and branches. If the man had been Welsh, he might have derived his character from Taliesin's poem *The Battle of the Trees,* in which rowans, elms, and willows came to life, but there was very little about this fair that was Welsh, having been conceived by the mind of King Edward himself.

Walking beside the jester was a heavily armored knight with a laughably massive sword resting on one shoulder. Rhys guessed he was supposed to be Sir Kay. For some reason, the English had latched upon Arthur's foster brother, a man known to the Welsh as Cai, as the member of King Arthur's Round Table responsible for making everyone else laugh.

King Edward had even ordered the construction of an actual round table for the event, around which he and his knights would eat and consult.

Catrin nudged Rhys again. "You could smile too, you know."

Rhys allowed his lips to twitch, more at her coaxing than because he was genuinely happy. He was happy to be with *her.* "I *am* trying."

She squeezed his arm tighter. "I know you are."

"It's just that *fun* is not all I see!"

"Oh really? I hadn't noticed." She rolled her eyes at him, refusing to be discouraged by his overarching gloom.

For her sake, he tried to shake it off. Even three months into his duties as one of the king's men, his lip still curled every morning when he put on his tunic emblazoned with the three gold lions of King Edward's coat of arms. He was well aware that the sooner he got past his regret, anger, and outright hostility, the better would be his life—and Catrin's, since she insisted on staying at his side whenever they were freed from their duties.

Although he knew she was trying to help him, he stopped her from poking him again by grabbing her finger as it was aiming for his ribs. On impulse, he kissed her hand, though as he did so, he was suddenly afraid he'd gone too far. She didn't pull away, however, so he kept her hand in his own. The two of them had grown closer as the months had passed, but he was not unaware that most of the time they endeavored to keep their conversation light and not presume too much of each other.

Not that this was something they'd actually discussed. Likely, if they had discussed it, they would no longer be doing it.

And sure enough, Catrin began gesturing to different areas of the scene before them. "I will tell you what you see. Those three by the cobbler's wagon are conspiring to murder the king with shoe nails; as soon as the man selling mutton on a stick over there closes his stall for the day, he intends to use one of them to skewer the king; and that woman with the bulbous nose got that way because she was testing poisons, searching for the best herb by which to do him in!" She laughed. "You know I have the right of it!"

In the face of her laughter, Rhys couldn't maintain his foul mood and allowed himself a chuckle. "I'm sorry, Catrin. I will endeavor to be a more cheerful companion henceforth."

Although he was still smiling, Catrin herself sobered and said softly, "It is all right, Rhys. I know what ails you because it ails me too."

"This is the world as it has come to be," he said. "Our task is to learn to live in it."

"Yes, but it's harder for you. That collar around your neck is new and still chafes. I was brought to heel long ago."

"My dearest," he kissed the back of her hand again, "we do what we can with what we've been given." Then he gave a low chuckle and said, very softly in Welsh, though there was nobody around them to hear, "Who would have thought that a man such as I, who hates with his entire being everything the king has done to Wales, would be trying so hard to keep him alive?"

2

Day One

Rhys

"The king thought it." Catrin gave him a wry smile. "He cares not at all what you hate about him because he knows you despise greed, treachery, and injustice more. When he enlisted you in his retinue, he knew exactly what he was getting: an upright, courageous, and absurdly honorable knight."

Rhys bent his head in acknowledgment of the compliment. Even with her use of the word *absurd*, he knew what she meant. "That may be, but I'm not entirely sure he knew what he was getting into with *this*." He gestured to the crowd of hundreds before them, at the same time recalling the moment he'd learned of the king's plans for the summer:

Simon, Rhys's commander and closest friend, faced him across the table that had been set up in the command tent. By the

remains of his breakfast that had been pushed to one side, Simon
had been awake for some time. The day had dawned fine after a
week of rain, so the sides of the tent had been rolled up, and the sun
was shining on the back of Rhys's legs, warming them and filling
the tent with yellow light.

"You cannot be serious!" Rhys stared at his friend.

"You know full well I'm serious. The king has declared he will
host a tournament after we arrive in Nevin, with jousting, archery,
and a mêlée on the final day."

A mêlée was a terrifying, all-out mock-battle that was more
battle than mock. In it, two opposing teams of knights charged into
one another and then, when unhorsed, fought on foot, with the intent
of capturing opponents so they could be ransomed.

"All the best men are to be invited, and it will be modeled on
the legends of King Arthur. The king has called it a Round Table.*"*

Rhys ground his teeth. "Arthur was Welsh. He didn't hold
tournaments. He led us against the Saxons and kept them at bay for
a generation."

Simon was entirely unaffected by Rhys's temper. "You for-
get, my friend, that our lord king has conquered Wales; he has built
a castle at Caernarfon, from which Emperor Maximus, King Ar-
thur's great-great-grandfather, ruled, and he has reburied Maxi-
mus's bones with proper ceremony. He is the heir to Arthur's throne.
You'd best remember it."

Rhys resented this reading of history, but it was useless to
say so—and possibly treasonous. Simon was telling him to keep any
further objections to himself.

"Is this before or after we ride to Llyn Cwm Dulyn?"

"After."

"Why does the king want to spend his birthday in a location that even I think is remote?"

"The lake is the hiding place of King Arthur's sacred sword, Excalibur," Simon said simply.

Rhys's hands clenched briefly into fists, knowing full well the king's notions about Arthur and his plan for a Round Table tournament were not Simon's fault. He also knew there was a limit to even Simon's patience with Rhys's rebellious tendencies. Nonetheless, he corrected his friend with the proper Welsh name for Arthur's sword: "Caledfwlch."

Simon ignored the interjection. "We will celebrate our lord's forty-fifth birthday with a magnificent party, and then we will journey to Nevin, where Prince Lewellen had a palace, and the chronicler Gerald of Wales discovered the writings of Merlin. All are to see as clearly as the noonday sun that King Edward is the return of Arthur."

Now Rhys groaned at the memory—and at the knowledge that he was in this predicament because he himself had agreed to it. "That I could be so predictable."

Catrin hugged his arm. "You are predictable, except when you're not. That is what makes you so good at what you do."

Rhys was again grateful for the accolade, and he supposed, if he closed his eyes, he could pretend the festival through which they were walking was something to be enjoyed. If it hadn't been for all the foreign crests and banners—and the constant reminder that everyone was pretending to be *chevaliers,* it could have been a market fair in the time of Prince Llywelyn.

Simon was right that King Edward had co-opted Arthur, wholly and without shame. All that was Welsh, except for the names of some of the heroes, had been swept aside. Instead, Arthur's men pranced about a foreign court, bleating about the beauty of women and their own prowess in battle, which no chevalier, however skilled, should ever do.

And Nefyn, as a location for a tournament, was as absurd as Catrin had labeled Rhys's honor. Located on the northwest coast of the Llyn Peninsula, it was a thriving market and port town, one of the largest in Gwynedd and second only to Llanfaes in population (or at least it had been before Edward had started building his castles and bringing in English settlers to inhabit them). But to the English, it was the ends of the earth compared even to Caernarfon.

If King Edward's men had been wondering, once they crossed the border from England to Wales, why the king had bothered to conquer the country, they were really wondering now. The shortest journey for any to reach this spot had been that of Richard de Burgh, the Earl of Ulster, who'd sailed to Nefyn in a day and a half from Ireland. Many others had needed to travel for at least a week—and that hadn't included the time spent at Chester to acquire the necessary gear for a tournament, supplies that were wholly unavailable anywhere in Wales, even in the planted English towns at Conwy, Caernarfon, or Denbigh.

"Stop, Rhys." Catrin glanced at him with a worried look. "You're doing it again."

Instantly, Rhys obeyed, shaking himself and putting his resentful thoughts aside. She was right that they did him no good. He would be well advised not to live in the past.

"You won't have to remind me again." He patted her hand. "Even if we are surrounded by foreigners, we are blessed with the fact that we are still in Wales."

Even better, he had Catrin on his arm. He needed to constrain his thoughts for no other reason than he wanted to keep her beside him. If he did otherwise, she would eventually leave him. She was strong enough to understand the need to protect herself.

"Why aren't you with the king right now, by the way?" Catrin asked.

"He is in conference in the great hall with his barons, sitting around that great Round Table like the *chevaliers* of old they are pretending to be, so Simon gave me the afternoon off."

"I thought the king wanted you standing at his back, regardless of how safe it seemed."

"He did—he does—except this meeting was to include Henry de Lacy. Simon said it would be better if I didn't come face-to-face with him so soon after the death of his brother. Apparently, I wear too many of my emotions on my sleeve."

"No, really?" Her response was immediate.

He widened his eyes, feigning surprise. "I know! So odd he thinks that."

Catrin touched Rhys's hand. "I don't think Simon's right, in point of fact. It's just that he knows you, as do I. Most noblemen don't bother to look any closer."

"I'm glad to hear you say that." Now Rhys spoke sincerely. "I was somewhat confused because, for over a year, I perfected the art of not allowing anything of what I was thinking to show. Could I have changed so much in so short a time?"

"I think you could have. I think you have." She looked up at him with that beautiful smile he liked to think she reserved for him. "And for the better."

They turned down one aisle and went up another, this one devoted to mundane household necessities, such as baskets, brooms, iron cookpots and the like.

"I think he was putting me off." Rhys wasn't concerned that his friend, in the guise of his commander, hadn't told him the truth. "The king prefers to plot with his barons in secret and tell me afterwards what new travails he has devised for our country."

Yet again, as soon as he spoke, he shook himself. Every conversation, no matter the source or subject, came back to King Edward's conquest of Wales. Rhys couldn't blame Catrin for being fed up with him and his sour attitude. Rhys was sick of himself too.

He was turning back to Catrin, genuinely apologetic, when Catrin's eyes lit at the sight of a young man striding towards them. As it was her son, Rhys wasn't jealous.

"Did you hear the singing?" Catrin asked Justin as he halted in front of them. "Wasn't it beautiful?"

Justin had close-cropped brown hair, a slightly lighter shade than Rhys's own, and a scant beard he appeared to be trying to grow, though without a great deal of success. It was his eyes, more than anything else, that were his mother's, with their similar shape and hazel color that could range from green to gray to brown, depending on what he was wearing and the weather. That and the intelligence that shone from them.

"It was, Mother. I had a moment to listen to other bards earlier, and that last one was by far the best." Justin's comment was made somewhat perfunctorily, and though he kissed his mother's cheek, his eyes were not on her but on Rhys.

Rather than scold him for disrespecting her, Rhys thought he recognized the concern in the young man's eyes, and a similar sentiment filled his own. "What is it?"

"I was sent to find you, Sir Rhys. You are needed in the king's hall. Will you come with me?"

Justin barely waited for him to agree before turning on his heel. As a kingsman, Rhys would hardly have refused, but still, he felt his curiosity rising as he followed Catrin's son.

Not one ever to be left behind, Catrin skipped a few steps to keep up. "Why did the king send you to find Rhys?"

"It is less our lord king, Mother, who has asked for Sir Rhys, than my lord Clare." He meant Gilbert de Clare, sixth Earl of Hertford, seventh Earl of Gloucester. Justin served Clare as his vassal, following in the footsteps of his father, Robert. "He wants to talk to you about the murder of his man."

3

Day One

Catrin

J ustin led them to Prince Llywelyn's former palace, in which King Edward had taken up residence. While the prince's *llys* at Caernarfon had been destroyed and others throughout Gwynedd were being dismantled piece by piece, parts of which were being used to build Edward's new castles elsewhere, the palace at Nefyn remained entirely intact. None of the fighting had taken place here, and it had never been a defensible site anyway. After Llywelyn's death, the English had simply marched in and taken it over.

Under normal circumstances, nothing here at Nefyn was on a grand enough scale for the king either. But, as he'd spent the last month living in a tent, when he'd arrived, he appeared quite pleased about the somewhat more comfortable and permanent quarters.

Queen Eleanor and her ladies had taken over what had been the guesthouse. The queen was three months postpartum, which, in the past, had meant she'd returned to her usual queenly duties by now. But because they hadn't left Wales, her son Edward remained with her. Astoundingly as well, Eleanor had insisted on nursing her baby herself much of the time instead of giving him up entirely to a wet nurse. Although little Edward was second in line to the throne behind ten-year-old Alphonso, the queen openly feared he would be her last child, and she couldn't bear to lose him as she'd lost so many others.

It might also be that a little bit of Welshness had rubbed off on the queen. Her determination to nurse Edward had arisen after Catrin had mentioned in passing the Welsh saying, *a child learns wisdom at his mother's breast.*

Catrin had visited Nefyn a few times in the company of her father, who'd been Prince Llywelyn's steward, and she experienced the same pang stepping through the palace gate at Nefyn as she'd felt when she and Rhys had entered the ruin at Caernarfon. Nefyn was not a ruin, however, and the king had spent a considerable sum enlarging the buildings and improving the amenities, having diverted a contingent of artisans from Harlech to do the work.

Today it was her son, rather than her father, whom she followed down the walkway from the gatehouse to the great hall. And it wasn't so much that she'd come full circle, but that she'd opened a door to a world she barely recognized.

Llywelyn's great hall had been set aside for King Edward's private use, having been deemed too small to accommodate the huge crowds of people who'd come for the tournament. Thus, the meals for most of the guests and participants were taking place in a pavilion set up in yet another nearby field, with a massive half-tented, half-open-air kitchen providing the food. The king's servants had even built a bread oven out there, just as they'd done at the lake where the king had celebrated his birthday.

Thus, the hall had become Edward's receiving room and the center of his personal and administrative activities at Nefyn—just as it had been for Llywelyn. Except now, a giant round table took up the center of the room.

Justin bid her and Rhys adieu, having duties of his own to attend to, so it was just the two of them entering the foyer. Beyond, in the great hall, the king sat on the dais in his royal chair. Like the round table, it had been made specially for the occasion and derived from a design found in one of the king's books on Arthur. Constructed in wood, it sported a high back and arms, with a red cushion upon which the king could sit.

What made it different from other thrones was the carved dragon on the headrest. The symbol of the King of England was normally three lions *passant guardant,* but as with the rest of the tournament trappings, Edward was making Arthur's crest his own.

Also in keeping with his role as the return of Arthur, the king was wearing a long ruby red robe, rather than his usual mail.

Still, both robe and throne were comfortable more than ornate, and the king sat relaxed, an elbow on the arm of the chair and a finger to his lips. Meanwhile, Gilbert de Clare was pacing before the unlit hearth. He was a tall man in his early forties and red-headed, hence his nickname, *the Red Earl.* As he'd arrived several days ago, Catrin was honestly surprised it had taken him until now to ask for this accounting.

Also present, in addition to various scribes and clerks on the margins of the room, was Simon, the captain of the king's guard and Rhys's friend.

Rhys strode down the hall towards the king, but Catrin hesitated in the doorway, all of a sudden unsure of her welcome. While she had spent as much time as possible with Rhys over the last months and was used to being at his side in the presence of the king and queen, this meeting looked a little different, more private, and thus perhaps something in which she shouldn't take part. *She* was not a knight of the Round Table.

The king saw her hesitating and motioned her forward, speaking to Lord Clare as he did so, "Lady Catrin was among those integral to discovering the truth of the matter, since we thought at first that it was she whom Cole had come to see."

Cole de Lincoln, the dead man, had once been a companion of her husband, which was why Catrin had aided Rhys in the investigation of his death. But the king and queen, once Catrin and Rhys had relayed to them what they'd discovered, had concocted a story to account for Cole's death, one which bore little relationship to the truth. Although it had been a necessary deception at the time, it still felt as if they'd done Cole a disservice. He had done his duty and had died because he'd been in the wrong place at the wrong time.

That Cole had ridden to Caernarfon at all had been mere happenstance. In the aftermath of his death, having sent word of it to Gloucester and received a reply, they'd learned that the king's regular messenger had fallen ill on the journey from London to Wales. Though he'd been well when he'd left Westminster, he'd been at death's door when he'd struggled into Clare's castle at Caerphilly. Earl Clare had deemed the news he was bringing to the king important enough to send Cole to Caernarfon in the messenger's stead. In retrospect, perhaps the news could have waited. That Pope Martin had declared the war against Aragon a holy crusade and conferred the kingdom upon Philip III of France's son, Charles, was not something the Edward could affect from Wales, even had he wanted to.

But nobody knew at the time what lay in wait for Cole on the road and that Caernarfon was saddled with its own cold-hearted, cold-blooded murderer.

Such was luck and a life lost.

In response to the king's introduction, Earl Clare, who had never looked at Catrin for more than a moment or two in all the years of her marriage to Robert, held out his hand. "My dear, Catrin. It is wonderful to see you looking so well. What an unexpected pleasure."

Immediately, Catrin's hackles went up, since his words were politeness only. He knew she was in the queen's retinue, since he had been the person from whom she'd had to seek permission—or rather, a blessing, since the queen outranked him—when Eleanor's summons had come. That conversation had been the first she'd had with him since her husband's death, and she couldn't remember the last time she'd spoken to him before then.

Even his condolences at the funeral had been perfunctory. At the time, Clare had been far more concerned about what Robert's death represented—namely, a loss of position and station in the eyes of the king, since he had been the one leading the king's army in the disastrous battle where Robert had lost his life.

Catrin could be gracious, however, and she came forward to take his hand as he wished. Gilbert de Clare remained a close enough companion to the king that he was not one to be gainsaid or snubbed if it could be helped. "Thank you, my lord. I am so sorry for the loss of Cole." She bobbed a curtsey. "It was an ignoble ending for an honorable man and not what he deserved."

Clare bowed over her hand. "What we deserve is something few of us ever truly achieve."

She was so surprised at this comment that she almost laughed, for he spoke a truth that was perhaps slightly impolitic, especially in the king's company. Then, reverting to form, Clare looked past her to where Rhys had stopped a respectful distance away. Although the earl had known Catrin for twenty years, Rhys should have been new to him, or so Catrin supposed, up until Clare's eyes narrowed and he said, very stiffly. "Thank you for coming. Once I learned you were involved in the investigation of Cole's death, I found it easier to accept the conclusions."

"How observant of you, Gilbert, to recognize the boy in the man Reese has become." King Edward made a lazy motion with one hand in Rhys's direction. "Sir Reese is my quaestor and a member of my personal guard."

"Yes, my king, I heard as much upon my arrival in Nevin."

Rhys bowed in return, evidently not nearly as befuddled as Catrin. "It is kind of you to remember me, my lord."

"How did you—" Catrin stopped, realizing she should not be interjecting herself into their conversation.

But Clare did not take offense and, as he was still holding Catrin's hand, he turned to her again. "I first met Reese twenty years ago when his father was serving in Prince Lewellen's personal guard. This was before your marriage to Robert."

"I remember, my lord. It was a long time ago." Catrin could do little but nod. It was another astounding comment for Clare to make in the king's presence, since that was a period of time, however short, during the Second Baron's War when he'd been allied with Llywelyn instead of with Edward. It struck her as either unthinking or an attempt to create a bond between him and Rhys—for reasons Catrin in this moment couldn't guess. In her experience, Earl Clare never did anything he hadn't thought through very thoroughly in advance.

And then the earl added, "We have met several times since, back when he was serving in Prince Edmund's retinue. No murder went unavenged when Reese was in charge. I feel somehow that the capriciousness of Cole's death is mediated by the fact that it brought Reese back into the king's service."

"Thank you for saying so, my lord." The tension in Rhys's shoulders told Catrin he longed to move on from any discussion of the past.

King Edward nodded. "I agree, Gilbert. The Lord works in mysterious ways, which we are not to question."

Catrin shouldn't have been surprised the king had missed nothing of their conversation. He noticed everything.

Rhys welcomed the king's intercession with a barely perceptible nod. "Catrin's son tells me you desired an accounting of the circumstances of Cole's death?"

"I did wish for that, but Simon has explained in sufficient detail such that I have had all my questions answered. At this juncture, I am more interested in your services on another matter."

"Services, my lord? In regards to what? Justin said you wanted to see me about the murder of your man." Rhys glanced at the king, who nodded at Rhys in that same barely perceptible way Rhys had just nodded at him. It was odd, really, the extent to which these two enemies understood each other.

"This is about the murder of my man, but it isn't Cole I'm speaking of. This man was found murdered in his tent today." Clare tsked under his breath at their surprised looks. "My first act upon finding the body was of course to ask the king for you."

4

Day One

Rhys

There was no *of course* about it.

Rhys would do as the king asked (of course), but it was making him more than a little uncomfortable to be loaned out to someone like Clare, whom Rhys trusted not at all. Though Justin hadn't intended to deceive, Rhys felt as if he'd been brought to the palace under false pretenses. Yes, Rhys hated King Edward. But he wore that emotion comfortably these days, like a shirt that had been washed so many times it was soft to the skin. It was such a part of who he was that many days (though admittedly less this last week as they were preparing for the tournament), he forgot he was wearing it.

Clare's treachery and lack of character were another matter entirely. The king was doing what he thought was right for Wales, heinous as that was. Rhys had to respect his forthrightness and his motives, even as he detested the result. Clare truly cared only about himself and his own power.

Rhys might hate the king, but Edward had always dealt fairly with Rhys himself. Rhys had no expectation he would get the same treatment from the red earl.

He had no alternative but to agree, however, especially after the king said, "Go with him, Reese." As was Edward's habit when he was amused, he spoke laconically. Likely he knew full well the desperation Rhys was feeling in this moment and didn't care to appease it. "Others can see to me for now."

"My lord." Rhys bowed first to the king and then to Clare. "I am at your disposal."

His words were polite but at the same time no less than the truth. Rhys would have been lying if he'd said something along the lines of *I am happy to be of service*. Whatever his failings on a daily basis, he endeavored never to lie.

But before he could follow the earl, who himself had already bowed and started walking away, the king said in a much softer tone, "Keep me apprised of what this is about, Reese."

Rhys glanced back at him. "I will, my king."

Now Edward leaned forward and spoke even more softly, though, since Clare was already at the door, he couldn't have heard him from that distance, "I refer to more than just this investigation."

Out of the corner of his eye, Rhys saw Clare stop and turn, fixing his eyes on the two of them at the far end of the hall. "Yes, my lord."

He knew what Edward wanted, and the fact that he felt the need to speak of it showed the depth of his concern. Rhys was his quaestor, when murder was the order of the day, but he was also Edward's new spymaster. Rhys hadn't had to investigate a murder since Caernarfon, so most of the last few months had been spent sussing out animosity against the king, which grew like an unchecked weed extending fingerlings under the soil.

For the most part, the Welsh populace remained well and truly cowed, and he hadn't yet had to inform on any of his fellow countrymen. The real threat came from unsatisfied lords like Clare, who lived and breathed conspiracy and served it at every meal. Since the end of the war, many had been bought, appeased, or otherwise rewarded with new lands in Wales. They weren't necessarily plotting against the king, but their antipathy for their fellow barons was untamed, and sometimes their machinations rebounded on, or affected in some way, the royal court.

Seeing that his message had been received and understood, Edward leaned back and flicked out his fingers, as if to say *get on with it, then.*

Rhys was used to these casual dismissals. Thus, after another bow, he turned smartly on his heel and headed down the length of the hall, scooping Catrin up on the way to the door, through which Clare, having seen him coming, had already progressed.

Rhys had known, in renewing his service to the king, that he would come into contact with men from his past, some of whom he'd known very well. He had no problem renewing his acquaintance with former crusaders over a pint of mead in one of the outdoor, makeshift taverns that had sprung up to slake the thirst of hard-working fairgoers. But he had nonetheless been unprepared to come face-to-face with lords he could not respect and yet had to feign that he did.

Clare was one such man. Facing him brought back memories of a time long before Llywelyn's death.

But when William de Valence had walked into the hall two days ago and bowed before the king, Rhys had felt like puking on his shoes. It should have been no surprise he was present, as he was Edward's uncle and closest adviser in all things. And his rewards for that service had been commensurately great.

It had been Valence who had taken command from Clare of the English forces in south Wales after the disastrous battle of Llandeilo Fawr that had killed Catrin's husband—and Valence's son.

Though both earls were in service to King Edward, they despised each other so completely they didn't speak. Clare thought Valence was an interloper from the Continent and resented the way Edward had bestowed the best parts of the March on him in the aftermath of the victory over Llywelyn; Valence viewed Clare as arrogant, incompetent, and responsible for getting his son killed.

To add insult to injury, Clare was working to annul his marriage to Valence's niece, Alice de Lusignan. It was rumored that she had once been a favorite of Edward himself, which was why her marriage to Clare had foundered. But it was also rumored that King Edward was finally supporting Clare's request to the pope for an annulment.

While Rhys could appreciate Valence's position, more damning to Rhys's mind were the stories coming out of Pembroke of his cruelty to the people he was supposed to be ruling. Although brutal acts had been perpetrated on both sides during the war, they hadn't ceased in Valence's domain once the war was over and were enough to turn any Welshman's stomach. King Edward had ordered Llywelyn's brother Dafydd hanged, drawn, and quartered, but since then, and especially since the birth of his son Edward, he'd been in a much softer mood towards his newly conquered people.

And yet, he wasn't bothering to curb Valence's activities. Valence had been on crusade with the king too, along with an even worse nemesis, one Vincent de Lusignan, a relation of some kind, who was exactly Rhys's age. When Rhys had known him, Vincent had been Valence's strong right arm. By the looks, nearly fifteen years on, he still was—and likely it was Vincent who was carrying out Valence's orders in Pembroke. Even Simon had hissed at the sight of him in Nefyn's hall.

It occurred to Rhys only now that Vincent was to Valence as Valence was to the king, and Edward was giving Valence free rein to oppress the Welsh within his domains so he himself didn't have to and could float above the fray, a magnanimous King Arthur.

It was by no means a comforting thought. Still, Rhys ruthlessly suppressed it, knowing it did him no good to rail at what was or long for what could have been.

Once outside, as he walked across the courtyard to the palace gatehouse, Clare didn't glance behind him, a fact which Rhys decided was just as well, since by the time they arrived wherever they were going, Catrin's presence would be *fait accompli*. Rhys was aware that people assumed their relationship was closer than it was, and while he did nothing to dissuade them of those assumptions, he was also cognizant of the fact that those selfsame people would look askance at her presence at his side during a murder investigation.

But as was often the case when dealing with nobility, better to act first and deal with any questions later. After all, it was what *they* did.

Upon leaving the gatehouse, they were instantly engulfed in teeming humanity. Rhys was quite certain that he hadn't seen so many people in one place since he'd ridden away from London many years ago. There were, quite literally, hundreds of people in and around the palace, and Rhys wasn't at all clear as to what they were doing, beyond socializing and drinking. Perhaps that really was all, though he couldn't help looking for more suspicious activities, as Catrin had implied earlier. None appeared to be set on murdering the king, but conspiring against their fellow man, or stealing from him, was practically the order of the day. Not everyone here was noble, and if Clare was anything to go by, nobility was hardly a barrier to nefarious dealings.

The land around the palace, and around Nefyn in general, was quite flat, so the guests and participants in the tournament had been allowed to spread out across a large area. Llywelyn's former *llys* was located to the east and slightly south of the ancient church and priory dedicated to St. Mary, around which the village had grown up. The tournament fields were even farther east and south, and everywhere bright banners streamed above tents and pavilions that had been set up as far as the eye could see. Now, in the middle of the afternoon, the sky was a deep blue with no clouds on the western horizon, which boded well for the next few days. The sky was clear enough, in fact, that he thought he could see Ireland across the sea.

Rhys had half-hoped for a continuation of the rain that had thundered down on them in the night, but he decided he could be glad not to be walking about in it if it meant Catrin was happy. And, as he'd learned in his years of service to princes and kings, men smiled more often under a blue sky than when it was raining and cold, and smiling men were just that much less likely to be contemplating mischief.

The Gloucester contingent had set up camp directly east of the palace, though a full hundred yards from the front gate.

"Clare could have set his tents closer," Catrin said as they crossed the distance. "It's almost as if he's daring another lord to establish himself between his camp and the king's."

"Nobody has so far."

"None would dare." Catrin had spent twenty years in Gloucester, so she would know better than most how other lords viewed Clare and of what he himself was capable.

And she was right, as usual.

"I have my theories about that actually," Rhys said.

"You do think it's deliberate. Why?"

"Two reasons: first, it implies respect for the king not to encroach on his domains. And second, amidst the endless jostling for power among his fellow barons, it indicates Clare doesn't *need* to sleep closer to the king to show what a close companion he is."

"I imagine you're right. You'll note too that Clare's pavilion is the farthest of any from the fair and the tournament field. He's saying he's above the petty squabbling of everybody else."

"Or, it could be he just liked the spot," Rhys added with a grin.

Catrin laughed, as he meant her to. "Or that!"

Like the other lords who'd come, Clare had brought a small army with him, composed of household knights, of which he had half-a-dozen, and men-at-arms, squires, servants, stable hands, and the families associated with each. This wasn't a war; it was a party, never mind that Nefyn was as far from London as it was physically possible to be while still within Edward's kingdom. Though the tip of Scotland was farther, so far Edward hadn't managed to wrest that land away from the Scots.

Rhys also didn't necessarily accept Clare's easy *of course* in regard to asking him to investigate this murder. He had capable men available. He had to. Rhys had appeared in the king's service only a few months ago, and Clare had been the Earl of Gloucester for nearly thirty years. Rhys furthermore didn't understand why Clare was personally showing him the scene of the crime.

But show him he did, wending his way through his assorted tents and wagons, ignoring the bows and gestures of obeisance sent his way by all and sundry, until he stopped near the edge of the encampment and ducked through a tent flap. A man holding a pike stood guard outside. As had been the case with his men up until now, Clare didn't even look at him as he went by. It did seem that everyone was used to it, since the expressions left in his wake were not resentful. Rhys had been looking too, but all he saw were people doing their work with some level of contentment.

Unlike Clare, as Rhys passed by, he did look at the guard, who proved to be an older man with a full gray beard, who stiffened to further attention and kept his eyes straight ahead. There was something familiar about him, and a memory itched at the back of Rhys's head. The man was old enough to have been on crusade, but Rhys had met many men, and couldn't remember all of them, and he'd been seeing ghosts all week.

Rhys and Catrin found Clare standing with an arm across his chest and his finger to his lip, looking down at a dead man, approximately fifty years of age, lying flat on his back on the bare grass of the tent floor. Because it was afternoon, it hadn't occurred to Rhys that the man wouldn't be clothed, but he was wearing only his undergarments. Rhys supposed they were lucky, given Catrin's presence, that he wasn't naked. Many men slept without clothing in summer, and Rhys should have thought of that before he'd allowed Catrin to come with him.

That said, she was a widow, with more freedom than at any other time in her life and greater leeway in what was socially acceptable for her to encounter, and she came to a halt near the man's head. His eyes were closed in death, and he looked for all intents and purposes to be sleeping peacefully. While there was some puffiness around the eyes and mouth, and the skin on his torso was unusually mottled and darkened, something like a sunburn that had browned with time, Rhys couldn't see any blood. The dead man did have a lesion on his inner forearm that looked ugly, but if that was the cause of death, it should have been redder with striations reaching out from it, indicating it had suppurated.

Clare sighed and dropped his arms. "Dead, as you can see."

"I do see, my lord." Rhys stepped into Clare's line of sight and gestured towards the body. "May I?"

"That's what you're here for."

Rhys ran his eyes up and down the corpse once more before lifting one wrist to check for a pulse, just to be safe, and then for stiffness. The arm did not want to move, indicating the man had died at least twelve hours before. The body was still warm too, a fact which wouldn't be entirely attributable to the heat of the day and the further warmth inside the tent. On the other hand, because the weather was warm, the body might be decaying faster than usual, compressing the timeline.

"What do you see?" Clare demanded into the silence that had fallen during Rhys's initial inspection.

"Pardon, my lord, a few questions first." Rhys glanced back in order to see Clare's nod, indicating he should continue. These lords, from the king on down, stood on ceremony, demanding at every turn their due from underlings. "Can you tell me what you know of him?"

"He was Rollo d'Honfleur, the captain of my guard."

The bluntness of his words and the close relationship to Clare himself (and thus to the king) caused Rhys to hesitate and take in a breath, accepting that this death would also be delicately political.

He covered his dismay by rising and walking around the body. "Was he worried about anything? Fearful for his life?"

"Not that I was aware." Clare stepped back to let Rhys pass, but otherwise was not being helpful, which was odd since he was the one who'd brought them here in the first place.

Normally, Rhys would have arranged to move the body to a laying out room before he examined it, but the instant he called for a board to move the body to the church, everyone in Nefyn would know of the death and that Rhys was involved. By now, even the meanest camp follower knew that meant murder.

"Was he ill?" Rhys asked.

"Not that he said."

"Would he have said?" Catrin asked.

It was a genuine question, one that Clare took seriously. In general, fighting men were the last to seek out a healer, not until whatever was wrong with them was well past dangerous.

"I don't know," he said slowly.

"From the stiffness of the corpse, he's been dead since sometime early this morning. When was his death discovered?" This was from Catrin again. Although she had been involved in just one murder investigation before this one, back at Caernarfon in April, it had involved three deaths. And while he couldn't say that she knew entirely what she was doing as yet, she knew enough to start asking questions while Rhys worked. Anyway, she wasn't one to examine a body with Clare looking on.

"What you're really asking is why are you being called in only now." The corner's of Clare's mouth turned down.

"That is the second half of my question. Yes," she said, undaunted by Clare's possible disapproval.

"His body was discovered this afternoon. Once I realized he was dead, and died in this position, I concluded that discovering the whys and wherefores was beyond my people and went to the king to ask for you." And then, at Catrin's lovely raised eyebrow, Clare added, finally, "You may think I'm being miserly with information. Perhaps I am, but it's because I can explain nothing of what you see here. He was healthy and well last night when I retired to bed."

Rhys was genuinely confused too. "Did nobody miss him sooner than this afternoon?"

"We all missed him. I myself stood right where you are standing not six hours ago." Clare tsked under his breath as he'd done in the king's hall. "He was lying as he is now, but I did not see him."

5

Day One

Catrin

"My apologies, my lord, but I am confused," Catrin said. "It doesn't seem as if you're saying he was brought inside the tent only an hour ago, but that he was here all along. Nonetheless, you didn't see him?"

"Don't apologize, Catrin. You did not mishear, and I confess to being deliberately cryptic, in large part because I'm still trying to make sense of things myself." Clare gave a minute shake of his head and pointed to the bed that occupied one side of the tent. "When I looked inside the tent this morning, he was underneath the bed, hidden by the blankets, which were draped so as to cover the open side. It was only when the launderer brought fresh linens in order to remake the bed that his foot nudged the body. He ran for me, and that's when I sent for you."

That was a much longer speech than Clare had delivered so far and much more in character with the man she knew. It had been many months since Catrin had seen him, but her husband had served

Clare his entire life and died in his company. While she thought Clare's behavior had been somewhat odd this afternoon, she was wondering now if that was because he felt some guilt towards her—and that was also the reason he was pleased to see her attached to the queen's retinue.

"Is that the definitive order of events, my lord?" Catrin asked. "The servant found the body and went straight to you?"

"Not exactly." Clare's lip twisted ruefully. "As you might imagine, he ran away, screaming that Rollo was dead. At least a dozen of my men came in here before we managed to establish order and come to terms with Rollo's death."

"Where is that servant now?"

"In the laundry area. I left it to his overseer to determine when he was fit to continue his work."

"We will be sure to speak to him in due course," Rhys said. "If I may confirm, you said you spoke to Rollo last night?"

"Indeed." Clare looked searchingly at them both. "Are you aware of how King Edward has set up this Round Table with two teams, one headed by Richard de Burgh, Earl of Ulster, and the second by Henry de Lacy, the Earl of Lincoln?"

Rhys and Catrin nodded, and Catrin added, "Many of King Edward's barons are also to be *chevaliers,* playing the role of one of the knights of the Round Table. Lacy is Gawain and Burgh is Galahad. You, I understand, are to be Bedivere."

"That is correct, with one important caveat: I am not actively participating in the tournament myself. Rollo was to joust and lead my knights in the mêlée in my name. That was the topic we were discussing."

Neither Catrin nor Rhys reacted with anything but understanding that Clare had bowed out of the actual competition, though not the play itself. While it was a great honor to be chosen to participate in King Edward's Round Table, it was quite another matter for Clare, at the age of forty-one, to risk his life in the events. Catrin was thankful Rhys himself hadn't been asked to participate—not that the king would ask him, since Rhys was a low-ranking Welshman. Her brother Tudur, however, had told Catrin at breakfast only that morning that he'd been elevated to a member of the Round Table, with a name of his own, Gornemant. It revealed the extent to which the king was truly in a magnanimous mood.

"Who, by the way, is playing Lancelot?" she asked. "I hadn't heard."

"Nobody," Clare said. "King Edward did not feel that character was appropriate."

Since, in the French versions of the legends, Lancelot had run off with King Arthur's wife, Catrin could understand Edward's reluctance to include him.

"Rollo was a great warrior," Catrin said simply, speaking no less than the truth as she knew it. He hadn't been her husband's superior, since Robert had been of the comparatively elevated rank of household knight and had inherited estates of his own. For his part, Rollo had earned his knighthood on the battlefield, and thus had been promoted to the captain of Clare's guard.

"He was one of the best," Clare agreed. "We no longer live in the time of William Marshal, when a man could parlay tournament victories into an earldom, but Rollo had won more than enough to retire very well when he chose. He had told me, in fact, that this would be his last tournament."

"How old was he?" Catrin asked.

"Thirty-eight."

Catrin looked ruefully down at the body, acknowledging that Rollo's scars and weathered features were what a lifetime of soldiering did to a man. But even so, for someone the same age as Rhys, for all of Rhys's own hard living, Rollo looked a decade older.

"My lord, did your captain have any enemies?" Rhys had returned to a crouch beside the body.

Yet again, Clare tsked through his teeth. "Many ... and none. When a man has been the captain of my guard as long as Rollo, and if he has fought in as many wars as Rollo, he has made enemies. How many are at Nevin or within this camp, is another question, one I perhaps cannot answer. How many men could have such animosity towards him that they would murder him while he slept? That I also couldn't tell you." He made a gesture with one hand. "I can't imagine Rollo hiding himself under his bed of his own initiative, so it *is* murder, isn't it?"

"Very likely, my lord."

"Can you tell me how he died? There's no blood that I can see."

"He was suffocated," Rhys said flatly.

"You're sure?"

"My lord, if you care to look, his eyes are bloodshot, a telltale sign." Rhys lifted Rollo's closed lids one after another. "He also has a slight bruising around his nose and mouth where pressure may have been applied. And finally, if you bend closer, you can see fibers in his beard and mustache from the fabric used to smother him."

"Such as his own pillow?"

"Possibly," Rhys cast around the tent, "though he seemed to sleep without one." He fingered a rolled up blanket that had fallen to the floor. "This would have done it. If I'm wrong about the fibers, the murder could have been done by hands alone, but the bruising on Rollo's face is not as pronounced as I might have expected if that were the case."

"How could he have been overpowered by anyone? He was a warrior!"

"I can't say as yet, but there's this—" Rhys half-turned to show Clare and Catrin Rollo's left hand. The dead man had no defensive wounds, no cuts or abrasions on his knuckles. Nonetheless, they were swollen and disjointed, as one might find in a very elderly person. Far more dramatically, the tip of his forefinger had been cut off.

If it hadn't been sweltering inside the tent, Catrin would have shivered.

Clare, meanwhile, recoiled. "What is this madness?"

"I cannot say, my lord."

"Have you ever seen anything like it?"

"Only once before in murder, when a ring was taken from a dead man's finger." Rhys gently put down Rollo's hand. "That's not what happened here."

"No." Clare's expression was like a thundercloud. "Why isn't there more blood?"

"The fingertip was taken post-mortem." And then Rhys continued as Clare's brow furrowed and he opened his mouth to ask how Rhys knew: "As soon as a person dies, his heart stops beating, and thus his blood stops flowing."

Rhys then moved around the body to the bed and threw back the wool blanket, revealing a linen sheet over a wool-stuffed mattress. A few red drops spotted the sheet, but it was otherwise clean. The servant who'd intended to change them had discovered the body first and not completed his task.

"That's about the right amount of blood for the wound."

Clare's expression smoothed. "So he wasn't tortured?"

That made both Catrin and Rhys blink, and caused Rhys to ask, very carefully, "Would Rollo have had information that someone might have tried to torture out of him?"

"He was the captain of my guard."

And really, that was all Clare needed to say. Catrin herself knew many of the queen's secrets because she was a member of her household, slept in her room at times, and sang her to sleep. Every high lord or lady surrounded him or herself with companions and lived with the risk of betrayal because to do otherwise was not to live. Rhys now played that selfsame role for the king, and it was Rhys's personal honor that kept him there.

"Why take the fingertip after Rollo's death? Who would do such a thing?" Color rose in Clare's face, matching his hair. "Are you saying he was killed by someone crazed?"

"I can't say as yet." Rhys cleared his throat. "Some murderers like to take trophies."

Clare blinked rapidly three times. "I did not realize I had so much to learn about murder."

"Was anything taken from the tent, besides the tip of his finger?" Catrin asked.

As the captain of Clare's guard, Rollo would have been well-paid, both because he deserved it, in order to have achieved his station, and to maintain his loyalty, about which Clare was clearly concerned.

"His armor and sword are still here," Clare cast around the tent, "but we couldn't find his purse."

Catrin began searching too, though beyond the chest that Clare had already opened, there was little of substance through which to search. As she went to kneel to look again through his trunk, she hesitated, a handspan from the yellowed grass, noting a reddish discoloration on a small patch of it.

"Rhys, is this blood?" Tentatively, she put out a hand to it. Much had soaked into the ground, but liquid came away from a few grass blades onto her fingers. Hesitantly, she sniffed it.

In two strides, Rhys was at her side, bending to put his own hand to the discolored patch. Catrin's fingers smelled sweet, but not of blood, and she stuck out her tongue to lick her finger.

Before she managed it, Rhys caught her wrist. "Don't!"

He didn't speak the word *poison!* out loud, but she could tell he was thinking it.

"It doesn't smell like blood. I'm thinking wine."

Rhys sniffed her fingers, and then got down on all fours to put his nose to the ground. What Clare thought of them, Catrin didn't know. Regardless, all he said was, "Have you found something else?"

Rhys sat back on his heels. "Wine was spilled here, but I don't see the cup or carafe that contained it."

"His steward could have taken them," Clare said.

That was the first they'd heard of a steward, but naturally Rollo had one. "We will speak to him too," Rhys said.

"In addition, Rollo's sister kept house for him since her husband died," Clare said. "He was squired by one of my men-at-arms, or by Hugh, his second-in-command."

"Does his sister know he's dead?" Catrin's stomach clenched at the thought of having to tell her. If unmarried, she would have been dependent on her brother for her living, but wouldn't necessarily inherit his wealth if he had a male heir somewhere. Catrin's situation had been different when her husband had died because she'd had a grown son of her own.

"I told her first, before I went to the king." Clare frowned. "So is it thievery? Rollo was killed for his purse? Or his finger, heaven forbid?"

"Again, I can't say for certain until we discover more than we know right now." Rhys turned one hand palm up. "But yes, it's perfectly possible that a thief snuck into the tent in the night, intending to rob your man. Rollo woke, saw him, they fought, and the thief got the better of him, unlikely as that seems on the surface. Still, the motives and character of a thief versus a murderer are very different."

"How so?" Clare said. "They're both criminals."

"A thief steals," Catrin said simply. "If that's who murdered Rollo, we won't be looking for someone who had a grievance against him."

"I don't know which I would prefer." Clare gave a shake of his head. "A thief strikes me as easier to catch."

"Not necessarily, my lord," Rhys said. "Thieves are not known for their courage. He might now go into hiding."

Then Catrin's own brow furrowed. "I didn't see defensive wounds on Rollo's hands, Rhys, did you?"

"No."

"Why does that matter?" Clare asked.

"It could be a sign he knew his killer," Rhys said.

"It also indicates Rollo didn't mark his attacker." Catrin swept a stray hair that had come loose from her chignon out of her face. She understood why they were keeping the tent flaps closed, since prying eyes were the last thing any of them wanted. Still, it was hot.

And then, as if drawn by her desire for fresh air, a slight breeze swept across her face. The opening to the tent had started to flap. Frowning, she crossed the room to the opposite seam. It had begun to gape at the bottom, and when she touched it, the two pieces separated easily, though they also left a residue on her fingers. This she sniffed as well, resisting without Rhys's intercession the temptation to lick her fingers, and then turned to look at the men. "Someone made their own entrance and then tried to seal it closed again with wheatpaste."

"As in what is used to bind books?" Rhys came over, and she held out her hand again to him so he could sniff her fingers. At least neither of the smells were putrid.

"It's a quick and easy glue," she added, as she pulled the seam farther apart to reveal the sunny afternoon outside, "which doesn't last long on any substance but paper, but it was enough to keep this hole hidden until now."

Clare grimaced. "Rollo liked to have his tent on the edge of the camp, the better to keep his eyes on the sentries, or so he said."

Catrin swung around to him. "You are placing sentries?"

"Of course," and she heard him *tsk* yet again. "The Round Table is a perfect opportunity for rebels to attack."

Catrin herself couldn't imagine a worse moment. Yes, a band of rebels could gather themselves to the east of the encampment, possibly in the remains of the old settlement on top of Garn Boduan, and surprise the tournament participants. But the Round Table was a gathering of the most notable warriors in all of Britain. They might initially be taken unawares, but they were here *because* they knew how to fight.

As Clare had learned at Llandeilo Fawr, the Welsh were much better at ambushes and raids than combat on open ground. With most of their warriors and all of their leaders dead in the war, she doubted any Welsh lord could muster even a hundred who would risk an attack on Nefyn. If they were to be successful, they would need many times that number.

None of that did she say, though a glance at Rhys told her he was thinking along similar lines. Although in the initial days of her return to Caernarfon, she'd been suspicious of Rhys and his motives, those concerns had long since disappeared, and she cherished the way she knew what he was thinking much of the time—and he seemed to know her thoughts as well.

Rhys fingered the split seam and spoke to Clare, though his back remained turned to him. "My lord, it looks as if the murderer took pains not to be seen entering the tent by normal means, and even greater pains to hide his departure. Could a stranger have been roaming the camp in the night without being stopped by your sentries?"

Clare's eyes narrowed. "What are you saying?"

"For someone to have entered the tent and murdered Rollo, he would have had to fit in well enough not to be remarked upon. He could even have been well-dressed and well-armed. He might possibly have been someone Rollo knew." Rhys spread his hands wide and turned to face Clare—bravely, Catrin thought, since those narrowed eyes were daunting at the best of times, all the more so after his captain had been murdered. "My lord, Catrin is right. Our most important fact may be that *Rollo didn't fight back.*"

6

Day One

Rhys

"I can't imagine you are usually in the habit of making proclamations in the first hours of an investigation, Rhys. Why did you today? And to Gilbert de Clare of all people!"

Rhys made an *ach* sound at the back of his throat. "Clare gets my hackles up." Then he smiled ruefully. "You're right that it isn't my habit. Even so, I don't think I'm wrong in what I said."

"I don't think you're wrong either, but I have a few more points for your consideration."

They had moved out of the tent into the field between Rollo's tent and the sentries. Here, they could not be overheard, and the cooler air was a relief.

Rhys turned to face her. "I am open to anything you suggest. You know full well how much I value your company."

He was skating very close to a real truth, and it was on the tip of his tongue to tell her flat out how he felt about her.

But she spoke again before he could, and he told himself it was just as well. Now was not the time. "My first thought is that Rollo could have drunk to excess, such that he was insensate. My second is that someone dosed him with an herb to make him sleep, something like poppy juice. If he shared that drink with his murderer, that would be a reason to dump the remainder in the grass and take the carafe and cup."

Rhys grunted. "My fear of something along those lines was why I didn't want you to lick your fingers."

"But you didn't feel the need to share that with Earl Clare?"

"Why muddy the waters just yet with guesses?"

Catrin pursed her lips, canting her head as she studied him. "You want him thinking about who he can and cannot trust, don't you?" She blinked as clarity came to her. "You *want* him suspicious!"

"Indeed I do. It's always easier to tell oneself that a murderer is someone outside the social circle of the victim, a random stranger, in other words. We saw that in Caernarfon. Everyone wanted Cole to have been killed by a masterless man." Rhys swept out a hand. "How many masterless men do you see here today?"

"None." Catrin coughed a laugh. "Hangers-on, yes."

Rhys nodded. "And one of them may not be all that he seems. Unfortunately, that quality can make him that much harder to catch."

"Unless and until he strikes again."

"But will he? If his target *was* Rollo and the theft of Rollo's purse was secondary, then this may be over. Not everyone takes a life as easily as Guy fitz Lacy."

"I can't believe I'm hoping for a second murder!"

"Or maybe I'm wrong and this really was a thieving gone wrong."

"Once a thief, always a thief, or so I've heard you say." Catrin frowned. "I am curious now about Clare's secrets that Rollo knew."

He studied her, pleased at how much she'd learned in so short a time. "Did you have another issue for my consideration?"

She smiled. "We keep speaking of the killer as male, saying *he* because it's convenient, but Rollo could have been murdered by a woman. While few women would be strong enough to hold him down and suffocate him, with or without a pillow, if he was drunk or dosed with an herb to make him sleep, the task would have been comparatively easier."

"I don't like to think of the murderer as a woman." Rhys shook his head. "It's wrong somehow. Even more wrong than murder."

"But possible. Rollo has a sister, don't forget. She's a suspect, whether we like it or not. He was also unmarried and could have entertained a lady in his tent last night."

Rhys opened his mouth to comment, but Catrin was deep into her thesis and continued, "It seems to me that idea was also not something you wanted to discuss with Clare immediately."

Rhys gave her a crooked grin. They were out of earshot of anyone and had been speaking in Welsh, but he lowered his voice even more anyway. "You and I both learned long ago that our superiors don't need to know everything we know, at least in the short term."

"You are a devious man, Rhys ap Iorwerth." She grinned. "I admire that about you."

Rhys stuck out his lower lip in a feigned pout. "And here I strive every day to be honorable and upright in all my doings."

"You are all those things too, my dear," she took his arm, "there can be no doubt."

"Jesting aside, I am concerned about the scope of this investigation." Rhys began walking slowly with her back into the encampment. "I can understand why Clare came to me if he is concerned about the culpability of his own people. My skill aside, it's logical to think he might prefer an outsider investigating."

"That would be even more true if he was concerned about his own people finding out about the secrets Rollo kept for him," Catrin said.

"Though why he would think I will be more discreet than one of his own men, I don't know."

"Well, you might," Catrin said. "You are not one to run at the mouth."

Rhys bit his lip. "Clare has given me *carte blanche* to act and question as I see fit. But, unlike the king, I don't think he really knows what that means."

Catrin laughed. "He will as soon as you start poking your nose into his doings and disrupting the lives of his men, in just the way he came to you to avoid. The question then will become *how badly does he want this murder solved?*" Her eyes were on the ground as they walked, trying to navigate the burrows and divots hidden in the turf. "By then it will be too late to stop you, since you will proceed to solve the murder regardless of what he wants." She stopped suddenly and bent to the ground.

He bent with her, since she was holding his elbow for balance.

"Look what I found!" She held up a ring, one meant for a man, in that the band was thick gold and too big for any woman Rhys had ever met. The signet was a garnet, etched with the image of a hawk, and worn with age. It wasn't a real sigil, he didn't think, or at least it didn't display the usual flourishes. "Could it be Rollo's?"

Rhys's heart started to beat a little harder, feeling the excitement of the chase once again. "Clare didn't say anything about a missing ring."

Far more urgently than they'd been moving before, they threaded their way through the tents, crossing half of Clare's encampment in their quest to find his second-in-command, a man named Hugh. Because of Rollo's death, he was suddenly promoted to captain.

While Rhys had been overseeing the removal of the body, Clare had left them alone in the tent in order to tell Hugh of his promotion and to warn him that they would want to speak to him. Once Clare returned, he'd assured Rhys that Hugh would answer all his questions and give him every accommodation.

It was further proof, if they needed it, that Clare was intent on him finding Rollo's killer.

"What do you know of this Hugh?" Rhys asked Catrin.

"Very little. Most of the time when Clare called, Robert rode to Bristol or Gloucester Castle alone or with his men or Justin, once he was old enough, while I stayed on our estate. I haven't seen him since Robert's funeral."

Catrin and Rhys arrived at the encampment's command tent to find Hugh standing in the cleared space in front of it, with his hands behind his back and his legs spread. A dozen soldiers stood in formation before him, and he was telling them of his rise in station and their duties. To Hugh's credit, he didn't look gleeful.

He was also relatively young, perhaps thirty, tall and handsome, a supposition which Rhys confirmed when he glanced at Catrin and saw an admiring expression on her face. Rhys was amused rather than jealous, and didn't need to remind himself that Catrin had spent these last months on his arm and showed no signs of wanting something different.

After answering several questions succinctly and with confidence, Hugh dismissed the men and turned towards the command tent, at which point he spied Rhys and Catrin waiting for him near the entrance.

He took in a visible breath before coming forward to meet them. "My lady, I am glad to see you are keeping well. My condolences again on the loss of your husband."

"Thank you, Sir Hugh."

Hugh turned to Rhys. "May I presume you are Sir Reese, sent by the king to investigate Rollo's death?"

Sent by the king was an interesting way to phrase it, rather than *invited by Earl Clare*. Perhaps Clare himself had used those words in order to ward off any resentment Hugh might feel over the fact that he himself wasn't in charge of the investigation.

"You can."

"Is it certain it wasn't an accident?" Hugh asked. "Or that Rollo didn't die in his sleep?"

"It is certain," Rhys said. "Didn't Earl Clare say?"

Hugh spread his hands wide. "Not in so many words. He merely confirmed you were here to investigate. May I ask—" he hesitated, almost stammering, "—*how* he died?"

"I'm sorry." Rhys made his expression rueful, not wanting to offend. On the whole, he was pleased Hugh was being so civil. "We have reason to keep that to ourselves for now."

Hugh blinked. "Excuse me?"

Rhys put out a hand to appease him, though in this, he had the full confidence of experience to know not to share information with suspects and witnesses right away. "Did you see the body yourself? Earl Clare said a dozen people entered the tent before order was established."

"Yes, I was one of those people. Others had already moved the bed that lay over the top of Rollo to expose him lying on the ground."

"Did you touch him?" Catrin asked.

"I felt for pulse and breath, yes." Hugh was looking defensive, which wasn't what they wanted. "I had to!"

Rhys's hand was still out. "I am in no way passing judgment, and I agree completely that you had to determine if he was breathing. I was just trying to establish the order of events."

"Then how can I help? Earl Clare said I was to extend you every courtesy."

"You can tell us about Rollo," Catrin said immediately.

"I probably don't have to tell you this is the last thing we needed," Hugh shook his head, "and by no means the manner by which I wished to be promoted."

"What other way would there have been?" Catrin said.

Hugh's chin wrinkled. "I hoped Rollo would retire soon. He was growing older, and he was less able to keep up with the younger recruits. He'd already said this was his last tournament."

"What would he have done if not this?" Rhys said.

"I believe my lord Clare would have made him a castellan of one of his castles, which would have given him a good living and wouldn't have been a demotion." Hugh drew himself up to his full height. "I can hope that I might be so blessed, when my time comes." Then he deflated. "That Rollo is dead is terribly unlucky."

Although things had turned rocky a moment ago, Hugh was proving to be quite talkative, possibly his normal state, and Rhys wanted to keep him that way. As with withholding information about the way Rollo died, he deliberately hadn't shown him the ring yet, wanting to get the measure of him first. "Unlucky for him or unlucky for Clare?"

"Well ... both." Hugh's eyes nearly crossed as he thought. "Obviously, that Rollo is dead is terribly unlucky for him, but it is also unfortunate for all of us, since Rollo was the best commander here."

"Does that mean the men responded to him well and trusted him?" Rhys asked.

"They trusted him, certainly. Though—" Hugh raised one shoulder in a partial shrug, for the first time qualifying his effusiveness. "Rollo was less one of them than I, since his family came with the Conqueror. But they didn't need him to be one of them to follow him."

"He was that good a soldier?" Rhys said.

Hugh nodded. "The best."

Catrin tipped her head. "It looked as if you handled the men well."

"They trust me too. Or at least I hope they do." Hugh turned to her, his expression hopeful, making him appear younger than ever. He was talking not only with no apparent resentment, but with genuine openness. "Though my family came later, from Gascony, I have proved myself to them."

Gascony was a province of Aquitaine, which had come to the English crown in the last century when Henry II had married Eleanor of Aquitaine.

"How so?" Catrin paused and what she asked next was gentle but genuinely curious. "Were you at Llandeilo Fawr?"

"Madam, I was, and a worse hell I could not imagine. We were beset and lost many men. I am grateful to have escaped with my life and the lives of the men under my command."

"I'm guessing that some of them are alive because of your leadership," Catrin said.

He bent his head in modest acknowledgment of the accolade. "That may be. I would be grateful to think so." But then he frowned. "What does this have to do with Rollo's death?"

Rhys gazed back at him, not wanting to stem the flow of information and deliberating how to convey to Hugh without offending him that he himself was a suspect.

In the end, he didn't have to explain because Catrin stepped in, still with that gentle manner that made it hard to take offense. "We'd be grateful to hear anything about Rollo that could help us understand why he was killed."

Hugh made a *hum* sound deep in his chest. "He had lived long enough to make enemies. Isn't that enough? It could be anyone!"

"But could it, really?" Rhys said. "Murder isn't perpetrated lightly, even for soldiers. It is one thing to kill a man on the battlefield, but quite another to suffocate him in his sleep."

Hugh blanched and took a step back, which was why Rhys had withheld that specific information initially and told him now in the hopes of eliciting a genuine response.

"That's awful." Hugh's voice, like his face, had drained of color.

His emotion was genuine. It had to be, or Rhys had lost all ability to evaluate men.

"Likely it was quick, and he didn't fight back." Catrin glanced at Rhys, who understood what she was asking and pulled out the ring.

"Do you recognize this?" he said.

Hugh's imagination was distracting him still, but he glanced at the ring as required. It made Rhys think again that his responses were genuine. "No. Whose is it?"

"Not Rollo's?" Rhys said.

Hugh shook his head, frowning. "Not that I ever saw. His ring, when he wore one, bore no stone. His sigil was carved into the gold."

Both Rhys and Catrin made a disappointed face, though truly, there was little to be disappointed about. The ring gave them a new lead to pursue, one they would not have had if the ring was Rollo's. Perhaps the ring wasn't related to their investigation at all, and an entirely unrelated person had dropped it in the grass. But investigations weren't concluded by dismissing evidence within the first hour of starting.

"What more can I tell you?" Hugh glanced away, towards Earl Clare's tent, perhaps impatient to get on with what must be a list of duties the length of his arm.

"Just a few more things, if you please." Rhys spoke hurriedly, not ready to lose him yet. "In hopes of establishing a timeline of events, we need to know what he was doing in his final hours. When did you last speak to Sir Rollo?"

"Last night," Hugh said promptly. "We were discussing his role in the tournament—" He broke off, his brow furrowing. "I suppose it will be my role now."

Rhys recalled his earlier conversation with Clare. "Are you ready for that?"

"I am!" Hugh's eyes lit, as well they might. As Clare had said, the great knight William Marshal had been the son of a minor nobleman, with no lands or title to inherit, and had risen to an earldom and the regency of England in part based on his victories in tournaments. "It is a moment I have dreamed of and never for one moment thought I'd see!" Then he put out a hand, hastily amending his words. "Not that I had anything to do with Rollo's death! It would be absurd to think it!"

He still wasn't understanding that he was a suspect. Catrin might call such innocence endearing.

Rhys could hardly blame Hugh for being excited about his new role and promotion. Wars during King Edward's reign had been a constant, but with the strict control he had over his men, it wasn't always the case that a soldier could become rich—not like in the old days when the spoils of war belonged to the victor. Raping and pillaging were forbidden now, as they should be.

It was only when one knight captured another knight or nobleman that he could ransom the captive back to his family. The deaths of so many noblemen in the war against Llywelyn had been the exception rather than the rule. It was one reason the English had heaped such scorn and hatred upon the Welsh for what was viewed as their dishonorable tactics—and meted out such cruelty at their defeat. To ambush one's enemy rather than attacking them on an open field was seen as ignoble, never mind that ambushes had almost won Llywelyn the war.

Ironically, in their own country, time and again these barons had fought amongst themselves with passion and prejudice for the throne of England. In their wars, no crime was too heinous or betrayal too extreme to commit in the name of their cause. For all their talk of the Welsh lack of honor in war, they themselves would do anything—*anything*—not to lose, but then claimed not to understand why another people might hate losing just as much.

So here they were, in the midst of an Arthurian play, acting as if anyone in the royal court had a hope of living up to the ideals manifested by Arthur, a Welshman.

The further irony was that Llywelyn had lost his life and his war when the Mortimers had ambushed *him*.

Rhys suppressed these thoughts along with all the others today. "Nobody was suggesting you did. Animosity against Rollo might not even be the primary motive. His purse is missing from his tent, along with a cup and carafe, so theft—"

Rhys broke off at the disconcerted look that crossed Hugh's face.

Catrin saw it too. "What is it?"

"It's funny you should mention thieving." Hugh chewed on his lower lip for a moment before finishing his thought. "Some of the men are missing items."

"Valuable items?" Catrin said.

"Yes. A missing shirt would be one thing, but these include a gold cross, a ring, a cup, and a knife." Hugh grimaced. "Taken separately, each is small and easily lost, so we haven't known how seriously to take their disappearances."

"We?" Catrin asked.

"Rollo was looking into it." Hugh's frown deepened.

"And now he is dead," Catrin said.

"I confess it never occurred to me that Rollo's death and these thefts could be related," Hugh said.

"Lord Clare did not mention this to us," Rhys said.

"That's because he possibly didn't know. Rollo was an experienced commander. He didn't feel the need to take every matter to our lord."

"I can understand that," Rhys said, because he did. "But now we have no choice."

Hugh looked as if he didn't relish having this be the first thing about which he spoke to Clare in his new position as captain of his guard. Still, he squared his shoulders. "I will see to it. What else do you need from me?"

"I need access to all of your men, to question them about their whereabouts last night and what they might have seen."

"Anyone in particular whom you would like to see first?"

Rhys looked at Catrin. "Would it be possible for Lady Catrin to speak to Rollo's sister?"

"Of course."

"Meanwhile, I need to return to Rollo's tent."

Hugh nodded, agreeable as always, but still asked, "Why is that?"

"It is in my mind that I recognized the man standing guard there. And I think I know him because he was once a thief."

7

Day One

Catrin

S peaking to a sister about the loss of her brother was never
going to be part of the job of being an investigator that ap-
pealed to Catrin. At the same time, it was a role to which she
was suited—in this case more than Rhys. That wasn't just because
she was a woman. She'd lost her husband too, and both parents. She
knew loss, and Joan, Rollo's sister, would be feeling the full impact of
it right about now.

Or so Catrin thought right up until the moment she finally
tracked her down in the church in the center of the village of Nefyn,
north of the palace. Catrin was surely earning her dinner tonight with
all this trekking about. St. Mary's, as with nearly every church in
Wales, had an ancient Welsh origin, but it was now an outpost of the
Augustinian abbey of Haughmond near Shrewsbury. This change
from native control to English control had taken place even before
Nefyn had been conquered by King Edward's forces. A prince of
Gwynedd with a Norman wife had endowed the abbey over a hun-

dred years earlier, and its authority had remained the same through-out Nefyn's changing fortunes.

When Catrin arrived, blinking back the bright sunlight so her eyes could adjust to the candlelit church, Joan was kneeling at the rail before the altar. Nobody was about that Catrin could see, so she squared her shoulders and walked straight down the length of the nave to come to a halt within a few paces of Rollo's sister.

Joan didn't turn around.

Catrin stood there for a count of ten, and then cleared her throat. "My apologies, madam, for disturbing your prayers."

Joan still didn't respond, and Catrin had a moment's spike of fear that she was dead too and the murderer had propped her up against the rail so nobody would discover it for a time and allow him to get away.

But then Joan's shoulders lifted and fell as she sighed.

"You are so polite." Joan rose to her feet and turned to look at Catrin. She was about Catrin's age, in her mid-thirties, with dark hair and eyes. In the dim light of the church, her face was pale, making her coloring even more contrasting. Catrin was very conscious of her own unruly red hair, which never stayed longer than a few hours in any device meant to contain it.

"I am Catrin. I am so sorry to disturb you, but the lord Clare has tasked me with speaking to you about the death of your brother."

"You don't need to apologize to me nor pretend not to know the truth." Disdain dripped from Joan's lips as she spoke.

Catrin was genuinely confused, and she quickly rearranged her features away from pity to something more matter-of-fact. "Excuse me, madam. I am not understanding."

Joan tsked through her teeth in a similar manner to Earl Clare. "I was not praying for my brother's soul but thanking God for my deliverance." And then at Catrin's unintentionally wide eyes, she added, "You are shocked I would say so out loud? Believe me, it is hardly the worst thing I could say about my brother."

Catrin worked to wrestle her expression back to neutral, attempting to imply, as Joan expected, that her hatred of her brother wasn't wholly new information. Catrin was quite certain she wasn't entirely successful and decided she had to reply with the truth. "I'm sorry. I didn't know."

That prompted another scoff from Joan. "You expect me to believe that? Everybody knew and turned a blind eye. How dare you insult my intelligence by telling me you didn't know!"

Catrin shook her head uncertainly. "It has been only a few days since you arrived—"

Joan cut her off with a slice of her hand. "I recognize you. You were wife to Lord Robert, who died at Landelo Var." Like every non-Welsh speaker, she said the name of the place the English way, without any of the Welsh accent or pronunciations.

"Yes, I am Catrin."

"And you never heard rumors of how he treated me? Not even from your own husband?"

"No, madam. I'm sorry. If I had, I would not have stood by silently."

Joan studied her for a moment. "I suppose that might be true, because even if you haven't ever heard of me, I have heard of *you*. Your husband was quite proud of you, you know."

Warily, Catrin shook her head. "I-I-I suppose I did know that, after a fashion. He wasn't one to be effusive in his praise."

"He was an honorable man. One of the few. It's easy to see the father in the son."

At Catrin's surprised stare, Joan scoffed one more time. "You have been away from Gloucester too long, my lady, to have lost touch with so many of your people."

They were never my people was on the tip of Catrin's tongue to say, but to do so might antagonize Joan further and for no reason, so instead she glided forward to put a hand on her arm. "Please, I would very much like to hear your side of the story."

"Why?" Joan was not to be appeased. "Clare knew full well what kind of man Rollo was and didn't care. All he regrets is that, with Rollo's death, he has to find someone else to replace him in Edward's precious tournament."

Her words were bitter, unapologetic, and left Joan too open to censure not to be her true feelings. Catrin very much didn't want to dissuade her from speaking her mind, since more truth in a murder investigation was always better than less. But not here. She urged her back down the nave towards the exit. "Perhaps we should find some place to speak where there are fewer echoes."

"I don't care who knows my feelings." Joan's derision was nearly palpable.

Still, she came with Catrin, somewhat stiff-leggedly, through the churchyard and out the gate. Once in the street, she walked a little more easily, and they settled upon one of several makeshift taverns that had sprung up at the edge of the fair. This particular vendor had arranged for patrons to enjoy their drinks at tables and benches, many of which were occupied. One small table had been set apart from the others, and the two people sitting at it stood just as Catrin and Joan arrived.

"Would you like some wine?" Catrin made a beeline for the table.

"I prefer mead." Joan settled on the bench and looked up expectantly at Catrin, who was still standing.

"Really?" Catrin blinked her surprise. "It is my preference as well, but I would not have thought someone from England would view it favorably."

"Over the wine at this place? For certain."

Catrin laughed. "That's a fair point."

While she waited in line for the proprietor to provide a carafe and two cups, she kept her eye on Joan, whose mouth remained turned down as she studied the gathered people with disapproval. Her morose expression deepened further at the sight of a blonde woman ahead of Catrin who was carrying on a lively conversation with the man behind the counter and holding up the serving of the mead. Catrin couldn't blame Joan for being angry at everyone around her, if not the delay. If Rollo was as much a tyrant as Joan had so far implied, daily abuse could give anyone a jaundiced view of the world.

Then the woman ahead of Catrin swung around so quickly, she almost spilled the contents of her cup down Catrin's front.

"Oh! I'm so sorry!" The woman's face went pink. She was younger than Catrin, and prettier, and appeared genuinely contrite, her blue eyes wide with horror. "Did I get any on you?"

Catrin swept away the few drops with a brush of her hand. "I stepped back just in time." She smiled. "Please don't concern yourself."

"Again, I'm so sorry." The woman bent her head and moved away from the area of tables entirely, heading down the road at a rapid walk. Apparently the proprietor trusted her to return the cup when she finished the mead inside.

Once supplied with her own mead, Catrin settled herself across from Joan, who reached unabashedly for the carafe and poured herself a cup. She was in the act of setting the carafe down when she glanced at Catrin, made a face, and poured a portion for Catrin as well. Catrin was quite sure that mead was not the answer to Joan's problems, but at this place it would be very watered down. Even if Edward hadn't ordered it done to quell the expected drunkenness amongst the tournament participants and spectators, watering down the mead turned a better profit.

Though Catrin could hardly blame Joan for wanting to drown her sorrows in drink, she felt that if she herself had just been released from bondage, she would have been more light-hearted. Joan's brother *was* dead, and she was free.

Or was she? Catrin herself, widowed for two years now, had hardly been *free* at Robert's death, though admittedly she had more freedom now than at any previous time in her life.

After several hours of investigating, Catrin was thirsty too and was pleased to discover that the mead they'd been served was better than average, whether or not water had been added. She took several sips, noting that in that time Joan had drained her own cup and filled it again. The other woman then proceeded to drink an entire second cup before sharing out the last of the carafe evenly between her cup and Catrin's.

And, at last, Joan found the grace to be polite. "Thank you for the mead. I would have told you about my brother even without it."

"I didn't intend it as a bribe. I am allowed in the king's pavilion and could have drunk freely there, but I thought you would prefer fewer eyes on you, and more anonymous ones, besides."

"And fewer ears to hear my heretical talk against the sainted Rollo?" Joan rolled her eyes. "As you have no doubt heard from everyone else, my brother was the perfect *chevalier*: upright, honorable, and loyal. He was also rigid and uncompromising in his opinions, few of which coincided with mine."

"I'm sorry."

Joan gestured with her cup, which Catrin was glad to see she was now sipping rather than guzzling. "Everyone said it was kind of him to take me in after the death of my husband, who didn't live long enough to leave me more than a few trinkets to see me into old age."

"How long ago was this?"

"Ten years." Joan shook her head at the enormity of that number—and perhaps at the waste. "I have served him for ten years."

Catrin didn't know how to ask her next question delicately, so she said it straight out. "No other man caught your eye?"

"Oh, more than one did, but Rollo refused to let me go."

"But as a widow—"

Joan cut her off. "Earl Clare is Rollo's lord, and thus mine. Rollo did not want me to remarry, and he was the captain of Clare's guard. Of course my requests were denied. Rollo made sure of it. He said the men were not good enough for his sister, but really, he didn't want to give up his slave." She fixed Catrin with a beady eye. "That last afternoon, before the evening meal, I had mended one of his tunics with the smallest stitches you have ever seen. I'm quite good at stitchery. But did he thank me? Of course not. He took the tunic from me without looking at it. Then his upper lip lifted in disdain as he looked at me and pointed to a smudge on my cheek, sneering that I would never find a husband at this rate and that if I expected his help in that regard, I had better mend my ways as well as his shirts."

The story came out all in a rush. The scene had clearly been unpleasant, but in and of itself perhaps hardly the worst Catrin had heard or experienced herself. Compounded daily over ten years, however ... "Did he ever touch—"

Again, Catrin didn't finish her sentence before Joan interrupted. "Of course not. For him to beat me or touch me in a manner unseemly to brother and sister would imply he had actual passions. He was correct in all things, but without compassion, love, or a thimbleful of human feeling." She raised her cup in salute to Catrin, drank it to the dregs, and set it down with a clap to punctuate her sentiment.

"Did you kill him?" They'd come far enough in this conversation that it didn't seem strange or offensive to ask.

"You are correct to think I could have. I have come to realize that I have it in me, thanks to ten years serving Rollo." Joan's chin wrinkled. "But, no. I did not kill him. I hated him, it's true. The sad thing is that I don't think he was aware of my emotions—or that I had any. And yet, he had a soul, even if I can't bring myself to pray for it just yet."

"I am glad you are telling me this. My sense is that you haven't been able to confide in many people."

"In no people. I had food and shelter, and nobody could see why I couldn't be grateful for that. He didn't beat me, after all."

"I won't insult you by asking if you tried to leave. I can tell you did."

"Twice. He sent out men to find me and bring me back." Joan smiled sadly, becoming calmer and less angry as the moments passed. Maybe that was the mead, but Catrin might really have been the first person to listen to her in a long time.

"I focused my energies on seizing a way out if the opportunity ever presented itself." She paused, and something crossed her face, an expression Catrin couldn't read.

So she leaned forward. "Did something present itself recently? Or ... someone?"

Joan pressed her lips together, but then she smiled for the first time. "Maybe."

"A man?"

Joan lifted one shoulder, smiling into her cup and tipping it back before she remembered it was empty.

"Would you like some more?" If mead hadn't been the answer before, it surely wasn't now, but Catrin was still hoping for additional answers.

"This time I'll pay." Joan lifted a finger, the proprietor came over with another carafe, and Joan paid him. After he left, she poured out two more cups.

"Will you tell me his name?"

"It may be you'll know soon enough. I dare not say as yet."

Catrin tried not to harrumph.

Even so, Joan saw her discontent and put out a hand. "I assure you, he had nothing to do with Rollo's death."

"But surely, from what you've said, Rollo would have objected to you seeing a man."

She shrugged, no longer rising to anger at every mention of her brother's name. "But he's not here anymore, is he? At least I have his wealth. He had no other heirs."

Catrin bit her lip. "I fear your inheritance will not be as great as you hoped. Lord Clare could not find your brother's purse."

"That's because he didn't have it. I do." Real light entered Joan's eyes. "My brother had few vices. He never drank to excess, and he never lay with a woman in all the years I lived with him. But he would occasionally gamble. When he felt the urge coming on, he gave his purse to me to hold, leaving only a few pennies to himself until the feeling passed. He had just such a feeling yesterday. With so many contests, large and small, at this tournament, he was afraid he wouldn't be able to resist."

Catrin sat up straighter. "When did he give you his purse?"

"It was before the evening meal. You knew he was to joust in the place of Lord Clare?" At Catrin's nod, Joan continued, "He feared there would be wagering on the outcome, and his honor would require him to bet on himself."

"Did he want to avoid all betting, or was he afraid he wouldn't win?"

Joan laughed. "My brother always won. Lord Clare must be having kittens at having to settle for someone else."

"That would be his new captain, Hugh, or so I understand," Catrin said.

Joan's smile turned sweet instead of sardonic. "Now there is a true knight." Then she sighed. "He is too honorable to back out even though he's outmatched and has far less experience than many of the men he'll be facing. I'm afraid Hugh is going to get himself killed."

8

Day One

Rhys

In any investigation, Rhys believed it was important to at least make the attempt to keep a tight hold on the information discovered, so he could bring up bits of it to those interviewed at an appropriate time, as he'd done with Hugh. Watching faces when the details of a crime were relayed could be a shortcut to determining who knew what when, and how they knew it.

But in this case, Rollo's tent was part of Clare's camp. According to Clare himself, a dozen people had been inside, stomping all over the scene, before it was contained. As with the servant who'd discovered the body and, in Clare's words, *had run screaming from the tent*, those witnesses all would have told what they'd seen to someone. That's what people did. Thus, too many people already had detailed knowledge of the circumstances of Rollo's death for any attempt to be made to swear them to secrecy.

These witnesses included, perhaps especially, the man who was posted outside the tent. Clare had arranged for the body to be taken to the monastery's laying out room so it could be prepared for burial (and in case Rhys needed to examine it again), but even so, the guard remained to prevent anyone else from poking in a nose where it didn't belong. And even with the guard, a steady stream of curious onlookers craned their necks at the tent as they passed by.

With Catrin departed to find Rollo's sister, Hugh introduced Rhys to the guard. "Thomas, I will expect you to answer Sir Reese's questions in full."

"Yes, sir." The man's spine stiffened, as it had when Rhys had approached him the first time.

Rhys thanked Hugh, suggested that he could go, and then stood looking at Thomas for some length of time without speaking. His intent was to discomfit him, and his tactic was successful since, after a short wait, the guard said, "Was there something you wanted, sir?"

"Please remove your helmet."

Clear reluctance crossed Thomas's face, but he did as he was bid, revealing the craggy features of a man in his forties who'd spent too many years in the sun. That surely was going to be Rhys soon enough. It already had been Rollo.

"You remember me, don't you? We fought together in the Holy Land."

"No, sir. I don't know what you mean, sir."

"Are you really going to lie to me … *Finnian*. I can see why you changed your name in your attempt to disappear, since some members of the king's company have no love for Irishmen, and your name is far too memorable. I commend you on the taming of your tongue."

Finnian visibly warred with himself for a count of ten before breaking his own silence. "Yes, sir. I recognized you the moment I saw you."

"Vincent de Lusignan was your commander then, in the service of William de Valence. And now here you are in Earl Clare's service. I suppose it can't be a coincidence that you chose Clare as your master this time, since he and Valence are mortal enemies, and you assumed they would have little to do with one another. The only baron whom Clare hates more is Humphrey de Bohun."

"I really couldn't comment on such great matters, my lord."

Rhys scoffed his disbelief, but decided he didn't need to force Finnian to agree with that particular truth, as it was plain as day. "As I recall, you were arrested for … thieving, wasn't it?"

Finnian swallowed hard and bowed to the inevitable. "Yes, sir."

"I remember now. You escaped from custody before Vincent could cut off your hand." Rhys himself was no more happy at the reminder than Finnian appeared to be. "He would have enjoyed that. Instead, he raged around the camp for three days, making miserable everyone who came in contact with him."

"I have mended my ways, sir. I've never been caught thieving in all the years since."

"*Caught* being the operative word." Rhys studied him. "You do realize that Rollo's personal carafe and cup are missing from his tent, along with his purse, and he is missing a fingertip to boot."

If Finnian could have stood straighter, he would have. "Yes, sir. I did hear that."

Rhys couldn't be surprised he'd guessed right about the extent of Finnian's knowledge. None of the three—Rhys himself, Catrin, or Clare--would have talked, but somehow, Finnian knew the details of Rollo's death anyway. Perhaps his hearing was as good as his new accent, and he hadn't needed to listen to gossip from the men who'd moved the body or gone in and out of the tent over the last hours.

"And yet you stayed at your post, even though you knew who I was and what I was here for." Rhys canted his head. "Why?"

"Because I didn't do anything wrong."

It was a brave stance. Admirable, even.

"Go on."

"When I saw you, and our eyes met, I was afraid. I admit that. I was ready to run. But then I decided I didn't want to leave if I didn't have to. I have a good life here. I've kept my nose clean. I have friends and companions I don't want to abandon." He snorted. "Especially here! Where would I run to if you don't mind me saying? How far would I get amongst these savages?"

He meant the Welsh, even knowing (if he'd taken a moment to think), that Rhys was one of them.

And because he'd spoken so honestly, he had Rhys believing him, much as he'd believed Hugh, and even more so as Finnian elaborated: "I do remember you, my lord. You were hard on those you caught, but you were fair. You didn't arrest someone you didn't think was guilty, and you kept looking for the guilty man, even after everyone else thought they had the right man in custody. Or when it was easier to think so."

Rhys's superiors hadn't always appreciated that quality. However, common Englishmen, or half-Irishmen in Finnian's case, knew what many lordlings born in a manor did not: that battles weren't won with knights. It was men like Finnian, common men, who fought for pennies and paid for their commanders' mistakes with their lives, who did the hard slog of war. Not for them were legends of chivalry and round tables. They developed a clear-eyed understanding of every man under whom they served, and Rhys couldn't be sorry he had found favor amongst them—despite the fact that Finnian had just labeled him a savage. It was a general prejudice against the Welsh, and Rhys chose not to take it personally.

"You landed on your feet too, my lord. The king's guard." Finnian shook his head. "I suppose we should have expected it after Qaqun."

Finnian was referring to the time Rhys had saved Prince Edmund's life and been knighted afterwards.

"I've had my own journeys." Finnian couldn't know about the circuitous route he'd taken to reach this spot, and it wasn't something Rhys cared to share. So he began anew with his questions. "Where were you last night after midnight?"

Their moment of camaraderie had passed, and Finnian knew it, stiffening to attention once again and looking past Rhys's shoulder rather than at him as he answered. "In my bed, sir, legless drunk. My woman can attest to it. I snore, and she said I kept her up the whole night. I didn't know anything of Sir Rollo's death until I came on duty this afternoon."

"We'll check."

"Of course, my lord."

"Since you are innocent of wrongdoing, do you remember anything that went on yesterday or in the past few days that struck you as somehow *off* or wrong?"

"This whole place is wrong, my lord. All this water and wind, mountains everywhere you look. It isn't right. And the people—" He shook his head. "It's worse than the Holy Land. At least there I picked up some of the language, but this—" Again he broke off, still shaking his head.

"So speaks an Irishman from London," Rhys said, not unkindly, since Finnian was not the first soldier to express that sentiment.

Finnian's head came up. "Begging your pardon, my lord! I forgot you are one of them!" Then he leaned in to speak conspiratorially. "You're the best of them, I'm sure, and I didn't mean you when I was speaking just now."

This was base flattery, and Rhys told him so. "Stop talking, Finnian—I mean Thomas—before you do yourself an injury."

"Yes, my lord." He straightened his back one more time, but his eyes were amused, and his mouth twitched towards a smile.

Rhys had gone into the interview distrustful, but even though he didn't trust the circumstances that had him meeting outside Rollo's tent a thief who'd changed his name to avoid punishment, Finnian had Rhys believing him. Maybe this one time, coincidences could be ignored.

Maybe.

9

Day One

Catrin

It was nearing the end of the afternoon by the time Catrin walked Joan back to Clare's encampment, since she wasn't entirely sure the other woman would make it on her own with as much as she'd drunk. By the time they arrived, Hugh had arranged for an open-sided tent in which to interview possible witnesses, suspects, and victims of theft, with a chair for Catrin, a table, and stools on which visitors could sit.

Catrin also asked for pen and paper to write down questions and answers. Rhys himself always carried a book in which he wrote about the bodies he examined and the investigations he conducted. As she put another rock on top of a paper she didn't want the wind to take, she was thinking of that book with envy and wondering if it was something she could ask for, either from Queen Eleanor's scribe or the monastery here in Nefyn.

Catrin didn't know how it had happened, but in the last hours, she had been promoted to full-fledged investigator in her own right, and the remarkable thing was that nobody so far had questioned it—except, typically, her own son.

"What are you doing, Mother?" Justin arrived as she was finishing her notes on her conversation with Joan.

She didn't know how much of what she had learned was going to be important, so she'd written down everything she could remember, and it had taken up an entire piece of paper with very small writing. Her hand hurt already. While she'd been working, she had been mentally cast back to her young girlhood when Rhys had shown off his writing and offered to teach her himself, before her father had given in and let her learn alongside her brothers.

Relatively few men were literate, but her father had been a steward to Prince Llywelyn. Reading and writing were required for the position, which her brothers would inherit. Though Rhys's father had been a member of Prince Llywelyn's guard, rather than in the guild of scribes, he'd insisted that Rhys acquire the skill, wanting his son to have abilities that would allow him to rise above other men.

"Working, or about to be."

"It is unseemly, Mother." Justin had a stubborn set to his chin she recognized from childhood and youth—even though he was a married man now—and a tilt to his head that was completely his father.

It hurt, actually, to have him looking at her with such disdain, as if he didn't believe she was capable of intelligent thought. She had hoped she'd raised him to know better.

But if he didn't, she was still his mother and saw no reason why his education shouldn't continue. Her work with Rhys was too important for her to be put off by disapproval, even that of her own son.

"Is it? I'm uncertain why you would say that, since neither the king nor the queen have objected to me accompanying Rhys in his work. I spent twenty years running my own household. I know how to manage people, so I am doing it, Justin."

Justin blinked fast three times, and before he could marshal another objection, she added, "Lord Clare himself showed Rhys and me Rollo's body and the circumstances of his death. Not only do I have the king's approval, but also that of Rollo's lord—and yours, I might add."

It wasn't fair of her, really, to use Clare against Justin, but she wasn't going to stop helping Rhys just because her son wasn't open-minded enough to appreciate his mother's talents. Truly, she would prefer he helped rather than hindered.

To that end, she softened her tone slightly, realizing she might do better with honey than vinegar. He was at that sensitive age when he was coming into his own as a man and assessing his own upbringing. He was also doing it without a living father, so any resentment he might have held for Robert had to be directed instead to her.

"Lord Clare himself made this accommodation for me so I may question witnesses and suspects. I could use your help, actually, if you are willing."

Justin rubbed his chin. "What would you have me do?"

She had the sense that he was asking this with a tinge of condescension, along the lines of, *If you are going to embarrass me this way, I'd better join you to temper the worst of it.*

"At this moment, Rhys is speaking to various men-at-arms within the encampment. You'll be happy to know that such a task was deemed less appropriate for me. I have already spoken to Rollo's sister, who kept house for him. Because theft might be an element in Rollo's murder, we are here now to talk to other men from whom items have been taken. As far as I know, they are all men of standing."

"I see." He nodded, his attention focused on her face. Catrin herself had known nothing about investigating murder before Caernarfon, and if her experience was anything to go by, Justin was in for something of an awakening.

"Sit with me." She pointed to one of the stools, indicating he should move it around the table so he could sit beside her, and then, as he obeyed, smiled to herself that she could still see her curious boy within the man before her. "It may even be that the knight you see approaching will feel better about talking to me with you here."

"It isn't—" He stopped, seeming to think better of his objections—for now. "I will assist in any way I can, Mother." He sat.

She gave no indication of her internal triumph. She loved and admired her son, but he was *oh so predictable*. Though not quite twenty years old, he was extraordinarily mature in some areas and such a boy in others. In encouraging him to stay with her, she had called upon his protective instincts, as well as his curiosity. King Edward's tournament had also hit him in exactly the right spot, as it highlighted all the qualities he was cultivating in himself as a newly dubbed knight: chivalry, loyalty, honesty, and valor. Thanks to the legends of Arthur, these ideals were everything to him now, and the notion that Edward was King Arthur returned, and each of his men a *chevalier* striving to be worthy of the Round Table, had infected the English court.

In fact, she couldn't have asked for a more perfect circumstance in which to try to solve a murder. Her son was living the Arthurian legend, and so were (at least on the surface) all the other knights participating, many of whom would be fighting in one of the events for money and prizes. It was a chance of a lifetime, and not one to be missed by being abrupt, rude, or crude even for a moment—and even if they were surprised to find a woman asking questions in a murder investigation.

Clare was a notable exception to the mood. As an earl, a knight in his own right, and having passed the age of forty, he'd seen too much war and death to believe in heroes anymore, if he ever had. But he appeared to be going along with it anyway, as he always did, barring that moment of independence and insurrection twenty years ago, which had lasted just long enough for her to marry Robert, who served him. Not that she could regret the son who resulted, but *her* life had not been what she wanted. Since then, Clare had decided that cynicism and truth-telling were not a pathway to royal favor.

Rhys might beg to differ.

Regardless, Catrin wasn't going to undermine her son's desire to be the best man he could be, even when the way Edward had stolen Arthur's story from her people offended her deeply.

The knight who'd been making his way towards them ducked under the overhanging edge of the doorway and bowed before her. He was of average height, with a thick neck, hidden by a full beard. He wasn't wearing mail, and she could see the bulge of his bicep through the thin, long-sleeved shirt he wore beneath his tunic, indicating he was well-muscled, as would be the case with any knight who spent his life fighting.

"I am Sir Eustace. Lord Clare asked that I come here." He came up from his bow, and his eyes swept assessingly over her.

"I am Lady Catrin, and I am assisting Sir Rhys, the king's quaestor, in the investigation of Rollo's death." She gestured to Justin. "This is my son, Justin, whom I believe you know."

"Of course." He nodded to Justin, who nodded back. Then he turned back to Catrin. "How may I be of assistance?"

"Please sit." She pointed to the chair on the opposite side of the table, pleased he'd spoken directly to her rather than assuming Justin was in charge. "We understand from Sir Hugh that you are missing a silver cup from your tent."

"Yes, I am." He visibly hesitated, having sat where she indicated, though on the very edge of his seat. "Excuse me, but I have to ask what this is about? I thought I was here to talk about Rollo."

Catrin took a breath, realizing that she was nervous and had launched into her questioning too quickly. She'd been relaxed when she'd spoken to Joan, but this was a different kind of interview, and having her son's observant eyes watching everything she said and did was upending her a bit.

So she bent her head. "Pardon me, Sir Eustace, I would be delighted to hear anything you care to tell us about him."

Eustace shifted backwards on the seat, his hands resting on his thighs, in a more relaxed position than before. "He was a friend, of course."

"You knew him long?"

"Since childhood. Our families held neighboring manors, and it was natural that we would rise together in Lord Clare's service."

"You were under his command?"

As she asked this question, she felt Justin's fingers on her thigh, telling her that either she shouldn't have asked the question or he already knew the answer. She endeavored not to twitch and just smiled sweetly at Eustace as she waited for his reply.

The knight himself didn't seem to think there was anything untoward in her query because he simply laughed. "Oh no. I was my father's heir; Rollo was a younger son. Though we fought together many times, I serve Earl Clare directly as a vassal. Rollo had to earn everything he had, in battle or in tournaments."

"Do you think he resented your divergent paths?"

Eustace didn't object to that question either, since his eyes twinkled. "My *easier* path, do you mean? I would never have said so. Though I must tell you that in recent years we weren't as close as we once had been. After the death of my wife last year I made a foray in his sister's direction, even though she would bring me nothing in the way of inheritance or lands, and Rollo told me flatly not to look that way, that she had sworn never to marry again. I confess it put me off him—and her—a bit."

"You didn't talk directly to Joan? I understand she herself is a widow."

"I did not. I thought to speak to Rollo first." He was implying that to speak directly to Joan would have been a social gaffe.

Catrin pressed her lips together, deliberating with herself as to whether or not she should say something to the contrary. While Joan had indicated she had a lover now, unbeknownst to her brother, who was to say how long that would last or if he was actually suitable. In the end, Catrin told herself it wasn't her place to interfere and merely said, "I spoke to her earlier this afternoon. Regardless of her vision of her future, she might welcome the condolences of a friend. She did just lose her brother."

"You are quite right." Eustace sat up a little straighter. "I will seek her out and ask if I can aid her in any way. We did grow up together too, after all."

Content that she hadn't violated any confidences, Catrin moved on. "When did you last speak to Rollo?"

"I wasn't actively trying to avoid Rollo at this point, you understand, but our circles are different these days, even within Earl Clare's retinue." Now Eustace frowned. "It had been months, perhaps, since I'd spoken to him more than in passing until two days ago when I told him about the loss of my silver cup. I brought few valuables with me to Nevin, barring my purse itself, but my own father won this cup in a tournament many years ago, and I thought it would bring me good luck."

"I'm so sorry." Eustace had segued into the topic on his own, so Catrin took the opportunity to continue her queries about the thefts. "Was Rollo himself investigating the loss?"

"So I understood. I honestly didn't expect anything to come of it. I can't lock my tent, nor is it guarded day and night. We exist on trust here. It is my own fault for bringing the cup in the first place."

"It is the fault of the person who stole it. No one else," Catrin said straightforwardly.

"Thank you. You're right." Eustace bobbed a nod in acknowledgment. "Was anything stolen from Rollo's tent? Is this a matter of being in the wrong place at the wrong time? Could his fate have been mine if I had returned to my tent too soon?"

"I couldn't say." Catrin put out a hand in case he thought she was putting him off. "We don't want to draw any conclusions as yet."

Eustace visibly wavered. "Could he have been killed *because* he was investigating the theft of my cup?"

That thought had occurred to Catrin too. "Again I am so sorry, but we don't know."

She had deliberately said *we* this time, to include Justin, who'd remained silent up until now.

Beside her, he noted the change and straightened in his chair. "If there is any connection between Rollo's death and the theft of your cup, we intend to find it. Time is of the essence if we are to discover Sir Rollo's killer before he can escape or strike again."

"I don't know what more I can offer you in the way of information." Eustace spread his hands wide in the universal gesture of uncertainty. "I myself don't know what to think."

"Is it possible you misplaced the cup?" Justin said.

"Rollo asked me that too, and I told him I didn't see how I could have. It was in my trunk, and then it was gone." He paused. "The trunk itself was locked at the time, and only I have the key." He patted his purse. "I still have it, and it was never apart from me."

"Was the lock forced?" Catrin didn't know enough about thieving to know if a locked trunk would be much of a barrier to a skilled thief. It was also possible a copy of the key could have been made at some point in the past.

"Not that I could see."

"Do you have a servant?" Justin said.

"Yes, of course. Several! But my valet was my father's before me, so he would not have taken it, and my steward has been with me for more than ten years. Neither would betray me that way."

Catrin had to take him at his word, and he was right that the value of a cup was far less than a living in a knight's household. "When exactly was the cup stolen?"

"I had it the evening we arrived, but then it was gone by the time I looked for it two days ago."

"Did you speak to Rollo about it right away?"

"Yes."

"When did you last see him, even if you didn't speak?"

Eustace's mouth pinched as he thought. "I noted him after the evening meal last night. He was mingling with the lower orders, as was his wont."

Catrin tipped her head. "What do you mean by *as was his wont*?"

It was Justin who answered. "Sir Rollo was of a noble family, but he knew trouble could be found at any time of day or night from those of lower birth if they were not kept in check. He saw it as his responsibility to stay apprised of what they were up to."

"Did any confide in him?" If so, it would be rather the opposite of what Hugh had told them, though she didn't say that.

The two men exchanged a look Catrin couldn't read. As vassals and knights in Earl Clare's service, they were of equal stature, though Eustace was twenty years older and therefore had seniority.

"It was more a matter of making sure they knew he was watching them," Eustace said finally. "And I just remembered he mentioned the cup to me earlier that day, during the noon meal. He stopped by my seat as he was passing among the tables and said he thought he knew who might have stolen it. He didn't want to say who it was until he was sure."

"You have no idea who that might have been?" Justin looked beyond Eustace to the camp, his eyes searching, as if he could spy the culprit if he looked hard enough. "Or why Rollo suspected him?"

"No, but this makes me fear even more that the thief knew he was coming for him and murdered him to keep him quiet." He looked hard at Justin. "You must ensure your mother is protected at all times."

Catrin opened her mouth to insist she would be fine, even as Justin nodded. "I will, I assure you."

Eustace now looked at Catrin. "I fear it is too late for you to be safe from this thief's vengeance, if that's the reason Rollo died. It is well known already throughout the camp that you and Sir Reese are involved." He paused again. "I will speak to Reese personally of my concerns as well."

He made to rise, as if he was going to talk to Rhys right then and there. Catrin herself was far less concerned about her safety. She honestly couldn't imagine anything happening to her under such sunny skies, but she supposed Rollo might have felt the same. She glanced down at her notes, trying to think if she had any more questions and wanting to keep him longer, but then Eustace himself settled back onto the chair of his own accord.

"Before I go, may I ask how Rollo died? Regardless of our differences, he was a mighty warrior, and it is dreadful to think of him dying alone in his tent rather than on the field of battle. Was it a fight?"

Catrin gave him a rueful look, thinking Eustace sounded like a pagan warrior of old, who believed the only way to gain admission to Valhalla was to die a valiant death. "I am so sorry, but I can't give you specifics until we know more."

"You're saying the killer surprised him." Eustace's hands clenched into fists. "Something more is going on here. It is not like Rollo to be taken unawares." He looked hard at Catrin and Justin. "When Hugh told me you wanted to speak to me, I was doubtful of what good it would do. I understand better now. We must find this killer before he ruins the Round Table for everyone."

10

Day One

Rhys

Simon, Rhys's friend and commander, rested his arms on the rail that tomorrow would separate the onlookers from the archery butts. At the moment, Rhys had the place to himself. Or would have had, without Simon's arrival.

"I should have known you'd be here, but I confess, this is the last place I looked."

"By definition, the place you found me would be the last place you looked. What you really mean is you looked in every place you could think of before you ended up here." Rhys drew the bowstring to his ear and loosed the arrow. The bell had struck two hours ago for Vespers, but the sun had not yet set, so he was able to follow the arrow's progress through the air and see it hit the target with a satisfying thud. "You're right. You should have known better."

"Can you really see that far?"

"I can." Rhys turned to his friend, his brow furrowing. "You can't?"

Simon squinted and shook his head. "I'm getting old, my friend."

"Good thing you will be fighting only in the mêlée then." Rhys loosed another arrow, to be greeted with another satisfactory *thud*, and then turned to Simon again, rolling his shoulders and shaking out his arms.

He had been shooting steadily for the last hour and had achieved such a rhythm that he'd hit the center target on all of the last ten shots, even with the sun setting directly ahead of him at one point so it shone in his eyes. The best archers claimed all they needed was to sight their target once, and they could shoot at it with accuracy thereafter. Sadly, the best archers were all dead, many on the field at Cilmeri in that last battle against the Mortimers. Those who'd come to Nefyn, Rhys among them, were the dregs.

With his quiver empty, Rhys started across the field towards the row of targets placed sixty yards away. Tomorrow was the initial stage of the tournament, in which Rhys was still scheduled to participate. He would be expected to loose arrows at twenty, thirty, and sixty yards, competing against men from all over Wales and England. Archery contests had never before been a part of an English tournament, never mind one as elevated as a Round Table. Archers were, in the minds of the English nobility, of the lowest order of soldier because they killed from afar. There was no honor in that.

Not that the Welsh cared. It had been skill with a bow that had brought the Welsh forces home time and again.

This week, King Edward was including archery in his tournament in an overt attempt to welcome the Welsh as his newly conquered subjects. Arthur had been magnanimous with his former enemies, and thus, Edward should be too. In addition, the Welsh citizenry of the region would form the bulk of the spectators, since few English common folk would dare cross the wilds of Wales, even from Caernarfon to Nefyn, in order to watch. The Welsh would little understand the jousting, and Catrin's brother Tudur was the only Welsh knight in the mêlée. The archery competition, then, would give them something to care about and men to root for.

Besides, the king had seen the power of the Welsh longbow many times in the war, at Llandeilo Fawr and other places, and he wanted to put that power to use on his own behalf. The competition was a means to identify the best archers left in Wales.

Over the course of three days, archers would shoot against one another in heats until two contestants were left. These last two would compete on the final day in front of the king himself for a hundred pennies and a silver arrow trophy.

Only a fool would turn down that kind of money. Welsh archers would come. And why not? It wasn't as if Rhys was doing anything different.

Admittedly, Rhys hadn't wanted to participate in the first place and initially had declined to do so. But he served the king now, and Edward had insisted. Once committed, it was a matter of pride that he do his very best. He didn't need to be among the final two, but at the very least he didn't want to be put out on the first day.

Simon had sauntered after Rhys across the field, and now he laughed out loud at the sight of the arrows clustered together in the white dot that formed the center of the target. "You're going to win, aren't you?"

"I hope not." Rhys started tugging the arrows out of the sacking. "It would be better if I didn't. While I don't want to embarrass myself or the king, I don't have time for this, not with a murder to investigate."

"I heard." Simon spoke in a dry tone. "I spoke to Catrin already."

Rhys glanced at him. "I am in a fretful mood today, aren't I?"

"I wouldn't say it was just today."

Rhys laughed. "It's a wonder you put up with me."

"I have known you a long time." Simon was still being serious. "It's Catrin I'm concerned about."

Rhys froze. "Has she said anything to you?"

"About you? No, but you might think about mending your ways before it's too late and one of these many eligible men catches her eye with laughter instead of grimness."

"I was working on it today already, because she did mention it to me." Rhys blew out a breath and put his heels together in order to bow to Simon. "The reprimand is noted and accepted."

"It isn't that you have to be happy all the time, Reese, but you could laugh like you did just now every once in a while." Simon flung out his arms. "It's a festival!"

"I do remember that." Rhys scratched at his hairline with the point of one of the arrows. "Was there a particular reason you sought me out?"

"Someone came to see me, in hopes of speaking to you in private."

Rhys found himself curious. "Someone? That's an odd way to put it."

By way of an answer, Simon whistled towards the viewing stand.

King Edward had put on tournaments before, but only one, to celebrate his marriage to Eleanor, had been a *Round Table*. As the first such event since then, and the first since his conquest of Wales, no expense was being spared this week. That included the building of a raised, two-story viewing stand, twenty-four feet by twelve, set on the edge of one of the fields that would host the tournament and adjacent to the market fair on the outskirts of the little village.

Edward, his nobles, and their ladies would be able to watch the martial events from the main level, some four feet above the grass and protected from sun and rain by a second story above them, on which lesser nobles, along with the judges, could observe the various contests. Cleverly, the field that would host the jousting and archery competitions was located on one side of the stand, while the mêlée would take place on the other, in a different field, oddly shaped like a herring. Thus, simply by turning around, spectators could watch one and then the other within the comfort of the viewing stand. It was also where the bardic competition had taken place earlier that day, with spectators standing fifteen deep on the ground below it.

After a few moments, a man appeared around the corner, the last rays of the sun gleaming off the silver in what had once been entirely black hair. "*Someone* meaning *an old friend*."

"By all that is holy! How are you still alive?" Rhys's mouth opened in surprise as the man came to a halt in front of him.

"Is that any way to greet a fellow crusader?" With good humor, the man gazed into Rhys's face. Despite his age, they were still of a height, and he was unbowed, even after all these years.

The crusades had attracted more than their share of disreputable types—some seeking absolution for crimes committed at home, some outright villains, and some merely picked up among the riffraff on the street, when the king had asked for recruits, and offered coin in exchange for service.

Finnian had been one of the latter, a petty criminal, but Ned had been a master thief—and as brave a man as any Rhys had ever known. While Finnian had been given ample opportunity to polish his craft amongst his fellow soldiers, Ned had used the skills he'd honed on the docks of London to become a spy for Edward, until he'd been recognized as such one day in a Saracen camp. He'd barely escaped with his life and spent many days in the desert before returning to Acre.

This had been before Rhys's elevation to quaestor, and he could still picture in his mind's eye Ned staggering through the city on the arm of Prince Edmund's old investigator, Henry, who'd ridden into the desert to find him. Unfortunately, Henry had suffered heat stroke on the journey, and the ironic aftermath was that Ned had lived, and Henry had died.

These events had occurred after Qaqun. It was because Henry had been ill and his second so inadequate that Rhys had taken it upon himself to track down a murderer, the doing of which had brought him again to the prince's attention.

"You look well, Ned."

It was no less than the truth. The man's liquid brown eyes and sprightly step belied his many years of hard living. After his near-death experience, he'd disappeared, never to be heard from again, at least to Rhys's knowledge—until now.

"Thank you, my lord. Though the name is Alard. I would be grateful if you would be so kind as to refer to me as such in future."

Rhys shook his head wonderingly at Alard's transformation—and wondered too how he was going to keep these name changes straight. Finnian had become Thomas. Ned had become Alard. Last he'd seen *Ned turned Alard*, he'd been wearing the robes of a Muslim. Now he was dressed in the tunic and boots of someone who was accustomed to prosperity.

"What are you doing here?"

"Reese, he is Sir Eustace's steward," Simon said.

Rhys found his mouth genuinely dropping open. "The Eustace whose silver cup was stolen?"

Eustace had sought him out after his interview with Catrin. Though Rhys had skipped the evening meal tonight in favor of a little archery, he'd made sure her son was watching over her, both of them concerned about her safety.

"The one and the same, my lord!" Alard bowed. "And I assure you I had nothing to do with it."

Rhys canted his head. "I am to believe you based on our old acquaintance?"

"Why would I endanger my place in the retinue of an honorable knight for the pennies I could make from thieving from my own master?"

"It's more than pennies, so you'll have to do better than that." Rhys's eyes narrowed, not trusting the way Alard had answered his question with another question. It was a noted practice of liars. "You were an accomplished criminal all those years ago. I need a better reason to believe you."

Alard closed the distance between them and lowered his voice. "I was never a murderer, my lord—or no more than the next man. No more than you! My life before the crusade is a distant memory, and in the Holy Land, I did nothing more than what my prince asked. I see you are here in his service once again and can say the same."

"On the whole, you are correct, though I am in King Edward's service these days, not Prince Edmund's." Rhys's shoulders fell. "And I am not the same man I was any more than you say you are."

"Better that you aren't," Alard's tone was light-hearted and implied unconcern, "and better for me as well. It was a blessing, really, to have been caught in that camp. After I escaped, I couldn't go back to it. I hired myself on to a merchant vessel, which took me home. I knew I had to mend my ways. I was getting slower, see. Life was no longer a lark."

"How did you end up in Sir Eustace's company?"

"That would be telling, wouldn't it, my lord?" He grinned mischievously. "I couldn't go to anyone who'd fought with the princes, so I kept moving west and ended up in Bristol. Since Lord Clare had taken the cross but then declined to go, I figured I was finally on safe ground. I put out that I'd had trouble finding work since my last master died at Evesham. As Eustace's father had died in the fighting, along with so many others, he appreciated my suffering."

Evesham had been the final battle in the Second Baron's War—the war that had split England in two and had sent Catrin into a marriage with one of Clare's men all those years ago. "So Eustace doesn't know you were in the Holy Land?"

"He does not, and I'd like to keep it that way, my lord, if you would be so kind."

Rhys glanced at Simon. "Why did you bring him to me if you think he has nothing to do with the thefts and Rollo's murder?"

"Enough storytelling, Alard." Simon gave Ned his new name. "Tell him what you know."

Alard seemed to appreciate that he'd reached the end of the rope Rhys had extended to him, and it was time he climbed up it or hanged himself. "I lived in the underbelly of London once, it's true. And though I have long since risen above those times and those men, I remember them. I can't tell you who is behind Rollo's murder or these thefts, but I have heard rumors of such men. You need to know that the one behind this is not like the rest of us."

"How so?"

Alard was standing a foot away now, as if he was afraid of being overheard, even in the middle of the archery field. The sun had finally gone down behind the houses to the west, though it had not yet sunk completely into the sea. Opposite, the moon was visible against the darkening sky. With the beautiful weather, they might not need a torch to see tonight.

"He has no honor."

Seeing that Rhys was about to scoff, Alard put out a hand. "It isn't what you think, my lord! There is honor among thieves! We don't steal from our own. We don't carry weapons beyond a short knife to cut our bonds if we are caught, and we certainly don't kill. It's bad for business." Rhys didn't necessarily disbelieve the rest of what he'd said, and he could well imagine Alard had glossed over a great number of sins to get to this point, but his use of *we* spoke true. "This thief of yours. He plans, you see. And he knows how to pick a lock."

Simon frowned. "What is this *pick a lock*? What does that mean?"

"The trunk in which Eustace's cup was kept was locked. Either he or I hold the key at all times, and neither of us left it about. But still, the thief got into it. No ordinary thief would know how to do that. He is skilled in a way few men are."

"Do you have that ability?" Rhys asked.

Alard bent his head modestly. "I do, and before you ask, I still keep in practice, never knowing when such a skill might come in handy. But as you can see, I would not have had to pick the lock to steal the cup, not when I have free access to the key."

Rhys continued to believe him, though not because he reeked of sincerity, nor perhaps for the reasons he'd so far put forward. It was not unheard of for a culprit to insert himself into an investigation. But if Alard had stolen the cup, Rhys couldn't believe he would have risked seeking Rhys out, even to head off later questioning.

"So who is he?" Rhys asked.

"I don't know. Truthfully, I'm surprised one such as he would come all this way into Wales. It's a tournament, yes, but the crowds are small compared to London or Winchester, and while the wealth represented here is significant, it is harder to hide amongst so few common folk and so many great men."

Rhys's eyes met Simon's, and slowly, Simon nodded, reading Rhys's expression correctly. "Unless he had to come because he's one of us."

11

Day One

Catrin

At first, Catrin was annoyed at Rhys for skipping the meal, but he redeemed himself later by appearing at her side and suggesting they remove themselves to the viewing stand on the tournament grounds where an evening of dancing had just begun.

"How is it that in all of the last months in your company, we have never danced?" she asked.

"You know I am capable."

"I do know." She herself had taught him all those years ago, though now she wondered if, in fact, he hadn't already been learning himself and had merely allowed her to think she was a good teacher.

"I would have if you'd asked, though it isn't as if there's been ample opportunity."

It was her own fault for assuming he had either forsworn dancing at some point in the last twenty years or decided he wasn't good enough to do it in public.

And he was right that there had been a shortage of dancing these last months in the king's company. Though the common soldiers who accompanied them to Llyn Cwm Dulyn enjoyed revelries nearly every night, these were not for the likes of Rhys and Catrin. And while there'd been dancing at the king's forty-fifth birthday celebration, that was the one night she'd been barred from the festivities—not because of something she'd done, but because little Prince Edward had been colicky, and the only way he would settle down was if she held him and sang to him in Welsh. The moment she put him in his cradle, he would wake and cry again, so she'd ended up holding him the whole evening until his mother returned.

"I'll have you know I was once considered to be a civilized man." Rhys bowed over her hand and drew her out of the pavilion.

The musicians had set up on one side of the main level of the viewing stand, with dancers filling the rest of the space and even more dancers thronging the floor above, which was entirely open to the night air. It wasn't cold tonight, and even if it were, the dancers were generating quite enough warmth on their own, to the point that the pounding of their boots on the wooden floor was almost drowning out the music itself. To the Welsh, that would have been considered almost sacrilegious, but the English had their own traditions. Sometimes dancing was an elegant affair, but today, Catrin found the exuberance appealing.

"Shall we go all the way up?" Rhys asked.

"There's too many people up there already. We'd get run over!" The beat of the drum was tugging Catrin to join in, and she led

Rhys to a spot that had opened up on the first floor in the outside circle of the three rings of dancers.

She and Rhys clasped hands with the other dancers, who were moving to the beat of the drum and singing at the top of their lungs in French and English, uncaring of the cacophony they were creating. It was exhilarating to be part of it, to be one with the crowd and with Rhys—up until a great creaking sound came from the ceiling, which was also the floor for the story above them.

"What was that?" At first Catrin thought she was the only one who'd heard it, because she was the only one who faltered, but then Rhys pulled her out of the circle of dancers, looking up towards the ceiling as he did so.

By now more people were looking up. Then another creak sounded so loud that the musicians stopped playing. In fact, everyone stopped, even those who hadn't heard, which probably saved more than one life, because there was a general flurry to back away from the center of the floor.

Then the air was split by a loud *snap*, like a thunderclap, and the ceiling collapsed, scattering the dancers below like seeds on the wind.

Afterwards, Catrin could only be thankful for the two creaking warnings, which had allowed Rhys's instincts to take over. In the instant before the ceiling fell, he'd grasped Catrin's waist, spun her around, and thrown them both towards the edge of the viewing stand. If he'd waited even a heartbeat longer, they might have been among those caught by the collapsing ceiling.

As it was, he managed to wrap Catrin up in his arms and fall with her the four feet from the first floor to the ground below. They hit the grass with a thud and rolled, ending up with Rhys flat on his back and Catrin on top of him.

For a moment, Rhys was so still beneath her that Catrin's heart raced even more to think he'd been hurt. She knew him well enough to know that his entire goal had been to protect her. But an ear to his chest told her his heart still beat, and then his chest rose and fell with a deep breath.

Then he moaned.

"Are you all right?" She touched his face, desperate to hear him speak.

"I had the wind knocked out of me, that's all. How are you?"

"Me? It's you I'm worried about." She patted him down, searching for wounds.

He grasped one of her hands. "I'm fine. I'm not hurt."

She didn't see any blood, so she was willing to accept he was telling her the truth. It didn't feel as if anything important was broken anyway. And he'd been clever enough to take the fall on his left shoulder instead of his right, which he needed undamaged to pull the bowstring tomorrow.

Catrin's eyes now went to the viewing stand and the people still on and around it. "What happened?"

Rhys pushed up on his elbows for a first look. Most of the people had already escaped, but even so, the viewing stand shuddered again as the last of the dancers on the top floor hammered down the stairs as quickly as they could. This stairway was external to the structure and provided direct access to the ground without going through the main floor first.

Once on her feet, Catrin found herself trembling, but rather than make known how shaky she was, she rubbed her arms to warm them. Now wasn't the time for weakness. Rhys himself had already made a beeline towards a four-year-old child who was standing on the very edge of the viewing stand, crying.

"Where's your mother?"

The little one pointed a finger, looking one way and then the other, and then started crying harder. Rhys grasped him around the hips and lifted him down. "We'll find her."

Ralph, another of the king's men, popped out from the crowd and ran the last few steps to where she stood. "What should I do?"

Catrin wasn't surprised Ralph was the first to volunteer. Just past thirty, he was thoughtful and even a bit wise, which was remarkable given that he was also nephew to Otto de Grandison, the new Justiciar of North Wales. Neither Otto nor Ralph spoke Welsh nor even English, being Savoyards from France. Catrin had a sick feeling that Gwynedd was going to suffer terribly under Otto's rule, but that wouldn't be Ralph's fault. And so far, the young man had proved to be an able officer in the king's guard.

The guards themselves worked in shifts, in a rotating schedule worked out by Simon, their commander. Rhys was off the duty roster for as long as this investigation was ongoing, as well as because he was competing in the tournament. It seemed that Ralph had been given the evening off as well.

Not for long.

"We need one of the king's physicians, if he can be given leave to come. And Simon."

"I will see to it."

For her part, Catrin found a toehold two feet off the ground and hoisted herself into the viewing stand. It was a terribly unlady-like move, but a small crowd had gathered around the stairs to gawk, and she was afraid that if she used the steps to enter the viewing stand, others might decide to follow. By now, all the participants on both floors had scattered except for those who stayed because they were unable to leave.

"Careful, Catrin." Rhys had approached without her noticing, and now he levered himself up beside her by the mere strength of his arms. If she'd waited another few moments, he could have given her a boost. "You don't know how much more could come down."

The ceiling had been supported by seven big beams, but one end of the center beam now rested on the floor before her. It had brought down with it an eight-by-twelve foot section of the second story.

Thankfully, the whole structure had not collapsed or the number of casualties would have been much greater. As it was, danc-ers on the second story had fallen with the beam, or slid down the slope it created. Some had even rolled off the first floor onto the grass four feet below.

Where a moment before a hundred people had been dancing, now lay broken boards.

And five bodies.

12

Day One

Rhys

"**H**arry!" A woman peered down at them from the story above.

"Stay away from the edge!" Rhys waved her off, but then reconsidered. "Please come down. You shouldn't be up there anymore."

He heard a faint, "Yes, my lord."

She retreated to reappear a few moments later on the stairs, hurrying down them to the ground. Then, without asking permission, she elbowed her way through the crowd and came up the steps Rhys and Catrin had eschewed to reach the main floor.

Typically, in the brief moments Rhys had been talking to the woman, Catrin had left the safety of the post by which she'd been standing and knelt beside the nearest of the fallen dancers, a woman in a green dress, which was cut low enough to reveal the swell of her breasts. Her blonde hair was tinged with blood.

Catrin put a hand to the woman's neck. "She's alive!" Then she draped a length of her own hair, which was in its usual disarray, across the woman's lips. As Rhys watched, the ends of Catrin's hair wafted upwards, indicating the woman was breathing. "I think she's just knocked out."

"Which one is Harry?" Rhys turned to the woman who'd called down from the second story.

"Over there!" The woman made to move towards a man lying on his stomach, but Rhys stuck out a hand, blocking her progress across the floor.

"Stay back. Please!" It made no sense to injure more people in the rescue of those already hurt.

Rhys assumed the man was dead, but as Rhys patted his sides and then gently rolled him over, he elicited a moan.

The woman screeched with joy, prompting the man to open his eyes. "Elena?"

Two other victims had started making noise as well. One of these also had an anxious woman on the sidelines. In her case, however, rather than sobbing in relief as Elena had done that her husband was alive, once her man started moving, she shrieked invective, "I told you not to stand there, Tom! Didn't I tell you not to stand there!"

Leaving Harry to Elena, Rhys moved to crouch beside the beleaguered Tom.

"It's my leg," he said, blinking himself more awake. "I can't move it."

The leg in question was turned underneath him at an awkward angle, so Rhys gently shifted the injured man so he could lie flat on his back. Once straightened, the leg turned out to be merely wrenched. It was his ankle that was the bigger problem, since it was swelling up in a way that turned Rhys's stomach.

A fourth person, an older man with a beard shot with gray, lay barely conscious on his side, with the whole of the right side of his body bloody. Rhys was almost afraid to touch him, and a quick look under his shirt revealed a side full of splinters. None seemed so deep as to have severed a vein, and he didn't want to bandage him out of fear of further driving any of the splinters into his flesh.

Really, everyone in the whole place, not just the injured, were lucky to be alive.

"I sent Ralph to get a physician, but we could probably use the village healer too." Catrin covered the unconscious woman with her own cloak and then rose to her feet, ready to head off into the night on a quest to find her.

But she pulled up short at the sight of Simon coming up the steps into the viewing stand and nodded when he said, "I have already sent someone."

"Thank you for coming personally," Rhys said.

"I come when you call," Simon said simply, though truly the statement was as profound a one as could possibly be made about their relationship. Rhys hoped Simon knew that he himself would come if it were Simon doing the calling—and not just because Simon was his superior officer.

Simon took in the scene with a sweeping glance, and then took charge, barking at some of the onlookers to make themselves useful by acquiring stretchers. These would be a tarp slung between two poles and available in the storage shed located at one end of the viewing stand. The medical tent wasn't far away either, ready and waiting for the great number of men who would be injured in the jousting that started tomorrow. Hopefully, the archery competition would be a much safer event.

Typically prepared, Simon had also brought a force of men to disperse the crowd, or at the very least to push them back. Now that the initial shock had passed, people were pressing close all around the viewing stand. Some had climbed the exterior stairs that led to the second floor in order to give themselves a better vantage point from which to observe the injured people and the damage to the viewing stand. Fortunately, none had been so foolish as to actually walk across the upper floor and look down through the gap, though likely they would have done so soon enough if Simon hadn't brought men to stop them.

By now the injured, those who were conscious anyway, were starting to want to move even if they shouldn't. Trying to be reassuring, Catrin hovered between the still unconscious woman and the man with the splinters in his side, who was continuing to moan in pain.

Meanwhile, Rhys went to the fifth victim, a boy of fifteen, who was clutching a drum to his chest. He had been leaned against a post this entire time, to all appearances unharmed, though neither had he stood up. Rhys decided it was past time to pay attention to why he hadn't.

"Sut wyt ti?" *How are you,* he asked in Welsh.

His guess as to the boy's origins proved accurate. "Dw i ddim yn gwybod." *I don't know.* The boy's eyes had widened as Rhys had spoken, and now he added in Welsh. "You're the kingsman."

"I am." In the presence of others, Rhys no longer masked his concern for his own people to the extent that he once had, but he still eyed the boy a bit warily as he added, "Do I sense disapproval in your voice?"

"No." The single word was said so flatly, Rhys didn't know if he should believe him. But then his explorations under the boy's coat revealed a jagged, foot-long splinter that had jabbed itself through the tissue along the his right rib cage and come out the other side. It wasn't a life-threatening wound necessarily, but at the sight of it, Rhys cast around for a cloth to stem the bleeding. Noting his quest, Catrin tossed him a woman's headscarf, which had been discarded on the floor.

Rhys began to sop up the blood, keeping his attention on the wound instead of the boy's face. "Is there something you want to say to me?"

"I want to say *thank you.* Actually, I need to say it, and I am ashamed that I have not done so until now."

That brought up Rhys's head. "You know me?"

"I know everyone." He was holding himself very stiffly, which Rhys would have been doing too if he had a giant splinter shoved through his skin. Then the boy tipped his head, "Old Dafi is my uncle. I'm named for him. He told me what you did."

Rhys bent his head to the wound again, any remaining wariness leaving him like air departing a popped soap bubble. Young Dafi's uncle had been falsely accused of murder in Caernarfon and been released because of Catrin's and Rhys's efforts to find the real killer.

That Rhys was meeting Dafi's nephew in Nefyn was far less of a coincidence than seeing the fellow crusaders Thomas and Alard (formerly Finnian and Ned) had been. Gwynedd had a small population relative to almost anywhere, and everybody knew everyone else—and likely was related to most everyone else. "Give him my best the next time you see him."

"Will I see him again?" Dafi was trying not to look at his wound, but his eyes kept skating to it.

"Ach." Rhys tucked the boy under his chin with a gentle forefinger. "Once I get the healer here, we'll pull this out. In a day or two you'll hardly remember how you got it."

Dafi attempted a laugh, but his hand came up to his belly at the pain it caused. "Don't!"

Rhys grinned, pleased to see the boy's mood improving. Over the years, he'd found that at times the attitude of a wounded man had as large a say over whether or not he survived an injury as the wound itself. Rhys was capable of removing the splinter, but he would prefer to have a discussion with a healer first. What he didn't want to do was pull it out and leave even a single fleck of wood behind that could fester and lead to death.

To keep Dafi talking, he asked, "When you said you knew everyone, you meant that literally, didn't you?" After the boy nodded, Rhys indicated Simon. "Who's he?"

"The captain of the king's guard, Simon Boydell."

It was a good start. "Tell me the name of some of the injured."

"The blonde woman Lady Catrin is tending is called Alice. She's married to a big fellow named Bob." He proceeded to relate the identity of everyone within hailing distance, on sight, with no hesitation.

"How do you know all this?"

He shrugged. "I remember people. Their faces. Their names. I'm terrible with numbers though."

"You can read?"

"My father is a bard."

Which was all the explanation needed. Even the lowest bard was among the more educated Welshmen, and a free man to boot.

"I can also speak French."

That *was* a skill, but no surprise given Dafi's prodigious memory. He'd probably learned it in the last three days from listening to the people around him.

Simon's orders proved sufficient to move the gawkers farther away, and soon Rhys too was edged out by the gentle hands of a more knowledgeable healer. The king retained three physicians, all trained outside of England, and all deemed the best in the world at their craft. Alexandre, who was from Gascony, was the king's personal physician, and the other two administered to the royal household and were there for Alexandre to consult if needed.

One wore a yellow badge marking him as a Jew, and Rhys nodded to him in acknowledgment as he crouched beside young Dafi. Rhys and Josef were each unique to their kind within the king's retinue, and Rhys liked the older man very much. He also thought he was the most skilled healer of the bunch, despite Alexandre's reputation, and he was glad that Josef had made for Dafi's side.

Rhys showed Josef Dafi's wound, stayed until he was sure he didn't need to translate the conversation between them, and then held Dafi's hand as he was loaded onto a stretcher. The splinter would be removed once they repaired to the hospital tent. Although a few torches flared—they were honestly lucky the collapse hadn't taken a torch with it and caught the structure on fire—the light inside the viewing stand was too dim for a painstaking procedure like Dafi needed.

Suddenly surplus to requirements, Rhys glanced towards Catrin, who was crouched on the edge of the stand, speaking softly in Welsh to Wena, Nefyn's village midwife and healer, who was standing below her in the grass. They'd introduced themselves to her the first day they'd arrived in Nefyn, since they made a point to acquaint themselves with the local people wherever they went. Rhys vaguely remembered her from his visits to Nefyn as part of Llywelyn's *teulu* (his personal guard, in the same manner Rhys now served King Edward), but they'd never spoken before a few days ago.

Not wanting to interfere in their conversation, Rhys made his way to where Simon was standing in the middle of the floor, looking up at the starry sky through the newly made hole in the ceiling. His hands were on his hips and a frown on his face. "How could this have happened?"

"The dancing *was* vigorous. I myself was witness to it."

Simon dropped his gaze to look at Rhys. "Don't placate me. You don't believe this was an accident any more than I do," he stomped a foot, "especially knowing that tomorrow the king would have been sitting right here!"

13

Day One
Catrin

From behind her, Catrin heard Simon speculate that the failure of the second story floor wasn't an accident. She translated the French, which Simon and Rhys had been speaking, for Wena.

"Can you tell us anything about this, anything at all?"

For a moment, Wena stayed silent, her eyes on Catrin's face. "You can't be asking me to inform on one of our own people. I wouldn't, even if I knew anything, which I don't." Her refusal would have been clear on her face, even if it hadn't been in her words.

Catrin had to acknowledge Wena's dilemma, and she herself would feel the same conflict if she and Rhys had to bring a Welsh culprit to justice. If they did, would their own people ever trust them again?

No, they would not.

"Murder is murder, Wena. I don't care if the murderer is a farmer, a herder, a member of the king's guard, or an earl. Nobody has the right to take another person's life in cold blood, and this—" she gestured behind her, "was sheer cowardice."

"Some would say war makes its own rules."

"We lost the war," Catrin said flatly. "Our prince is dead, and there is none to take his place."

Wena's chin jutted out. "So you say."

Catrin flung out a hand to point to the Welsh boy, who was being carried from the viewing stand. "Is he merely a casualty, to be accounted towards the cost of freeing Wales?"

"Some would say so." Wena pressed her lips together. "There's a price to pay for cooperating with the Saxons."

She was speaking in Welsh so used the word *Saesneg*, what the Welsh had been calling the interlopers from the east long before today. To the Welsh, there was little difference between a Saxon and a Norman, never mind that the Normans had conquered the Saxons too.

It was in Catrin's mind that her people had spent so many years at war with men beyond Offa's Dyke that they'd become inured to it and couldn't tell when the tenor of it had changed. In drive and ability, Edward was unlike all of his predecessors, with the possible exception of William the Conqueror himself. For the Welsh, those qualities had been a deadly combination many hadn't recognized until far too late.

"Some *would* say so, but I don't think that young boy thought by coming here today he was enjoined in battle."

"Some would say by coming here today he was consorting with the enemy."

Catrin nodded. "They would say that, in the same way they would accuse Rhys and me of betraying our people because we also serve the king."

Not everyone, especially this far out on the Llyn Peninsula, where there had been little to no fighting, realized how few choices she and Rhys had in the matter.

"But I don't agree that we can focus only on the goal and not on the means to achieve it. We would lose too much in the process." She leaned closer. "Wena, we are all subjects of the king now. Until the king's arrival in Nefyn, you here could pretend that nothing had changed, but there is no prince in that palace anymore."

It was the truth, harsh as it might be, but likely Catrin shouldn't have said it, because it made Wena's chin jut out stubbornly again. "Then what do we do? Roll over and die?"

"I didn't say that. At one time I wondered the same thing." She paused, watching Wena's face. "I can tell you what Rhys has said, to me and to others: *We win by surviving. Even more, we win by living.*"

Wena looked away. "What if I say it isn't living to live like this."

"There's an argument for that. And if a Welshman sabotaged the viewing stand, it might be his: kill the king, and they'll leave us alone. And if he dies in the attempt, so be it." She raised one shoulder. "What that possible Welshman doesn't acknowledge, however, is that the future he creates could be far worse than what we have up until now experienced."

Wena shot her a disbelieving look. "How could it be worse?"

"Oh, Wena." Catrin shook her head. "It can always be worse. Just ask all those Welsh lords who betrayed Llywelyn for Edward because they objected to how Llywelyn ruled and what he demanded of them." She laughed outright. "Not so happy now, are they? Not quite the land of milk and honey under Edward's rule they thought they were getting, is it?"

"Is that how you see it? I am not the only one who's wondering how Rhys alone survived Cilmeri," Wena's eyes had already narrowed, but now they turned to slits, "Or how it is that your brother, alone of all our Welsh lords in Gwynedd, landed on his feet."

Catrin pressed her lips together, knowing neither Rhys nor her brother wanted her to explain. Rhys was too scarred by those events to want to speak of them, and Tudur had commanded that his continued loyalty to Llywelyn, even in death, *not* become common knowledge.

She'd begged her brother to let it be known, but he'd refused.

"When people look back on this time, they will see you as a traitor, a Judas!"

"As they should. I am a traitor."

She'd stopped begging then and stared at him as comprehension dawned. "You're punishing yourself."

He hadn't replied, but she could see in his face that she was right.

"I do what I must for the survival of our people."

Deep down, Catrin understood.

Her entire adult life, she too had walked a narrow path between her duty to her husband or the Queen of England, whom she now served, and the needs of her own people. It was one thing to help a young woman find employment as a nanny for a noble family, or to suggest to the cook in the castle kitchen that he purchase eggs from a local source she knew. She sat in a position of privilege and authority, and she always helped when she could. Truthfully, she helped disadvantaged English people too. But the stakes were greater now. In Caernarfon, she and Rhys had focused their efforts on protecting members of the Welsh populace, sometimes with real risk to themselves.

Saying anything along those lines to Wena, however, would come out sounding defensive. "What's done is done. What matters now is that we survive as a people."

"Is that why you think this can't have been an accident?" Wena indicated the fallen pieces of ceiling and floor.

"Others have tried to kill the king before. We don't know enough yet, and we shouldn't begin by dismissing the possibility this was another attempt."

"You mean someone has tried to kill him before he came to Wales?" Wena's lip curled. "The Saxons want him dead too?"

"Some do. Any royal court, even Prince Llywelyn's in its day, is a hotbed of competing interests and rivals. Nobody else has a more legitimate claim to Edward's throne, but some might find a weaker king, and particularly a younger one, more amenable to suggestion.

Others might go so far as to aspire to the regency. Edward's heir, Alphonso, is ten years old. The regent would have many years to establish himself powerfully at court and in England before the prince came of age."

"You know so much about these *mochyn*." There it was, the Welsh word for *pig* and the near universal epithet to refer to Normans.

Catrin made a shushing motion with her hand, looking around at who might have been close enough to listen. Simon, for one, understood it to be a derogatory term.

"You really are cowed, aren't you?"

"I suppose I am, but I am also smart. What purpose does being overt serve, other than to call attention to yourself? Better to be quiet and subtle. I can do more good for longer if I don't offend."

Wena wrinkled her nose, unconvinced, but then she said. "I respect what you've told me, and I will not speak against you to our people, but you are on your own in this investigation. If this was done by one of us, I would never say so."

"I understand, believe me, I do, and I appreciate you telling me so directly." Catrin let out a breath. She also appreciated that Wena had said *our* and *us*. Catrin hadn't become completely foreign in her people's eyes, not yet. "I must warn you, however, that if it comes to light that a Welshman did this, the whole village will be punished, if not all of Gwynedd."

"That's what they always say to get one of us to betray our own people."

She wasn't wrong, and Catrin bit her lip, regretting her frankness, because Wena now drew visibly away.

"I'm sorry." Catrin put out a hand. "I won't ask you about this again, but I do hope you will go to the tent where they are taking the Welsh boy. I hope you won't punish him for being in the wrong place at the wrong time."

"As if I would." Wena looked indignant. "What do you take me for?"

Catrin's expression was full of regret. "You did say that he was a casualty of war."

"I said *some* would say he was. I did not say I was one of them, and even if I did, I have a sworn duty to heal, not harm." She abruptly turned on her heel and marched away.

"Please let me know how he does," Catrin called to her retreating back.

Wena waved a hand, indicating she'd heard, but such was her disrespect for Catrin personally that she didn't turn around. Regardless of Wena's pledge not to speak against her directly, the healer's attitude would be more common than not, and the rest of the citizens of Nefyn might close themselves off to her as well.

With a sigh, Catrin straightened, grimacing to find her knees stiff from crouching for so long, and moved back to where Rhys and Simon were still talking. By now, all of the injured had been removed to the healer's tent, and the spectators had finally dispersed. There wasn't anything exciting to see any longer, and few things were more boring than watching people talk quietly to one another. Several soldiers remained on watch on the periphery of the viewing stand, giving Rhys, Catrin, and Simon privacy. Simon took up a position against one of the posts, near where Catrin herself had stood earlier, and Rhys circled the fallen planks.

"What did she say?" Simon asked Catrin as they watched Rhys bend first to one broken board and then another.

"If Wena knows something about what happened here, she isn't telling. And won't tell if she learns something new."

Simon turned to look at Catrin fully. "Not even to you?"

"She made it clear that if a Welshman is involved, she will never say."

Simon continued to give her a disbelieving stare, so Catrin sighed again and added, "This isn't Caernarfon, Simon. Rhys and I have no history here, and we are with you, which puts us immediately under suspicion. Wena welcomed me initially, as one Welsh woman to another, but I am in the queen's service, and Rhys is a kingsman. Many nights I sing Prince Edward to sleep! Far worse, Rhys's job is not only to protect the king but to seek out anyone who might want to harm him. All those here, to the youngest child, would much prefer Rhys fail utterly."

Simon rubbed his chin. "Without the king, there'd be chaos."

"In England, maybe." Catrin studied him. She didn't know him as well as Rhys did, but she'd spent many months in his company and felt she knew who he was now, even if, unlike Rhys, his past was the realm of stories. "But Wena thinks—and likely she isn't wrong—that *someone* would rise to lead us here in Wales and hold off your forces for a time, since they'd be leaderless. Henry de Lacy would attempt to carve out a kingdom for himself, as would Bohun,

Mortimer, Valence, Clare, and all the rest. But those Marcher lords would not unite, and it would be more likely than not that they'd be too busy fighting over the throne or the regency to do more than defend what they already have. Nefyn would be free, for a time at least." She paused as Simon ran a hand through his hair. "You know it's true."

"I do know it." He dropped his arm. "You trouble me."

"Such was not my intent, but you *are* here, and if you are to protect the king, *that* is the reality. In Nefyn, even a thousand years from now, you and your kind will be viewed as foreign."

"Is she right?" He glanced at Rhys, who'd straightened from a crouch.

"Yes, she is right," he said without emphasis.

Catrin and Rhys exchanged a look, in which she read Rhys as really saying, "She'd *better* be right, or everything we're doing for our people will come to naught."

He didn't say that, even to as close a friend as Simon, and instead added, "I'm surprised you had to ask."

Simon continued to look a bit put out by their conversation, and Catrin debated whether or not to elaborate further. On one hand, the more people like him knew the truth of her people, the better they would be able to control them. But on the other, talking to Simon about them would also mean he, as a friend, would better understand her and Rhys. While the two of them had survived for a long time on their own, this was a new world they were living in, and at least a small part of the reason they had agreed to serve the king and queen so closely was to facilitate understanding between their peoples.

They couldn't stop Wales from being conquered by England, but they could mitigate the effects. When the big things were out of one's control, the little things started to matter more. Which was essentially what she'd try to explain to Wena.

"The hatred Wena bears for Edward and every *Saxon*, as she calls you, when she isn't calling you a *mochyn*, isn't going away any time soon, Simon. You have conquered Wales, and the people are well and truly cowed, as Wena herself just accused me of being. Clare thinks the encampment is vulnerable to attack, but he's wrong. The Welsh are too scattered and leaderless.

"Then again, he isn't wrong in principle. The Welsh have fallen under the king's boot, but someone, sometime, will seek to rise again."

Catrin just stopped herself at the last moment from saying *we* instead of *the Welsh*. As one of those conquered people, she still had to observe the forms.

"For you, the war is over, Simon," Rhys said. "For the Welsh, it's just beginning."

Simon drew in a breath, prompting Catrin and Rhys to share another long look, acknowledging that this conversation was one they could have had with Simon months ago and deliberately had not done so because he hadn't asked. Their conquerors' inability to see the impact they were having on the people they'd conquered was a bit staggering, but they believed, all of them, to the deepest recesses of their hearts, that they were *good* and *just,* and that the government, laws, and way of life they'd brought to Wales were *right*. They decried the Welsh people's willfulness and stubbornness, and could not understand their inability to see the benefits of being incorporated into the Kingdom of England.

Rightly thinking it might be better to move on from this topic, Rhys drew Simon's attention to the beam that had come down. One end remained attached to its support nine feet above Catrin's head, but the other end had come to rest approximately two-thirds of the way across the main floor. If the king had been under it when it had fallen, there was no doubt it would have killed him.

"Since it's unlikely the master craftsman decided the central beam didn't actually need to stretch the full distance across the viewing stand, I'm not at all surprised to see a straight edge where there shouldn't be one." And then he explained what was suddenly obvious to all three of them: "Someone sawed through this beam almost all the way. I'm no carpenter, but even I know that these seven beams supporting the second floor are all that hold it up, and with all the stomping that was going on, it was no wonder it couldn't hold."

"So it's attempted regicide." Simon crouched in order to run his finger along the straight edge, his expression more drawn and tight than before.

"Only if the murderer didn't know about the dancing tonight," Catrin said.

Simon began to move methodically from one beam to the next, craning his neck upwards to make sure no more were sabotaged. He was just tall enough to tug on some of the bunting that decorated the viewing stand, moving it out of the way so he could see where all the crossbeams rested on the long support beams that ran the full length of the viewing stand.

Rhys had already done exactly what Simon was doing now, but he let Simon work in silence for a moment before adding, "Am I correct in recalling that the master craftsman was from Harlech?"

"Yes. And all of the workmen."

"They are English, then." Rhys waggled his head. "We need to talk to them."

Simon gritted his teeth. "The master craftsman is back in Harlech, along with most of his men."

"Already?" Catrin would have thought any number of workers would have been kept onsite for emergencies, even if nobody had contemplated one this dire. Within an encampment this large, there was always something that needed building or repairing.

Simon spread his hands wide. "They were here for nearly two months, what with repairing the palace and preparing for the tournament. They were needed back at the castle."

Catrin thought, but didn't say, *I bet they were*. The establishment of castles as a permanent symbol of, and means for, King Edward's domination of Wales was another sore point, but one they didn't need to get into right now.

"A few remain, Catrin. They are housed amongst the villagers." Rhys grumbled deep in his chest, as aware as Catrin of the resentment engendered among the Welsh by having to host English people for an extended period of time. "I can speak to them, as well as to any Welsh carpenters, of whom there are several." He paused.

"Those men will need assurances they won't be blamed if they come forward."

"I can make such assurances, but only, of course, provided none of them are responsible for the sabotage," Simon said.

Both Rhys and Catrin gazed at him impassively until Simon threw up a disgusted hand. "What do you take me for? Don't you know me better than that?"

These were essentially the same words Wena had thrown at Catrin earlier.

"We do, Simon," Rhys said, "but it is our reputation on the line too. Catrin and I are skating on thin ice with these people, as Catrin saw with Wena. One wrong move and they will turn away completely. You can't afford, if we are to actually get to the bottom of this, to alienate them."

Catrin put out a hand. "There's going to be pressure brought to bear to resolve this quickly."

Simon was standing straight and stiff. "I am not Guy fitz Lacy."

"I didn't mean you were, Simon," Catrin said, fighting the urge to revert to formality and call him *my lord*, "but what Rhys is trying to say is that powerful lords are in abundance here, and while they will follow the king's lead in the main, they will surely go their own way at times if it suits them, as long as they aren't defying a direct order. Your orders, if not clearly backed up by the king, won't mean much, if anything, to them."

"A sheepdog learns very early in his training that he can't herd cats," Rhys said, attempting a grin.

"I could choose to be offended that you are comparing me to a sheepdog," Simon's eyes were still narrowed, "but as they are clever, loyal creatures, I will take what you said as a compliment instead."

"A cat, though—" Catrin tipped her head.

"As another name for *Lord of the March*?" Simon let out a snort of laughter, easing the tension further. "I find it more applicable than *pig*. You truly do know them well."

14

27 July 1284

Day Two

Rhys

As a member of King Edward's personal guard, Rhys had become intimately acquainted with the king's routines and moods. He'd stood guard during the king's sleep, meetings, ablutions, and as Edward cuddled his newborn son. Rhys's familiarity with the king these days also meant that he could no longer defer entirely to Simon when bad news had to be conveyed and instead had to take on the responsibility himself. Thus, he was the first to arrive in the great hall of the palace the next morning, in time for the king to break his fast.

Fortunately, he didn't have long to wait, and when the king appeared, he was accompanied by the three men of his guard on duty at the moment, plus Simon, who drifted into the hall in their wake a few moments later. One glance told Rhys that he hadn't yet informed the king of the events of the night. Simon could be as judicious as Rhys about the best way to impart information. The royal temper was well known, even if it had been mostly—and likely deliberately—banked these last months.

The moment he came in, the king spied Rhys loitering near the far end of the hall, but when Rhys raised a hand to request an audience, the king held up one finger. "Whatever it is, I don't yet want to know."

Rhys subsided, settling back on his heels to watch as the king took up his chair, and the servant set out his prepared food (which the food taster had already sampled). Then the king slaked his thirst, downing a goblet of water and then a goblet of wine.

Setting down his cup, he motioned Rhys forward. "Do you know why I made you wait?"

This was a game they often played, where the king would ask Rhys a question about why he'd implemented a certain policy or treated a courtier in a certain way. Sometimes it would be a matter of state, along the lines of *What can Philippe of France be thinking?*

Rhys would attempt to answer as truthfully as possible, according to his own observations. And if he didn't know, he was to say so. This particular question was a little more fraught, in that he was being asked to comment on the king's own behavior.

But he thought he knew the answer. "If the matter was so urgent that it couldn't wait, I would have woken you with the news, or Simon would have. If it was a matter of immediate life or death, I would have had Simon at my side rather than arriving in the hall separately. As it is, I was here, waiting for you, when you arrived, indicating that I wanted to speak to you, that the matter is of some urgency, but I was willing to wait for the proper moment."

A slight smile hovered around Edward's lips, indicating he was pleased. "Thus, you were chosen for your current position." He waved a finger at one of the guardsmen, this one named Edgar. The man was descended from Saxons through and through, with a huge bulk and hair so blond it was almost white. "You may see to your own breakfast."

Edgar bent his head. "Thank you, my lord." He snapped his fingers, indicating to the other guards that they should converge on a side table upon which prepared food had been laid.

Rhys had already eaten, so he didn't begrudge them the moment of peace. One of the many benefits of having Simon as the captain of the king's guard was that none of the men with whom Rhys worked were awful people. Over the last months, since Simon had taken up the position, the several guardsmen who'd leaned that way had been promoted—or so they could say—to other positions within the king's court or returned to England to duties in far-flung castles. Simon wanted the men around the king to work harmoniously together. If they were to protect him, they had to trust one another. Anyone who didn't *fit,* as Simon himself had said, had to go.

At first, Rhys had suspected that he himself wouldn't last long—and at the very least would be resented by the existing guardsmen. But Simon was far smarter than that—and probably smarter than Rhys had ever given him credit for. Over the last three months, he had put together an eclectic crew of men, each with strengths from which the team benefited, and, even if they had glaring weaknesses, as all men did, these didn't distract from the whole.

There was Ralph from yesterday, who'd initially been included in the king's guard as a favor to his uncle, but had proved himself to be quiet, capable, and fiercely devoted to the king's welfare. He had a little trouble with humor, being overly serious most of the time, but the ribbing from the other men was gentle, because he had a genuine, kind heart. Edgar, the burly Saxon to whom the king had just spoken, had come into the king's service with a very large chip on his shoulder, which Simon himself had figuratively knocked off twice before Edgar had settled down and stopped taking every comment directed towards him as an insult.

Simon had inherited three Frenchmen—Fulke, Jehan, and Bertran—who were from various regions of France where Edward had lands or wished he still did. Middling noblemen of a similar station to Rhys, they spoke only French, though recently Jehan had approached Rhys about learning Welsh. While Jehan was of Norman descent, he was from Brittany, where the local people spoke Breton, a language related to Welsh.

The remaining five guardsmen were from England proper, though one, Donald, had a Scottish mother. Though he could converse easily in French, Donald also spoke Gaelic, along with English with a Scots accent so thick it might as well be a different language.

In truth, they could use a few more guardsmen in their circle. Simon was on the lookout for likely candidates, if only to spell the others—particularly in situations like today where Simon was busy with organization and the king's overall security, and Rhys was occupied with the investigation. Men got sick sometimes, they needed sleep, and an occasional day off. These ten were working long hours to make up for Rhys's and Simon's respective duties.

In addition to Edgar, it was Jehan and Donald on duty this morning. Jehan had initially posted himself behind the king's chair, ready to protect the king with his own form if need be. But now, having helped himself to a meal, he had retired with his fellows to a table near the door, beyond the great round table which took up the center of the room.

King Edward wasn't listening to petitioners today, so no other diners were in the hall. Certain close members of the court, those named as *chevaliers* of the Round Table, such as Prince Edmund or high lords like Gilbert de Clare or Humphrey de Bohun, would have been welcome. The rest of the court would find food in the pavilion, along with more amusing company and possibly music. A man didn't last long in the royal household if he wasn't flexible about the king's wish for a quiet breakfast.

With Simon a few paces away, Rhys placed himself on the opposite side of the small table on the dais at which the king sat this morning and related everything he'd learned about Rollo's death, as well as what he'd witnessed and observed the previous night at the viewing stand. At any point during his recitation, the king could have blared *what?* or castigated him. It wouldn't have been because he was the bearer of bad news but because he hadn't anticipated the possibility of sabotage and had failed to inspect the beams in advance.

It would have been an unreasonable expectation, but kings had no obligation to be reasonable, and Rhys and Simon *were* charged with his safety. Instead, the king continued to eat while Rhys talked, and Rhys supposed that daily he digested some sort of bad news along with his food. Every once in a while, the king glanced at Simon, and Simon nodded his confirmation.

After Rhys finished, the king put down his bacon and settled back in his chair. "I want you to read something for me, Reese."

Rhys was also used to the way King Edward shifted topics without notice. Very often, he would pursue one line of inquiry and then change course without warning halfway through the conversation. Rhys supposed it was a means to keep everyone around him on the back of his heels, but Rhys also thought he'd been doing it for so long it was a habit.

"My lord."

Edward snapped his fingers at one of his clerks, who'd been working away in silence in the far corner, waiting for the moment the king wanted to turn to business. With alacrity, he brought over a book that had been set to one side.

The words were written in Welsh on one side of the page and Latin on the other, and Rhys recognized the work instantly as that of the great Nennius, a Welsh monk writing over four hundred years earlier about the exploits of Arthur. In his past life as a member of Prince Llywelyn's *teulu,* Rhys wouldn't have known of it. But he'd had a slow six-month recovery in the monastery of Abbey Cwm Hir after Llywelyn's death, in which he'd availed himself of the monks' extensive library.

Edward indicated the book with a casual wave. "I want to know if my men are making a reasonable translation."

Rhys hesitated. "Sire, it is my understanding that Nennius himself wrote originally in Latin. It is the Welsh that would be the translated words."

"Reese," the king looked down his nose at him, and Rhys tried not to blanch or cower, "the monk was Welsh, and I am concerned that my transcribers may have misunderstood the full meaning of Nennius's text when they rendered it in French."

Rhys bowed to the king's wishes, as he must, unsure what Edward really wanted, but knowing it wasn't this. The king had an entire country full of Welsh clerics at his beck and call, now that he had reformed the Welsh church and brought it in line with Canterbury and Rome. Rhys also knew that the king knew he knew it.

But since King Edward was his liege lord, Rhys did as he was bid, first reading the Latin and Welsh to himself, and then relating the passages to the king as best he could in French:

Then it was that Arthur,
the great and magnanimous,
with all the kings and military force of Britain,
fought against the Saxons.
And though there were many men more noble than himself
by birth,
he was twelve times chosen their commander,
and was as often conqueror.
When Arthur faced his enemy on the hill of Badon,
nine hundred and forty fell by his hand alone,

no one but the Lord affording him assistance.

In every battle, the Britons were victorious,

for no man can go against the Will of the Almighty.

While Rhys read, Edward kept his head bent, as if in prayer, and didn't respond immediately after Rhys finished. When he did, his words weren't directed at Rhys. "It sounds different when he reads it, don't you think? The Welsh have poetry in their souls."

The clerk bowed and Simon, who'd been standing silently beside Rhys throughout, as was his wont, said, "It is as you say, sire."

The king looked at Rhys. "Thank you."

Rhys gently closed the book.

"What is the state of this viewing stand now?"

They were back to business. "We worked through the night to remove the offending beam and all the broken boards. The remaining Harlech carpenters, augmented by anyone in Nefyn or here at the tournament who is handy with a hammer, are putting it back together with new wood as we speak. They started at dawn, and nobody thinks it should take long. They could even have finished in the time we've been talking here. It will be ready before the archery competition is meant to begin."

Simon then augmented Rhys's answer: "We would have preferred to have kept the entire incident a secret, but regrettably, with all the witnesses, that was impossible from the start."

"You are certain the beam was sabotaged to fail?"

"As certain as we can be without interviewing the men who originally built it, though I have sent to Harlech for the master carpenter."

Now it was Rhys's turn to interject. "I, as well as more knowledgeable men, have concluded that the central beam was deliberately sawed through from the underside. It didn't matter that the boards that formed the floor of the second story were solid when the evening began. The beam could not withstand the pounding feet of the dancers and was bound to fail."

Edward absorbed this analysis with the same apparent equanimity as before. "When would this have been done?"

Back to Simon. "We cannot say, my lord, though one of the Welsh carpenters from the village guessed it had to have been within the last day or two, otherwise the ceiling wouldn't have passed inspection by the master carpenter responsible for its building."

King Edward gave a little snort. "How likely is it that the man you questioned did it himself?"

Rhys felt a little hollow inside, but still he answered truthfully. "It's possible."

"Unlikely, however, my lord," Simon said softly. "It would have been difficult for a Welshman to have entered the arena at any hour without being stopped. This craftsman also suggests that the entire endeavor could have taken as little as a quarter of an hour. We must remember that the sound of sawing is not so loud that it would necessarily have been heard and responded to in the middle of the night."

"Besides which, two nights ago we had a rainstorm," Edward himself said.

"Yes, sire, quite a substantial one," Simon said. "At the time, I was relieved the encampments surrounding Nefyn weren't blown away or washed into the sea."

Rhys was standing with his hands behind his back, trying very hard not to move, or he would have spread his hands wide. "Even if it was accomplished later, after the bardic competition ended yesterday, few people would have been out in the field to pay attention. A confident man, sure of himself and of his actions, can get away with most anything without being questioned."

"Thus I myself was taught." Edward was relaxed again in his chair, tapping a finger to his lip.

Rhys had learned that lesson too. Every man, at one time or another, had moments where he was afraid to act, to stand before other men and speak, or just plain afraid. It had been the captain of Llywelyn's guard, now long dead, who'd explained to Rhys that he needed to put on the cloak of his office, as one of the prince's men, straighten his spine, and act like he knew what he was doing. It didn't matter most times that he was mumming. Invariably, people responded to confidence.

Simon cleared his throat. "My lord, we must view this as another threat to your person, even if the attempt at harm failed."

Edward had taken a sip of his wine, and now he put down his cup. "Because I would have been sitting inside the stand today to watch the jousting and archery?"

"Yes, my lord," Simon said. "In fact, your chair would have been exactly under the beam that failed."

"You think this attempt on my life is in keeping with the others?"

"Yes, my lord," Simon said again. "I would also say that whoever is responsible is not a close member of your court, but he's close enough to be here."

"Which means, effectively, I brought him with me," the king said flatly.

Simon hesitated, but then he nodded. "Very likely so."

"The sabotage could be unrelated." Rhys paused, a new thought on his lips that he was hesitant to say.

Both Simon and Edward saw it, however, and Simon's warning tone when he said, "Reese," could not be ignored.

"In the Holy Land, when the Saracens were contemplating an attack, they often probed our defenses before settling on a strategy. Sire, this could be similar."

The expression on Edward's face was one of surprise—which turned almost immediately to the same intensity as in Rhys's own. "To me too."

Simon looked from one to the other. "Do you think the sabotage is unrelated to the murder and thieving in Earl Clare's camp?"

"We should assume nothing at this juncture," Rhys said. "I'm just telling you what is in my gut right now. We can't rely on it."

"There are few guts I trust more," King Edward said, being completely serious.

Rhys felt himself straightening, honored despite himself. "Thank you, sire."

"I agree the attempt was ineffective," Edward added, "since I am alive. But are we sure it didn't achieve what the saboteur wanted?"

"May I ask what that might be?" Simon said. "He can't be so naïve as to think he could stop the tournament."

"I can see others reasons for doing it." The king was back to tapping one finger, this time on the arm of his chair, which everyone in the room knew from experience indicated a burgeoning temper. Rhys tried to focus on the king's face instead. "One, to stop the dancing. In this he was successful, though I agree that it's hard to see why that might be important. Two, to distract you from the death of Rollo."

Rhys's expression turned thoughtful. "In this he was successful as well, though it isn't as if we have put that investigation aside."

"Three," the king wasn't done, "as Reese said, as a foray into our territory, to probe our defenses or even as a trial run, to see if cutting the beam would even work."

Rhys didn't like the sound of that at all, and he knew that he would now have to take ceilings into account when he made sure any room was safe for the king.

"Finally, the fourth possibility, to redouble your efforts to protect me."

Simon frowned. "Why would someone want that as a goal?"

The king met Rhys's eyes and nodded that Rhys should be the one to answer.

"Because if more attention is paid to the king, we have fewer men and resources to protect ... what?"

"Or whom?" the king said. "Don't forget, this is a tournament, and the stakes are very high for many men."

"It will be life or death for some," Simon agreed. "Riches or poverty for others."

"Including you," Edward said somewhat dryly, his eyes on Rhys, having changed the topic again. "The archery contest is about to start."

Rhys managed to refrain from rolling his eyes. "I was assuming, with the investigation, I would no longer—"

Edward cut him off. "You will not withdraw."

"As you wish, my lord." Rhys bent his head.

When he looked up next, a disturbing twinkle had appeared in the king's eyes, and he seemed to be hiding a smile rather than glowering with disapproval as before. "And I expect you to do your best to win!"

15

Day Two

Catrin

atrin's heart was racing as she clasped her hands before her lips. This was only the first round, and she was already a complete wreck. Most of the archers were Welshmen like Rhys, but a handful of Englishmen had joined the festivities, daring to match their skills against the natives. One of them had actually won the previous heat, to the jubilation of the English onlookers and the silent embarrassment of the Welsh who'd come to watch. Perhaps even worse, so far, none of the Welsh archers who'd won their heats had actually done what anyone would call *well*. They'd eked out a victory over inferior competition, and that was it.

The day had dawned beautiful, which King Edward and all the tournament guests took as a sign that God was looking favorably upon their event. Everyone had been in Wales long enough—what with the lengthy journey to get here—to know that even in late July it rained at least a little most days.

As she waited for the next archer to begin, Catrin glanced towards the viewing stand. It had been repaired to the satisfaction of all who inspected it, though nobody was being allowed on the top floor, and the staircase upwards was now blocked and guarded to ensure the rule was followed.

The first three heats had finished before the king arrived. Everyone had stopped what they were doing and bowed, and then he'd taken his chair, surrounded by nobles of his court, including Eleanor herself, who'd risen earlier than usual in order to sit beside her husband in another ornate chair. It might be that she was here specifically to cheer on Rhys.

For the Welsh onlookers, there wasn't much cheering going on otherwise, even when the Saxon archers did lose or their chosen hero won, as had been the case in four of the five contests that had occurred so far. Though they'd been dutifully respectful to the king, otherwise the Welsh spectators were nearly silent. Grim, even. Archery was serious business, and the pride of the entire nation was on the line.

Rhys was the next archer to take his turn, and as he stepped up to the line for his first shot, the air was heavy with tension. From the looks on everyone's faces, Welsh and English, Catrin wasn't the only one to feel it. Rhys himself was well aware of the weight on his shoulders. He'd tried to hide his emotions from her, but she'd seen how he'd picked at his food at breakfast, and how, before the competition started, his nervous stomach had him spending too long in the latrine.

He was upright now, however, and every line of his body spoke of confidence. Then, with one smooth motion, he nocked his arrow, drew his bow, and loosed. He was shooting only twenty yards, but anyone could miss a shot at any time. Catrin held her breath.

Bull's-eye.

She heaved a sigh of relief, and that same sigh swept through those around her. They didn't know Rhys well, not with how rarely Prince Llywelyn had come to Nefyn and with how far it was from Caernarfon and Anglesey, but they recognized a master when they saw one. Whatever happened now, he had comported himself well. It was going to be all right.

She glanced towards the viewing stand again. The king was sitting forward on his throne, his eyes intent and focused on the events before him. Edward fancied himself something of an archer, which may have been the most compelling reason in the end for him to have included archery in the tournament. She also saw in his face that he was invested in the competition itself and, what's more, wanted Rhys to *win.*

Rhys did.

The last *thunk* of the arrow into the white spot in the middle of the target prompted the first real sign of jubilation in his fellow countrymen, not to mention the king (who applauded politely and nodded as if he'd never feared otherwise).

Afterwards, she held back as Rhys received congratulations from the other archers. The top two participants in each of the ten heats would advance to the next round, which was tomorrow. The third day of the tournament would see the final contests in both archery and jousting, and the *Round Table* would conclude with the mêlée. One team would be led by Henry de Lacy, the Earl of Lincoln and Lord of Denbigh, and the other by Richard de Burgh, the Earl of Ulster.

Rhys had not been among those chosen to fight, a blessing as far as Catrin was concerned. Mêlées and jousts were for younger men, which he himself admitted. In addition to her brother Tudur, the only other man tapped to participate with even a claim to being Welsh was her own son, Justin. He would be in Clare's contingent, fighting for Henry de Lacy.

"Well done, sir," she said to Rhys, once he made his way over to her. She ignored his lifted hand dismissing Ralph, who'd been trailing after her all morning, supposedly protecting her from the killer who might want to do her in.

"Thank you." He grinned and draped an arm across her shoulders. "Were you afraid I would lose?"

"Terrified!" She laughed.

"Oh ye of little faith."

"I had faith that you would do well," she said. "But nobody can control the competition. It isn't even so much that it's fierce. It's the expectations on you."

"I have felt worse, believe me."

"Honestly, I am surprised so many came if they were going to do so poorly."

"Didn't you know?" Rhys's brow furrowed. "They didn't have a choice, Catrin. Each lord did a survey of the archers in his district, picked out the best, and sent them here."

Her shoulders sagged. "I should have realized. And each lord would know because everyone is required to practice on the green every Sunday. No wonder everyone is so het up."

"They are better shots than they've been showing too. I know the man who barely won the first heat. I've seen him hit the center of a target at three hundred paces." Rhys shook his head. "Everybody was just unsettled today, feeling a mixture of obligation and defiance. They know the king wants Welsh archers in his army the next time he fights a war."

Catrin came to a dead halt. "I should have realized. The jousts and mêlée have always been designed to be practice for battle. Why not archery?"

"No reason it should occur to you," Rhys said. "This is the first tournament ever to include an archery contest."

"Which is why you have to win it."

He barked a laugh. "Not you too!"

"Sorry." She hesitated. "Did you see the king's face when you won?"

"I did. He was pleased."

"What you didn't see, because you were focused on your shooting as you should have been, was his expression during your heat. He was rooting for you."

Rhys made a sound that was something like *"Gah!"* Then a curious expression came over his face, one she recognized as indicating when a new thought occurred to him.

"What is it?"

"You just said, *nobody can control the competition*, but what if that isn't true? What if Rollo was killed to give someone an advantage in the jousts or mêlée? Hugh called the idea absurd that *he* would murder Rollo to take his place in the competition, and maybe that's true for Hugh. But for someone on the opposing side?"

"No." Catrin stared at him. "It's absurd to think it."

"Or maybe not. This morning Simon and I discussed with the king what a serious business the tournament was to many men. Simon called it a matter of life or death for some."

Catrin swallowed hard. "I hate to think someone murdered Rollo to get him out of the way."

"It's my job to think it." Rhys looked down at her. "How did your inquiries go this morning?"

While Rhys had been speaking to the king, she had squeezed in several more interviews with people with missing items. It had been left to her because neither Simon nor the king had allowed Rhys to participate, even if he'd had a spare moment, as both were invested in his performance.

"In this, I have news you do not want to hear: these thefts are not limited to Clare's camp. Several other noblemen and knights are missing items. It isn't many, mind you. One of Bohun's men, two of Lacy's, one of Burgh's."

"Does it seem to you they're related?"

"I think so." Then she qualified her already hesitant conclusion. "I fear so. It can't be surprising we have thieves among us. It isn't just the lords' encampments either, with all the men-at-arms, servants, and camp followers, to consider. We also have a market fair with several hundred people that none of us know in attendance, and an entire Welsh village, which is packed to the gills with archers and spectators from all over Wales—though admittedly, the latter would have a hard time passing undetected through any of these encampments. Most don't speak any language but Welsh."

"Do you see a pattern in the thefts?"

They began walking through the tournament grounds, her arm hooked in his. Their progress was slowed because of all the congratulations Rhys received. For the first time in Nefyn, she heard someone refer to Rhys as *combrogi,* the Welsh word for *countryman.*

"Again, I don't know." She shook her head. "The stolen items are small and so far belong only to lesser lords. Our thief didn't steal from Clare or Bohun or Mortimer himself. He stole from Eustace."

"Any other deaths?"

"No. And we still don't know if Rollo should be counted among the victims of theft."

"His silver carafe and cups are missing."

"True." Catrin wrinkled her nose. There was still so much they didn't know.

"When did these other items go missing?"

"All the thefts have happened since everyone arrived at the tournament, the same as at Clare's camp."

"Which begs a number of questions," Rhys said, "first among them whether or not these other thefts are the work of the same person or persons."

"Secondly," Catrin lifted the hand not tucked into Rhys's elbow, "if Rollo was the latest victim, was his death a complete accident, or will this thief develop a taste for murder?"

"As I told Earl Clare, murder is a very different sort of crime than theft."

"To some, maybe." Catrin felt her mood lifting at being able to talk to Rhys, even if it was about murder. All morning, she had been feeling the burden of investigating the crime on her own. "Lacy's man is missing a ring that was given to him by the old earl and is *very* put out."

"Do the men from whom these items were stolen have anything obvious in common?"

"Other than being here?" She canted her head. "Other than being *men*? Not that I could find. While those within each earl's encampment are acquainted with one another, neither of Lacy's men know Bohun's. I spoke with Eustace again, and he is friends with one knight in Lacy's camp but not the other. And so on. They all knew of Rollo, naturally."

"Which signifies nothing. Either the thefts are exclusively a product of what each man possessed, or they have something in common we haven't yet found."

"I don't know what that is." She sighed. "I can say that none of the captains in any of the encampments have reported a theft since yesterday morning—nor a death, for that matter. And no thefts have been reported within the king's court in the palace."

Rhys rubbed his chin as he thought. "We had no problems when we were camped at the lake these past weeks."

"Meaning the thief came with one of the barons."

"See. We do know something." Rhys was starting to look pleased. "And we haven't considered yet all the ways Rollo could have been murdered for reasons other than theft."

"Neither Eustace nor Hugh could name any specific enemies of Rollo. Nor could Joan. I did ask."

"He was a gambler."

"Killing a man isn't a very good way to get money from him."

"Unless it means you get his purse," Rhys pointed out.

"His purse isn't missing," Catrin reminded him, "only his set of silver cups and carafe. As I escorted Joan to her tent, she told me they'd been part of a ransom from one of his first tournaments, and he kept them with him always."

"I'm back to thinking Rollo might be dead because of the role he was to play in the tournament."

"Do I need to fear for your safety? You're one of the best archers here. Does Ralph need to be protecting you instead of me?"

Rhys laughed. "My contest is worth little by comparison."

"A hundred silver pennies ..." her voice trailed off.

"I take your point." Rhys grumbled under his breath. "A hundred silver pennies is a fortune to some."

"To many."

He grunted. "A tournament, especially one called a *Round Table*, is predicated on everyone having honor. We know it isn't true, and there's a difference between outright murder, as with Rollo, and fighting too hard in the actual mêlée, such that a man dies."

"Would someone really murder Rollo because he was likely to triumph, and they wanted to give themselves a better chance?"

"Yes. Absolutely."

"How about using one crime to cover up another?" Catrin suggested. "It isn't as if we haven't seen that before. Maybe the killer stole Rollo's cups and carafe to make us think we were looking for a thief."

Rhys rubbed his chin. "If the killer is a man of rank, it would be that much easier for him to move about freely."

"Though that would also make him that much more likely to be noticed if he was somewhere outside his normal range."

Rhys acknowledged that was true too.

"By the way," she said, thinking the time was right to mention it, "you have a new apprentice."

"Do I? Who might that be?"

Catrin tugged on his elbow, bringing him around the viewing stand to a cleared area where knights were practicing for the mêlée. Justin was working with another young man, both stripped to the waist, their muscled chests and arms glistening in the sun with sweat. It was a continual marvel to her that such a perfect human being could have come from her own body, and all the more horrifying to think of him fighting again, even in the mêlée. During the war, she lived on her knees in their manor's chapel, praying for his safe deliverance, and she felt guilt to this day for not praying enough for Robert.

As they approached, Justin was finishing his bout and bowed to his opponent before coming over to where she and Rhys waited.

"You were well-matched, but I think you had the upper hand in the end," Rhys said by way of a greeting.

Justin had been taking a long swig from his water skin, and he lifted it to Rhys in salute.

"Should I know your opponent?"

"I don't know, sir. He is John Hastings, Lord of Abergavenny. He is married to Isabel, daughter of William de Valence."

It was a powerful lineage, one not to be trifled with, and an interesting match for Justin, considering the ongoing animosity between Clare and Valence.

"You are friends?" Catrin asked.

Justin gave a little laugh, knowing exactly where his mother was going with her question. "The sins of the fathers need not be laid at the sons' feet."

"I can only agree." Rhys gave Justin a slight bow.

Catrin was nothing short of delighted that her son and Rhys were not only being civil to one another, but getting along. She took it as a compliment that they would both care enough for her to make the attempt.

"We're here about Rollo's murder, Justin." Catrin made a gesture with one hand. "Tell him what you heard."

Something of a mischievous light entered Justin's eyes. "Valence is not happy with your activities. He is going to speak to the king to ask that *his* man should replace you as investigator."

Rhys laughed in surprise. "Why on earth would that be?" Then he frowned. "Who exactly would that be?"

Justin raised his eyebrows. "An old friend of yours, according to John, though I don't know how he knows. His name is Vincent de Lusignan."

16

Day Two

Rhys

"**A**n *old friend*, he is not!"

Before allowing his emotion to show, Rhys had waited until Justin had gone off to bathe and change, and he and Catrin had cornered Simon in his quarters in the guardroom. Simon had been standing beside the king before Rhys had started shooting, but he'd left immediately thereafter. Now he was standing over his table, studying the map of Nefyn he'd drawn earlier, X's through the places where a theft (or murder) had taken place. Simon had created the map because Rhys couldn't draw a straight line to save his life. He had a smirking thought that he *could* draw a bow in order to shoot an arrow straight, and that was the only drawing that really mattered.

"I am aware, Reese," Simon said, in something of a drawl. "You'll be happy to know the king put him off. More than what kind of job Vincent would do in pursuit of this criminal, the king and I are more interested in *why* Valence thought to supplant you with Vincent."

"Because Vincent hates me," Rhys said, "even after all these years."

"You were one of the few people ever to challenge him and get away with it." Then Simon put out a soothing hand. "Valence did not mention that piece to the king, and at present the king is not disposed to give the investigation over to anyone else, even at the request of his uncle and foremost baron. From his perspective, the murder victim is one of Clare's men, and Clare and Valence do not get along. It would be counterproductive to throw their men together more than needful."

"You have a gift for understatement, my friend." Rhys laughed, realizing he'd been laughing often since his round of shooting had ended—and that he was enjoying the feeling, even if that laughter was sometimes sardonic.

"I'm glad you're willing to claim *me* as your friend. I don't know if you will be so cheery about it after what I have to tell you next." Simon drew in a breath. "You are to fight in the mêlée. Alongside me."

Rhys was expecting to hear about the investigation, so at first what Simon said didn't register. And then when it did, he was back to staring. "No."

He didn't mean, *No, I won't do it*, but rather, *No, you can't be serious.*

"I'm afraid so." By his reply, Simon seemed to recognize the difference. "All the members of the king's guard are now expected to participate."

Rhys bent his head, hearing in Simon's tone that he was not to argue. Friends they might be, but Simon was still his superior, and King Edward was their liege lord. They would do what he asked, come what may. That was the oath each of them had sworn.

Catrin, however, had no such obligations and said, "Well, I, for one, not only *think* the idea is mad, I *know* it."

Rhys could appreciate her ire. While knights used blunted swords in the fighting (at one time they had not), men could still be severely injured.

"Why would the king ask you to join in?" Now Catrin's tone turned genuinely despairing. "And if you and Rhys are involved in the mêlée, who is going to be protecting the king?"

"*We* will, since he's going to be fighting too." Simon plopped himself down in his chair, in a somewhat despairing gesture himself.

Understanding had dawned in Rhys at the same moment Simon had spoken, and now he said, "At this point, I really am saying *no*. Catrin is right. Is the king mad?"

"I told him you would say that. He laughed, waved an airy hand, and said, *What could possibly be the danger with all of you around me? Let's see if I really have the best men protecting me.*"

"So it's a test, just like the archery tournament," Rhys said.

"Everything is a test," Simon said. "Besides, the king then added, *It has been too long since I fought in battle, and I need the practice as much as the next man.*"

Now it was Catrin's turn to scoff. "Somehow, I doubt that. He has not neglected his skills."

Rhys made a *hmm* sound. "Working with his men a few times a week is not the same as fighting in a real battle, as the king knows, though I was hoping he had thought himself too old for this by now. I know *I* am!"

Catrin looked at Simon. "How can King Edward possibly join a team? If he chooses Lacy's side, Burgh will feel snubbed and vice versa. That's another reason why he wasn't fighting in the first place!"

"The king has decided to fight with Lacy. His brother, Edmund, will fight with Burgh, to keep the mêlée as close to fair as possible."

"All right, then," Catrin made a dismissive gesture, "even I know that a major point of the mêlée is for individual knights to capture other knights for ransom. What if someone captures the king? He will be at once the biggest prize on the field and the one to avoid unless a man wants to lose everything to the king's wrath. And what if Edward were to die on an errant blade? He shouldn't be putting himself at risk."

"Catrin, I didn't know you cared." Simon's words could have been mocking, but he looked genuinely interested at the extent of her emotion.

"I hate the mêlée," she said softly, without responding to his observation about how much she might or might not care for the king. "I hate that the two of you will be fighting in it."

"Wealth and reputation is to be found on the tournament field," Simon said in a deliberately lofty tone.

Catrin snorted. "As if either of you need more of either of those."

"As much as I would never turn up my nose at money," Rhys's eyes were on Catrin, trying to see into her heart more completely, "Simon and I have little chance of such victories with a king to protect."

"About that." Simon lifted a hand. "Our lord has chosen the Earldom of Kent as his personal stake in the fight, while Edmund has put up Winchester. If someone captures either, their recompense will be commensurate with those estates."

"Whatever does that mean?" Catrin said.

"Neither Edward nor Edmund will actually be giving up Kent or Winchester, of course, any more than if Earl Clare loses he will give up Gloucester Castle," Simon said, "but some of the living from both of those estates would provide the ransom, were either to be defeated. The rules of the tournament are not the same as in war, as I think you know. A man has merely to remain undefeated for the allotted time. The faction with the most men left standing, coupled with those captured of the highest rank, wins."

"Those are huge prizes nonetheless," Catrin said.

Rhys nodded. "Clare would love to see himself gaining something from the Earldom of Kent, since his father's first wife was the daughter of the last Earl of Kent, never mind that she died without issue."

"He is fighting for Lacy's faction, though, so he can't win it from the king." She gasped a laugh as a realized the king's cleverness in setting up the sides. "And Valence very much would like to see the Earldom of Winchester at his feet, since he sees *it* as rightfully his."

"But again, he can't win it from Edmund since they will be on the same team," Rhys said. "Does the king *mean* to start a civil war?"

"He knows well what he is doing," Simon said.

Catrin took in a breath. "*This* is the point of the mêlée, isn't it? The king means to pit one baron against another, intending for them to work out their differences on the tournament field before the conflicts among them devolve into actual war. Clare and Valence are on opposite sides on purpose. And he very deliberately made other men, who might have designs on warring with one another, fight together." She shook her head. "Our king is too clever by half."

"No king could ever be too clever." Simon grinned. "But I confess I myself never thought about what he was doing in those terms."

"While I believe Catrin is correct in her supposition of what is in the king's mind," Rhys said, "I worry he is about to unleash something he can't control."

"Or maybe ..." Catrin paused, looking thoughtful, "... he knows he already has, and that's the problem he's trying to solve."

"Personally, as much as I distrust them both, I am not looking forward to seeing Clare and Valence openly at each other's throats." Simon met Rhys's eyes, and Rhys saw the same concern he felt mirrored in his friend. The entire tournament had suddenly become a pot left too long over the fire. It was going to boil over at any moment.

"Somehow, amidst all this intrigue, our job remains to protect the king." Rhys shook his head. "We really are too old for this, Simon."

"You are as strong and fit as you ever were," Simon said flatly. "We train daily to ensure it. Nobody wants to die on that field. Oh—" he put up one finger, "—one more caveat: the king has declared that any man who causes permanent injury or death to another man will also be ransomed, the money going to the dead man's family. Catrin is right that the king could die, but his killer would lose everything he owns to ransom. The watchword of the day is *skill*."

Catrin patted Rhys's shoulder. "Knowing this makes me feel much better."

"Disarm and capture a man without wounding him?" Rhys stared at Simon in surprise. "That has always been the ideal of the mêlée but was never made a condition of any tournament before."

"Ah, but this is a *Round Table*. We are *chevaliers* of King Arthur, and we will remain within the bounds of honor, dignity, and chivalry at all times. If we can't, the king will ensure that we pay for our transgressions." Then Simon's expression turned thoughtful. "Since we are in Wales, and King Arthur was Welsh, the king says it is fitting to abide by his rules. Do you know what he means by that?"

"I think so." Catrin and Rhys nodded together, before Rhys explained: "Welsh law, which the king abrogated in March mind you, required the payment of fines for major crimes like murder, rape, or theft, rather than imprisonment or hanging. In the case of murder, these fines would be paid to the victim's family and were dependent on the relative status of the one harmed. We called it *galanas.*"

"That *is* very civilized," Simon said, with something like amusement in his voice, "and not very Norman, truth be told, though I suppose the Saxons would understand."

"I guess we will see how much any baron hates another. For some, it still might be worth a fine and the king's wrath to rid himself of a rival," Rhys said.

"I just thought of something!" Catrin put out a hand. "This could be why Rollo was murdered in his tent!"

Both men turned to look at her.

"Rhys wondered earlier if Rollo could have been murdered to get him out of the way, since he was deemed the best fighter here, but what if it's more than that." She waved a hand back and forth, excited now by her idea. "In the past, the mêlée could be an avenue to avenge oneself on a hated rival. I've been wondering why Rollo's killer, if he is as high-ranking as we fear, didn't wait for the opportunity to kill him there. It's such a free-for-all that anything can happen."

"Because he was afraid he couldn't defeat him there. That's what Rhys was saying," Simon said.

Catrin shook her head. "What if he wasn't afraid, necessarily, but still wanted Rollo dead? What if he knew in advance about the king's decree, which made killing Rollo in the tournament too great a risk. Better to do it beforehand."

"I'm not sure how long ago the king—" Simon began.

But then he was interrupted by hurrying feet. Rhys had been an investigator long enough to distrust the sound and, sure enough, the door to the guardroom was flung open—in clear violation of protocol—to reveal young Ralph quivering with excitement on the threshold. "A villager has come forward, my lord. One of the carpenters is missing."

17

Day Two

Catrin

"Why did it take so long to report him missing?" Rhys glared at the youth before him, who was perhaps a year or two older than Dafi.

"We didn't like Adam much, see. It was better at home when he wasn't there, always bossing my mam around. We thought he'd gone off on a drunk, now that no work was being done for a few days while all the nobles are here."

Rhys understood completely what the young man was saying. In Caernarfon, the village headman had taken Rhys himself in so another villager didn't have to.

The intensity of the youth's emotions was perhaps also why he hadn't come to the guardroom alone, but had brought one of the monks. On the thicker side of middle age, Cadell was cleanshaven, like many churchmen, and entirely bald, which meant he had no tonsure either. He also had warm brown eyes and dimples, though he wasn't smiling now.

"Thank you for reporting it," Rhys said reassuringly. "How long has he been gone?"

"Two days," the youth said. "The last time I saw him, he was slipping out late at night. It was during that rainstorm. I assumed he was off to see a girl."

"What girl?" Rhys asked.

"I don't know about any girl. It's just what I assumed."

But the youth was shifting from foot to foot, prompting Catrin to look hard at him. "What aren't you telling us?"

"Nothing, my lady!" He'd been speaking in Welsh this whole time, which only Rhys and Catrin understood. "It's just—" He stopped.

Rhys waited through several heartbeats, but the youth didn't finish his sentence.

"Say what you need to say, Pawl. Nothing will happen to you." But then Cadell looked at Rhys. "Will it?"

"Not if he speaks the truth."

Cadell's encouragement appeared enough for Pawl to marshal enough courage to speak again. "Will he be coming back?"

"I don't know," Rhys said, "but by now it is perhaps unlikely."

The youth's expression cleared. "It's just ... he left some of his things. Clothes and-and ... tools." He said the last word softly.

"All of them?" Catrin glanced at Rhys, both of them realizing the significance of what the youth had said. Craftsmen brought their own tools to a job. They weren't supplied by their employer.

"No." The youth shook his head. "His toolbelt is gone. It's just some smaller things he didn't take with him on every job."

Rhys bobbed his head in understanding. "Let us know if he returns."

"Yes, my lord."

Rhys dismissed him.

"What did he say?" Ralph was standing rigidly beside Simon.

Rhys relayed the story the youth had told, this time in French. Simon's mouth turned down. "That isn't a good sign."

Ralph looked from one to the other. "What—what do you mean? Why not? We know now this Adam sabotaged the viewing stand!"

"We may know that, Ralph," Catrin said gently, "but we still don't know why."

"He must have hated the king! A few among the Saxons still resent our presence."

More than a few, most likely, though Catrin didn't say that. "What if he didn't collect his things because he couldn't?"

"I don't understand." For all that he was the nephew of the Justiciar of Gwynedd, Ralph was not devious.

Simon was the one to explain. "If Adam left his tools behind, it implies he either is on a bender, as the boy supposed, and is coming back ... or he is never coming back because he's dead."

Ralph took in a surprised breath.

Though Pawl had left, Cadell had stayed behind, and now he placed his hands on his well-cushioned hips. Life had been good to Cadell, living, as he had been, as an Augustinian at the edge of the Irish Sea and the world. "I didn't want to interfere with Pawl's story, but perhaps it's time I mentioned that I also know this man he spoke of."

"How?" Rhys said.

Cadell narrowed his eyes slightly. "We know everyone, Sir Rhys."

It was a bit of a chastisement, and probably deserved.

Once again, Cadell had been speaking in Welsh, but now he switched to French, for Simon and Ralph's benefit—and perhaps it shouldn't have been a surprise he knew it, since some of the monks in the monastery were Norman and the Welsh monks would need to know it to communicate.

"Adam came to mass almost every day these last two months. He was one of the men brought in to repair Llywelyn's palace." His voice hitched at the mention of Llywelyn's name, but then it steadied, and he continued as if it hadn't happened. The world had finally come to his doorstep, if not entered into his very house. "And something else. As the monastery's herbalist, after sunset two nights ago, I was checking on a tincture that had been cooking all day in my workshop, when he passed me heading for the church gate. In the distance, I could see another man disappearing in the opposite direction. Even at the time, I thought it looked like they'd been meeting."

Catrin thought, but didn't say, *And you didn't think to say anything until now?* But that would have been unfair because Cadell would have had no way of knowing before this moment that Adam had anything to do with any aspect of their investigation. She and Rhys hadn't known it until Pawl had come forward.

It was looking more and more like their assumption that Adam was the saboteur was accurate. And Simon was right that he hadn't returned for his belongings because he couldn't.

As the men continued to talk with Cadell, Catrin suddenly couldn't bear to hear another word about sabotage, thieving, or death, and she left the guardroom, to find a seat on a bench within the gatehouse. As she leaned her head back against the stones, she wondered how many such rooms she might inhabit and how many similar stories she might hear in the coming months and years if she stayed with Rhys.

If.

She thought about that for a long moment, acknowledging that she had a genuine choice before her: she could move forward with her relationship with Rhys, or she could end it. She knew by the way Rhys looked at her, sought her out, and talked with her that he cared for her. She couldn't say definitively that he wanted to marry her because they hadn't discussed it, but it was long past time she decided whether or not she wanted to marry *him*. Anything else would be unfair to both of them.

Unfortunately, nothing had changed in the last three months that had made the need for not advancing their relationship less compelling: she was lady-in-waiting to the Queen of England, and his duties and obligations to the king increased with every day that passed. For them to formalize their relationship with marriage might mean they saw each other less, rather than more, than they did now. None of the queen's current ladies were married, and Catrin had a real fear that the crucial reason she had been invited to join Queen

Eleanor's retinue was because she was widowed. The corollary to that idea was that any lady-in-waiting who married would find herself no longer part of the queen's inner circle.

Catrin didn't want to lose what they had together, when both of them had lost so much already. And really, what they had was a friendship that had lasted a lifetime so far. That, in and of itself, was worth living for.

But even as she rolled these thoughts over in her mind, she had to laugh. Rhys had brought sunshine to her rainy world, murders and investigations notwithstanding. She woke up every morning glad to know she would be seeing him, if only for a few moments. For all his occasional gloominess, which was hardly unique to him, being with Rhys was like throwing open the shutters on a sunny day and flooding the room—her life—with light.

Somehow the two of them had survived the end of the world. She never would have thought surviving the aftermath would be so much more difficult in comparison.

18

Day Two

Rhys

The three of them eventually made it to the pavilion where the evening meal was well underway and ran to earth a well-deserved drink. The tournament goers were celebrating the conclusion of the first round of jousts with song and revelry, which none of the three of them cared to join. Thus, they found a seat at the end of a mostly empty table, and the conversation coming from the diners all around them was so loud they had little fear of being overheard.

"If you'd come in second in your heat, I would have made you go practice," Simon said, "but as it is, at the same time you're pursuing the sabotage of the viewing stand you must proceed with Rollo's investigation. Who are your suspects?"

"Just as with the viewing stand, up until Adam so conveniently turned up missing, we have none." Rhys laughed. Again. "And I mean that literally."

"Nobody saw anyone entering Rollo's tent—or leaving it, for that matter," Catrin said. "Conversations with the other victims of theft have not borne fruit beyond what I've already told you."

"Any further thoughts on whether Adam was working alone or for someone else?" Simon gestured to where the viewing stand lay behind them. "I see it held up fine today."

The last joust had ended and the king departed, but it was still light out, so people were milling around it while other men sanded and raked the ground for the jousting that would take place tomorrow morning. Everything was in place for another day of festivities. To minimize the rearranging, though the archery competition had been first that morning, the jousting would be first tomorrow.

"It did, but there will be no dancing on the second story tonight." Rhys stomped a foot. "The ground will do very nicely."

"As it is, nobody heard or saw anything amiss, and I have asked." Catrin shrugged. "If Adam the carpenter is truly responsible, I find it unlikely he was working alone, but there are hundreds of people here. Anyone could be responsible."

"And we mean that literally too," Rhys said.

"I still can't decide whether we have one investigation or four." Simon rested his elbows on the table and leaned forward over them, his chin in his hands. "The sabotage of the viewing stand and the thefts are one and two, and then we have a dead man, three, who died within hours of the disappearance of another man, who could be number four if he's dead."

"If number four did number one, that would resolve the sabotage only to the extent we know who did the actual work. But if Adam didn't run away and instead was killed by yet another man?" Rhys put his chin in his hands too, suddenly exhausted.

"How credible is it, really, that Rollo's death, the thefts, and the sabotage are all related?" Catrin asked. "Do Adam and Rollo have anything in common?"

"Besides being dead?" Rhys's tone was dry.

"We don't know Adam is dead." Catrin wrinkled her nose at him. "If not for the sabotage, the fact that Adam is missing might have pointed us towards identifying *him* as the killer! Admittedly also, it is concerning that a single person could have murdered Rollo and sabotaged the viewing stand in one night and gotten away with it. That makes him good or lucky or both."

"Or dead," Rhys said again.

Simon harrumphed. "I don't like any of those options."

"Rollo's killer can't be lucky forever," Rhys said. "If he moves again, we will catch him."

"I'd prefer to catch him *before* he kills anyone else." Simon reached for the carafe and poured himself another cup of wine and then one each for Catrin and Rhys. The friends were silent for a moment as they sipped their drinks, and then Catrin looked at Rhys over the rim of her cup, "Are we going to talk about this—" she waggled the cup "—Vincent de Lusignan you so despise?"

Rhys bent his head, not ready for the change of subject, which left it to Simon to answer. He was sitting beside Catrin and made his voice so low Rhys could barely make out his words from across the table.

"In Acre, Vincent served Valence in much the same way Rhys served Prince Edmund and now serves the king, but was uncompromising in his application of the law. Rhys intervened before he could flog a man to death. I told him not to. Rhys didn't listen."

"I would have been surprised if he had," Catrin said, her eyes skating to Rhys.

Rhys remembered the day as if it were yesterday.

The heat had been oppressive, even after a year in Acre. Rhys had thought himself used to it, but it was driving all men, of whatever religion or creed, to madness. Rhys had just soaked himself in the sea, so had a cooler head than most, when Vincent arrived in the square with one of the soldiers, ready to string him up for abandoning his post on the wall of Acre. It was a serious crime, and one worth punishing, but as usual Vincent asserted that the only way to keep common men in line was to flog them and refused to believe that it taught them nothing more than fear and loathing for their superior officers.

Rhys had thought, even at the time, that if it had been Vincent in danger at Qaqun instead of Prince Edmund, not a single one of his men would have lifted a finger to save his life.

"We were friends," Rhys said under his breath. "Not friends like Simon and I had become, but more than acquaintances, at least at first. He is a little older than we are, and of a higher rank, but still a lesser lord, serving at the behest of a powerful relation. I thought him strict but fair. It was only later that he revealed his true colors."

"He felt threatened by you and your elevation to knighthood and Edmund's personal service," Simon said. "For a man who is at the same time proud and insecure, there could be no greater crime."

"So what happened?" Catrin looked from one to the other.

"I stopped him," Rhys said simply.

"He told Vincent," Simon said with exaggerated patience, chiding Rhys for being so miserly with details, "that his behavior was shameful. The soldier had made a grievous mistake and brought dishonor on himself, but Vincent was only compounding the poor man's error with one of his own."

"I perhaps spoke more harshly than I should have," Rhys said. "I regret that now, but it had been a long time coming."

"And after that? You're still here, still in favor. Or in favor again. What did Vincent do?"

"He stopped flogging the man, feigning magnanimity, and implied he intended to stop all along. Inside, he was furious." Simon took a long drink and then set down his cup. "Between one breath and the next, our friendship with him was over. Later, he threatened to kill Rhys at the next opportunity. Fortunately, we left Acre before that could happen."

Rhys slumped forward, feeling the heavy weight of the truth on his shoulders. Catrin noticed, as she would, and put her hand on his as it rested on the table. "What is it? Why the gloom? You look almost as if you're ... grieving."

"I am grieving." It was a truth he had never spoken, not even to his closest friends, even after these many months together. But under their scrutiny—and as Catrin's hand squeezed his—he couldn't hold back any longer. "He did kill me the next time he saw me." Rhys looked up and met his friends' eyes as they gazed at him. "It was Vincent who left me for dead at Cilmeri."

19

Day Two

Rhys

Simon cursed so loudly and with such fluency that their neighbors farther down the table couldn't help hearing. He put up a hand in apology and then continued in a softer tone, leaning forward again across the table. "By all that is holy, Rhys, no wonder seeing him in the hall was a shock."

Rhys knew Simon was truly moved because he said his name the Welsh way for the first time in months. For her part, Catrin was gripping his hand tightly, and her eyes were full of tears, which she brushed away with the back of her hand. She too said his name, "Rhys."

He wrapped both of his hands around hers. "I didn't mean to upset you. Truly, I didn't. It just seemed time you knew the truth."

"But Rhys—" Simon began.

Rhys looked at his friend. "I am well."

Simon didn't look convinced. "We've been concerned about Catrin's safety, but now I'm worried about yours. The two of you are going to be fighting on opposite sides in the mêlée."

"I have no interest in confronting him, believe me! At the same time, the more I've thought about it, the more I've begun to wonder if he knew it was me at Cilmeri. It had been twelve years since he'd seen me. It was dark and chaotic, and I was wearing a helmet and covered in blood. It appears he still hates me, given that he tried to get the king to supplant me in this investigation, but he hasn't gone out of his way to confront me otherwise."

Catrin was still looking weepy, though the tears themselves had stopped. "How can you bear to see him, knowing what he did?"

Rhys squeezed her hand again. "I would have killed him too, Catrin, if I could have. It was war."

"It was an ambush," she said tartly and in Welsh.

But at that point, the conversation couldn't continue because King Edward had arrived. They all stood as he took his place at the far end of the pavilion on the dais, constructed during the same fever of building that had created the viewing stand. The dais was just two feet high, however, so if its construction was faulty and the beams supporting the king's table broke, the diners wouldn't have very far to fall.

Simon had sent someone to check its stability anyway, just to be safe. It would be very much a matter of closing the barn door after the horse had escaped, but they were having trouble thinking like this culprit. As of yet, Rhys didn't understand his motivations, which made it hard to put himself in his shoes.

Once the king sat, the people returned to their meals. After a long look and a hand clapped on Rhys's shoulder, Simon left them, his strides taking him out of the pavilion towards the palace. As he left, his brow had been furrowed, and Rhys regretted giving him a new worry in addition to what he already carried. He had enough to be going on with, between Rollo and the sabotage of the viewing stand. He needed to let Rhys worry about Vincent, if anyone was going to.

With Simon gone, Catrin and Rhys left their more isolated seats in order to sit closer to the dais and the king. It had become a habit with Rhys, which he didn't try to fight. If anything, the sabotage of the viewing stand had confirmed the need for renewed vigilance.

"I'm looking forward to hearing the bard who won the contest," Catrin said amiably, evidently aware that Rhys didn't want to talk anymore about Vincent. "Many English participated, more than in the archery contest, but the Welshman we heard yesterday won."

"As with archery, in music the English are woefully inadequate." Rhys too kept his tone light.

"So says the winner of the sixth heat." Catrin actually grinned at Rhys before adding, "I'm so hungry," and setting to her meal with enthusiasm.

Rhys watched her for a moment and then found himself shaking his head. "Even without Vincent's presence here, I find myself unsettled and more than a little daunted. We have a Herculean task before us: somehow, within these hundreds of people, lies Rollo's killer, the carpenter's co-conspirator, and a master thief. The utter lack of conclusive evidence leaves me with an enormous amount of uncertainty. At the moment, I have no idea what to do next."

It was a baldly honest statement, and not one he would have shared with anyone but Catrin. Even with Simon, he might have tempered his doubt a little more.

Catrin set down the knife with which she'd been spearing her carrots. "You have felt that way during every investigation you've conducted, or so you've said. In which case, you shouldn't let it bother you. Something, or someone, will turn up. You have to trust the process."

"I have a process?"

She laughed. "You do, and it's working right now." She gestured to the empty places around them. "Do you think all these seats miraculously opened up near the end of this table as soon as we wanted them?"

He frowned. "I didn't think it was a miracle. I thought the people who'd been sitting here were done."

Still smiling, Catrin reached out a hand and rested it on his arm. "It is lovely that even after everything you've lived through, you can still be trusting. But no, they saw Simon leave us, and then they saw you head towards the end of this table, at which point two places became six. You may notice the other four haven't been filled while we've been sitting here, despite the fact that the pavilion is more crowded than ever."

Rhys gave a low grunt. "Are you sure people aren't avoiding us because we are Welsh?"

"If it was because we are Welsh, the men sitting here would have spread out more, so the two seats you spied would have become no seats. Besides," she gestured to where the bard was preparing to perform, "Welshmen are in favor today."

Rhys rubbed his chin. "I'm not sure how leaving us alone is going to advance the investigation. We need to hear things! We need people to confide in us."

"They'll come. You'll see."

And then, within the space of a few heartbeats and entirely proving Catrin's point, Miles de Bohun slid onto the vacant bench next to Rhys. Despite being Humphrey's uncle, Miles was only a year older than his nephew, making him two years younger than Rhys and the same age as Catrin. But as the eldest son of the eldest son, it was Humphrey who'd inherited the earldom, and whatever lands or station Miles possessed was thanks to Humphrey's largess.

Miles never appeared to resent the quirk of fate that had disinherited him. From birth, he and Humphrey had been close companions. By now, at thirty-six, he had been for many years Humphrey's perfect right-hand man: diplomatic, utterly dependable, and, with so many men between him and the title, completely loyal. In a noble family, there weren't too many men about whom one could say that.

He had also taken the cross in 1270, as part of the proof of his family's loyalty to King Edward and the Church. The Bohuns had been among the barons most active in the Second Baron's War, which ended in 1265 at the Battle of Evesham. Humphrey's father had been captured in the final battle and died of his wounds. In the process, the family had lost favor with the king. But with the death of Humphrey's father, the grandfather had made a deal, buying favor with the king through payment and—in Miles's case—the pledge to Crusade of his youngest son.

In the Holy Land, Simon and Rhys had served in the retinue of Prince Edmund, but they'd mixed with King Edward's men, and, since the three of them were similar ages, they'd been thrown together often. Miles was technically of higher rank than both Rhys and Simon, but he'd never stood on ceremony. And since he had no land of his own, being the youngest son of many, he'd acknowledged that Simon, who would inherit land from his father, could eventually end up more highly placed than he. Like Simon and Rhys, Miles had started out thinking the entire endeavor was a lark, and ended up, in the grit and desperation of Acre, a much older man than his twenty-two years.

As was the case with virtually every other man in Nefyn, Rhys hadn't seen Miles since before the 1282 war. Unlike at Evesham, in that war, the Bohuns had been on the winning side. Miles was also one of the few Marcher lords who himself had no Welsh blood, even if he had relatives who'd married Welshwomen in the years the Welsh kings and princes had been looking for alliances as a way to stem the bloodshed in the March.

"Reese."

"Miles."

"My nephew would speak to you." Straight to the point, as always.

"I would be pleased to hear whatever he has to say."

Rhys had conversed very briefly with Humphrey at Caernarfon Castle, in the first moments of his return to the fold, so to speak. In fact, Humphrey had been the first baron to step forward to grasp Rhys's forearm in greeting. He hadn't had to do that. Rhys's rank was many levels below Humphrey's, and they'd never had a relationship. It seemed that was about to change.

Miles snorted laughter. "How is it that I haven't spoken to you since we returned from Acre, and yet, from the way you look and speak, it could have been last week?"

Rhys had always liked Miles, and he quirked a grin. "I suppose I should be discouraged that I'm so predictable. I *am* older now, believe me."

"You are certainly smarter, given the company you're keeping." Miles turned to Catrin with a querying look on his face.

Rhys made the introductions, and Miles stood to bow over Catrin's hand. "Please advise me when you tire of this rogue's company."

His comment could have been *pro forma,* or even said with a leer, but Miles was looking at Catrin with utter earnestness.

"Are you saying you will watch his back if I let him go with you?" Catrin said.

Miles gaped at her for a heartbeat, having expected a more traditional response, and then he laughed openly. "As I was saying."

Then he leaned forward, both hands on the table, and said in a low tone. "St. Mary's Church. One hour. They're burying Clare's man Rollo this evening. I assume you were planning to attend?"

"I was." Rhys thought it disturbingly typical that nobody had told him about the service.

Miles gave Catrin another flourishing bow, nodded at Rhys, and turned on his heel to stroll back across the pavilion. He disappeared shortly thereafter amidst a crowd of men from the Bohun camp—at the very instant the bard launched into the first of his ballads. It was another one of Taliesin's about Arthur. Likely, he'd finish the evening with the song that had won him the competition.

"You seem to have been missed." Rhys indicated the front of the room, which was now filled with members of the royal court. The queen had put in an appearance tonight, wearing a rich red gown meant for Westminster Palace but didn't look out of place in Nefyn among this company. Her cousin Margaret was beside her, in a gown of dark brown, currently looking daggers at Catrin.

Catrin sighed. "You'll have to go without me. She doesn't approve of how much time I spend with you." She rose to her feet, prompting Rhys to stand too. Then, with a gleam in her eye, Catrin stood on her tiptoes in order to kiss him on the cheek.

Rhys's hand went to the place she'd touched, still feeling the warmth of her lips on his skin. "Catrin—"

She smiled up at him. "Is she still watching?"

His eyes flicked to the high table and Margaret's face. "I believe so. The queen too. Possibly we just had the entire hall as witness."

"Good." Catrin gave him a quick nod. "It's about time we put a stop to any uncertainty about what you mean to me."

20

Day Two

Catrin

Though she knew she'd shocked him, Rhys gave her a real smile. Then, with a slight bow to someone behind her, whom she assumed was Margaret, he strode from the pavilion. The mass for poor Rollo couldn't wait. What's more, neither could Humphrey de Bohun.

She could have pretended she wasn't entirely sure what had come over her to make her kiss Rhys in public or that she wasn't aware such a display of affection between two unmarried people was forbidden, even in such raucous conditions as a tournament pavilion.

But she knew.

She was tired of the back and forth. She was tired of uncertainty. And more than anything, she was tired of always watching herself and never allowing who she was inside to show.

Most people lived that way all the time, as she did and would again as soon as her heart stopped pounding at her audacity. For one moment, she had deliberately given in to impulse. Maybe she would pay for that. She hoped not, but even if she did, she couldn't regret the look in Rhys's eyes.

She'd seen surprise there. And a little consternation. But mostly joy. If that was all she could have from him because the queen was about to tell her she mustn't associate with him again, she could survive on that look for a long time—while she figured out how to change the queen's mind.

Margaret's expression was pinched, to say the least, and Catrin gave her a gracious smile as she made her way towards the high table and its associated smaller tables at which Eleanor and her ladies were sitting. But at her arrival, the queen merely nodded calmly at her in greeting, most of her attention on the bard and the music. And Margaret barely twitched in her direction, giving no indication of her disdain for Catrin's unseemly behavior.

Catrin sat beside Margaret in the chair the servant pulled out for her, suddenly confused. It was unlike Rhys to be so mistaken, but maybe for once he was. Catrin's kiss *had* been a quick gesture of affection.

Instead of chastising Catrin, Margaret was glaring down the pavilion towards several young women giggling together in an open space between tables, directly behind where Catrin and Rhys had been sitting.

Catrin cleared her throat to get Margaret's attention. "Were you wanting me?"

"What?" Margaret glanced at her. "No. Why?"

"I thought—" Catrin broke off, almost laughing now at how she and Rhys had constructed a reality based on guesses and their own fears. They'd assumed her kiss was momentous to everyone else because it had been so to them. "What's the matter?"

"Those girls." Margaret pointed at them with her nose and continued the daggers look Catrin had thought she'd been directing her way. "Do you know them?"

"No," Catrin said. "Should I?"

"I think I should."

Catrin knew well that she wasn't as young as she used to be. Queen Eleanor had a mirror that told her that every day, even if she hadn't been fully aware of the wrinkles around her mouth and eyes—and the stretch marks on her belly and thighs. In the last two months, she'd actually slimmed down some, as evidenced by a strange looseness in the waist of her dresses. But with marriage and child-bearing, at thirty-six she was hardly the lithe girl she'd been when she'd been given in marriage to Robert. More recently, when she tended her hair, she'd found white strands amidst the red.

Rhys thought she was beautiful and told her so with embarrassing frequency. But as Catrin looked at the three girls, who'd since been joined by a fourth, and then swept her eyes around the room, she realized these were four of at least a dozen unusually beautiful young women present that evening.

"Are they prostitutes?" she asked Margaret, a little embarrassed as to where her mind had gone first.

"Surely not!" While those were the first words out of Margaret's mouth, shocked to her very core, a moment later she reconsidered. "They can't be. The queen would never tolerate it. I don't care how beautiful they are or who brought them."

Maybe in prior royal courts, that of King John sprang to mind, the activities and tolerances of court life reflected the tastes of the king. While rumor had it that John had been faithful to his second wife, Isabella of Angoulême, his many affairs and improprieties earlier in his reign (before his first marriage was annulled) had encouraged the same behavior in the people who served him. Margaret was right that King Edward's court had a different ethic entirely.

"Maybe they're not prostitutes," Catrin said, "but they are *something*. While they are lovely and young, to me they have a look that goes beyond a girl searching for a husband."

Margaret turned her gaze on Catrin. "How would you know that?"

"I have lived in the world, Margaret." What she didn't say was *how can you* not *know that?* "Look past their outward demeanor to their eyes."

Margaret turned silent, surprising Catrin by doing as she bid her. For Catrin's part, the more she watched the young women, the more convinced she was that she'd judged them correctly. They'd separated now, two and two, and were moving amongst the diners, drawing the admiring eyes of every man present. Two of them had moved closer to the dais. While one had seated herself among several older knights and men-at-arms Catrin didn't recognize, conversing animatedly with them, the other had turned away, her eyes searching the faces of those around them. This woman's gaze wasn't general; she was looking for a particular person.

Because of the woman's focus, Catrin was able to look more openly at her. In so doing, she realized she'd seen her before: this was the blonde woman from the makeshift tavern who'd almost poured her cup of mead down Catrin's front. Within the space of a heartbeat, the woman caught the eye of the man she was looking for, he nodded, and she moved on, laughing merrily at something one of the young nobles at another table had said.

Catrin switched her gaze to the man. He was of average height and quite handsome, with dark hair, a clean-shaven chin, and the clothes of a courtier rather than a soldier, though many men had forgone their armor tonight, so that might not mean anything. He was seated at a table with several men in the party of the Earl of Richmond, who was not present himself, but had sent his eighteen-year-old son John to head the delegation in his stead.

John's mother was the king's sister, and while Edward held the family in high regard, John's father hadn't set foot in England in years. This man was not one she'd seen in John's company before, though perhaps that was only because John himself had just returned to England after a lengthy absence.

Margaret leaned in to Catrin. "You are right." Then she stood abruptly and made her way a few seats down to the queen.

Catrin had almost forgotten Margaret was beside her, focused as she'd been on the crowded pavilion. Now she looked past her neighbor to where the queen sat. Margaret was speaking too quietly for Catrin to hear what she was saying, but she didn't need to eavesdrop because, after a few more words, Margaret retook her seat next to Catrin.

"The queen wants you to find out who they are, how many they are, and in whose company they came to Nefyn."

Catrin had a pretty good idea of the latter answer already but didn't say so, not wanting to make any assumptions before she'd even started asking questions. "I will see what I can discover and report back."

"Thank you."

The conversation had been a far cry from the drubbing Catrin had thought she'd be getting for displaying affection to Rhys for all to see, and she and Margaret had suddenly achieved a level of accord that was unprecedented. Catrin decided to take it as the gift it was and not question it.

By speaking to the queen, Margaret had handed Catrin yet another mystery, but it was one she thought could be resolved quickly if she asked the right questions of the right people. Spotting her own son standing next to one of the poles that supported the pavilion, she left the dais for his side—though in doing so, she interrupted the conversation he was having with another man.

"Bertold," she said with a bob of her head.

"My lady." Bertold owned an estate near the one her husband, and now Justin, held. "Such a pleasure to see you so well."

"You are as kind as ever."

Bertold understood her words to be a dismissal. They were of equal rank so she didn't have the right or power to dismiss him, but she was Justin's mother, so he nodded and said to Justin, "We'll speak later."

When he'd gone, Catrin raised her eyebrows at her son, though he could have just as legitimately raised them at her.

"We want to survive the mêlée," he said flatly, "and we wouldn't mind winning a prize or two along the way."

"Bertold fights as well? How many men are going to be in this battle?"

"Fifty." He paused. "On each side."

His reply struck Catrin dumb. When she found her voice, she said, "Isn't that more than the usual number?"

"It is." Justin glanced at her, and his expression softened when he saw the worry in her face. "I can survive an hour on the field, don't worry. And truly, my role in the battle is to protect Hugh. If he falls, Clare will have to pay ransom to the victor for Hugh as well as for all of us. It will be a great sum, but it will not pauper him." His chin firmed. "We must not lose."

Catrin didn't want to undermine her son's resolve, but she had to ask, "Is there a greater chance of that now that you don't have Rollo?"

Justin had momentarily looked past her, but now he returned his attention to her face. "Yes." The word came out heavy, but then he lightened it with a cant of his head. "Hugh is an able warrior, but surviving the mêlée requires clever tactics as well as skill with a blade. Rollo had experience, in battle and in tournaments. Bertold and I were just discussing the desperate need to acquire more of it."

"You might stay close to the king," Catrin said. "Rhys and Simon—and the entire king's guard—is fighting to protect him. Rhys has never fought in a tournament, but he is older than you and looks upon injury incurred in the course of a mêlée with an even more jaundiced eye than you. His mandate to protect the king is equally great."

"And we are on the same side." A thoughtful look came into Justin's eyes, and the pinching around his mouth smoothed a little. "Thank you, Mam."

It was the Welsh way of saying *mother*, which Catrin hadn't heard come out of her son's mouth in two years, not since the funeral for Robert. She wanted to hug him, but she also didn't want to put him off using it again by drawing attention to what he'd said.

So instead, she asked him about what the queen had wanted her to discover: "Who is that man?"

Justin's expression brightened. "Bernard fitz Courcy. An able fellow."

"You know him?"

"Indeed. He is steward of Richmond Castle, overseeing the estates of the Earl of Richmond. It is a fine living, and he has wide influence." Now Justin's expression turned thoughtful. "No land of his own, of course. He's descended from a Courcy by-blow, not of the main line."

Catrin had understood that to be the case because of the *fitz* in his name. It meant *son of* and had come in many cases to reference an acknowledged son but one born out of wedlock. Back when Wales had been free, any son who was acknowledged by his father was seen as legitimate, but the king's new laws had swept that provision away, and now illegitimate Welsh children suffered under the same stigma—at least in the eyes of the law and the church—as their English and Norman counterparts.

"I can tell by your expression that you like him."

"He is very jovial, always willing to lend a hand. He's good at acquiring things, which in this encampment is helpful. Because of him, I found myself with a pair of excellent fitting boots when I tore a hole in the leather of my old pair the day I arrived." He wiggled his toes as Catrin looked down at his feet.

A frisson went through her. Such behavior reminded her of Rhys, since that was the kind of thing he had done for the conquerors when he'd been living in Caernarfon.

It didn't make her trust Bernard, however, since Rhys had been deliberately lulling his overlords into liking him.

When next she looked at her son, his attention had been caught again, and she turned to see what had drawn his eye this time. Somehow, she wasn't surprised that it was one of the beautiful girls. "Who is she?"

He blinked. "I don't know. I think she's a relation of—" he scratched the back of his head, "—the Earl of Surrey." Then he put out a hand to his mother. "Think nothing of it. Adele and I are doing well, and she bears my child."

Catrin gave a little squeak and threw her arms around her son's neck. "I had hoped one day to hear that news from you."

Justin smiled broadly. "It's a blessing it happened so quickly." Then his smile faltered. "Mother, I have never asked, and I hope you do not take offense that I do so now—but why did you and father have no other children?"

"I will never take offense at any question you ask me." She put a hand to his cheek, guessing that he was asking only now because he was facing parenthood himself. For the first time, he was able to place himself in her shoes. "I had three miscarriages after you were born." She shook her head. "It was so hard to—"

She broke off as her suddenly grown-up son wrapped her up in a hug. "I love you, Mam."

"Fy mab annwyl." *My beloved son.* "I love you too."

21

Day Two

Rhys

Rhys had spent the year he'd lived in Caernarfon working very hard to remain unassuming, as being underestimated by those he served meant he was free to go about his business as he saw fit. Since he'd begun his renewed service with the king, however, he'd deliberately cultivated the exact opposite persona. At long last, he could be open and above board again. With him, what you saw was what you got. And that was despite being the king's spymaster. Spying involved a very different form of deception than hiding at all times what was in his heart.

He found it personally refreshing, though it apparently hadn't improved his mood. It just went to show that a man took his happiness—or unhappiness—with him.

He had promised Simon he would do better, and even if it had been only a day, he thought he'd already made a good start. It helped that most of the people he worked with had no knowledge of who he'd been between Prince Llywelyn's death and when the king had come to Caernarfon in April.

"Where are you going?" Simon hailed him as he came out from the guardhouse at the palace gate just as Rhys was passing by on his way to the church.

It was unique in Rhys's experience to see so many knights walking, since, as a rule, they rode everywhere. Although as a member of the king's guard, Rhys had a horse of his own these days, he hadn't been riding her around Nefyn for the same reason Simon was walking now: there were too many people about and the distances were too short to warrant saddling up in order to travel a hundred yards.

Rhys had learned, in his year in Caernarfon, that walking helped him think, though he wished he had Catrin on his arm. They'd been walking together so often lately that, even in the short distance from the dining pavilion, he'd looked to his left with something he wanted to tell her before he remembered she wasn't actually there. He still couldn't believe she'd kissed his cheek in front of everyone. They were going to have to talk about that as soon as they had a free moment—investigation or no investigation. He had a thought also that they needed to do it before the mêlée, so he could wear her colors around his arm. He was in no way troubled by the fact that she'd made the first move. He had been biding his time, not wanting to upset the apple cart, and her kissing him would now allow him to tell her the truth.

He loved her.

By all that was holy, he'd always loved her.

There was something extraordinary about knowing someone as long as he and Catrin had known each other and finding themselves genuinely in love twenty years later. It made him believe the sun would continue to rise and set, despite the destruction of his country and his way of life. Here was a smidgen of hope in a world gone wrong. Here was genuine love as in the king's tales of Arthur.

He did not say any of that to Simon.

"Rollo's funeral is imminent." Rhys also didn't mention Humphrey's summons, not here, not out loud. If their conversation proved informative, he could tell his friend about it afterwards.

Simon frowned. "Why wasn't I told?"

"I wasn't told either. I heard about it just now when Catrin and I were at our meal. I left my food and came immediately."

"But not Catrin?"

"She was wanted at the high table." Rhys grimaced, thinking about the next steps if they were to formalize their relationship and deciding he didn't, in fact, need to keep his thoughts from Simon. "I fear the amount of time she spends with me has brought censure down upon her."

"Has it?"

"Hasn't it?" Rhys was genuinely surprised at Simon's surprise.

"Not that I have heard, and I think I would have heard." Simon matched his steps to Rhys's as they walked up the road to the church. Rhys hadn't actually expected Simon to come with him, and he was a little disconcerted as to how he was going to explain his meeting with Humphrey without offending Simon that he wasn't invited.

And then he mentally shook himself again. This was Simon he was talking to. He would understand the need for Rhys to meet Bohun alone and, what's more, encourage him to do so.

"Margaret told her once outright that she shouldn't spend so much time with me."

"That was in Caernarfon, when you weren't a kingsman. Before I left to visit my wife and children last month, I overheard her telling another of the queen's women that *of course* it made sense to elevate you to acting captain in my absence, and how appropriate it was that the two Welsh people in the king's service should find each other. It spared the queen having to find a man not of Catrin's own kind for Catrin to marry."

Rhys's step faltered, and he almost stumbled over a largish stone in the middle of the road. "She didn't say that!" He was practically gasping with laughter.

"On my honor." Simon put a hand to his heart, laughing himself at Rhys's astonishment. But then he sobered. "Leave it to Margaret to, at one and the same time, compliment you and disparage your entire people. I'm sorry."

"I have heard worse, believe me." Shaking his head, Rhys continued to stump along beside his friend, his eyes on the road before him. "Have I been a fool?"

"Invariably," Simon said dryly. "But what makes you ask me that in this moment?"

"I have been afraid to broach the subject of Catrin's and my future because I thought any relationship with her was better than no relationship."

"Do you want to marry her?"

Rhys swallowed hard that Simon would ask the question so openly. But it showed how far the two of them had come in a few months—and probably how obvious was his and Catrin's attachment to each other. Simon had been married for over ten years to the daughter of a baron who owned land near Simon's estate. Their marriage was a happy one as far as Rhys knew, an actual love match in that Simon and Jenet had been playmates from birth, much like Rhys and Catrin.

"Yes."

"Praise the Lord. I never thought I would see the day." Simon slapped Rhys on the back. "Well done."

"I haven't spoken to her about it yet! I haven't talked to the king."

"To tell you the truth, I have been wondering what you were waiting for." Simon came to an abrupt halt in the road, looking for all intents and purposes as if he meant for Rhys to turn around right then and there to fall on his knees before Catrin. Or the king.

Rhys took his friend by the arm, to keep him facing the direction they'd been going. "You had to ask permission to see your wife and children, after being separated from them for months. I don't want to marry Catrin only to find she cannot travel with me anymore. The whole point is to be with her all the time. You may have noticed that none of the ladies who serve the queen are married."

"I hadn't." Simon rocked back on his heels slightly. "Is that by design?"

"I don't know."

Simon made a *hmmm* sound deep in his throat and tapped a finger to his lips. "Perhaps a few subtle inquiries can be made."

Rhys looked at his friend, grateful beyond measure, but ... "It should be me who inquires. I want Catrin to be *my* wife."

Simon scoffed. "When was the last time you were subtle?" He shook his head. "I am your commander. It is only right that you should come to me first with your request, and I will look into the possibility for you. Leave this to me."

The thought had Rhys setting off at Simon's side with a lighter heart and less weight of emotion. During the first six months Rhys had lived in Caernarfon, respected by the Welsh but not trusted, while being sneered at or ignored by the Norman conquerors and their English subjects, he had not developed friendships per se. At one point, early in his sojourn, Gruffydd, the village headman had inquired as to the reason he always drank alone at the village tavern, and, when he did stop by, it was never for long. Rhys had been within a hair's-breadth from snapping back, "All of my friends are dead, and none of you want to be seen conversing with me in case I immediately report you to the castle. So yes, if I go to the tavern at all it's to drink alone!"

That had changed as time had gone on, and the villagers had learned to trust him. But the differences in their stations had continued to act as a barrier between them, and no other Welsh knights had survived the war—or at least none that Rhys wanted to befriend. He remained close to Catrin's brothers, Hywel and Tudur, and he and Catrin had been breakfasting with them every morning since their arrival at Nefyn.

However, her brothers' had both a higher rank than he and a more precarious one: they had survived Edward's purge of Welsh noblemen but were not necessarily accepted by their English and Norman brethren, regardless of Edward's assertions that they should be. Perhaps that would come in time. For now, they had set up their tents near Clare's and would be fighting in the mêlée beside his men—and the king. Rhys was feeling protective of them, and he didn't want to do anything that would in any way jeopardize their current relations with their peers or the crown.

So while Rhys and Simon would continue to disagree over the state of the world, Simon remained Rhys's closest (male) companion, never mind that he was Norman. If Rhys was ever so lucky as to marry Catrin, it would be Simon who stood up beside him at the church.

With that thought in mind, Rhys eyed Nefyn's church with a new eye, wondering how quickly the ceremony joining them could take place, and if they would want to do it here. Really, he would prefer Caernarfon, overseen by the beloved Father Medwyn. Or Conwy, where his sister lived. Caernarfon was a good day's ride away, however, and Conwy even farther. With Catrin's son here, as well as her brothers, perhaps there really was no time like the present.

The village had always had a church on this spot, but the Augustinian monastery had taken it over a hundred and fifty years earlier. While the church itself was used by both monastery and village, the monks worked from an adjacent cloister with the requisite monastic buildings that included a dormitory, chapter house, guest-house, dining hall, and abbot's quarters.

Unlike the Cistercians, who the princes and kings of Gwynedd had often favored, Augustinian monks were charged with going out into the world and seeing to their flock. This meant caring for people rather than sheep (though, here in Nefyn, the Augustinians did that too). Perhaps that was why the herbalist monk, Cadell, had known Adam's name and been out and about enough to recognize him when he passed him in the churchyard.

As they approached St. Mary's, the bell tolled at the gate, telling the people who hadn't witnessed the service inside the church that it had ended, and the burial service was about to begin. It was only then that Rhys realized Miles had meant what he said when he'd told him Rollo was to be buried within the hour.

"I am disconcerted that the mass for Rollo's soul is over, and we truly weren't invited. How is it that someone didn't ensure one of us knew about the service?" Simon leaned into Rhys to make his comment, though whispering wasn't really necessary, given the fifty people currently standing outside the church gate. They weren't a raucous crowd by any means, but fifty people speaking in low tones was more than enough to drown out any individual conversation, especially theirs, taking place as it was on the edge of the group.

Rhys didn't have to answer because, just then, Hugh spied them and wended his way among the onlookers in their direction. He halted in front of Simon and bent his head respectfully. "If I had known you were waiting out here, I would have ensured you had a place inside. I'm sorry you had to miss the mass."

"Please do not fret on our account," Simon said. "We had other duties and just arrived." This was partly true, and it made no sense to chastise Hugh about their lack of invitation. Charitably, everyone involved had a great deal on their minds, Simon and Rhys included.

But then Simon added, "What was the name of the man you sent to tell me when the service would take place? I would like to thank him again."

The prevarication came out of nowhere. Rhys couldn't remember the last time he'd heard Simon lie so openly, and he immediately dropped his eyes to the ground, initially unable to look at either of the other men in case his face revealed his surprise.

"My apologies, my lord. I was not involved in the planning of the funeral."

"I see." Simon was steadfastly calm. "Who was?"

"Lord Clare, as he was Rollo's lord. Once the burial is accomplished, he intends to open up his pavilion to anyone who would like to pay his respects and asks that we all join him there for the wake after the burial. As to the funeral itself, I believe it was Joan, Sir Rollo's sister, who spoke to the priest about the timing. She was quite adamant that her brother be buried as the sun set. As you can see, you're just in time. They're coming out now."

The timing of the service would have been the primary extent of the planning, since every funeral mass in every corner of Christendom was essentially the same. While a mass needed to be said for a man's soul, it didn't have to be especially scheduled and could take place before or after the burial. Possibly, Gilbert de Clare had provided an offering so it could happen now. Occasionally, if a man was very great, a friend or companion he'd left behind would stand at the gravesite and eulogize him, but otherwise all that was required was for a priest to say the proper words before the person was put into the ground.

"Why weren't you inside?" Rhys asked.

Hugh put a hand to his belly. "Upset stomach."

Rhys and Simon exchanged a thoughtful look Hugh didn't see because he'd turned towards the entrance to the church. Catrin had been concerned about Hugh's safety, fearing Rollo's murderer might target him next because he thought Rollo had shared with him his suspicions about the thefts. While Hugh might be a perfectly capable commander, Rhys worried that he didn't have the experience required. Rhys's private thought was that Clare might be well-served to see Hugh wounded in the jousts so that someone else could step to the fore for the mêlée. Who that might be, Rhys didn't know, but he was glad that the survival in the mêlée of any particular man, Hugh included, no longer needed to be of grave concern.

It was Rhys's thought as well that the king's decree should have eased Hugh's stomach instead of roiling it. Still, Rhys could hardly blame him for being nervous, since he himself had spent overlong in the latrine before his contest too.

As it turned out, it was just as well that Rhys and Simon had missed the initial service inside the church. With so many people coming to pay their last respects, the nave would have been packed to the rafters and then some. In size and shape, the church at Nefyn was not materially different from St. Peblig's. Unlike at Caernarfon, however, the Normans at Nefyn could not retreat to a church built in their own English town, since neither church nor town existed here. Truly, if the village of Nefyn hadn't been one of the most prosperous in Gwynedd, the king would never have come. As far Rhys knew, he had no plans to build a castle here.

Then again, all services were mostly in Latin, and, if Cadell was anything to go by, the priest at Nefyn spoke French too. As Rhys had that thought, the abbot of the monastery exited the church with Clare beside him, both following immediately behind the casket. Behind them walked Joan on the arm of none other than Vincent de Lusignan. Rhys would recognize that trimmed black beard and long nose anywhere, even if he hadn't come face-to-face with him at Cilmeri a year and a half ago and then again a few days ago in the great hall.

Rhys studied the pair, more than a little taken aback. In fact, he was speechless.

Simon, meanwhile, was grinding his teeth, though his tone, when he spoke, was perfectly level. "Why is Joan with Vincent?"

"Did you not know?" Hugh said, in a manner that implied he was unaware of any negative thoughts his audience might be directing towards Valence's servant. "Not three hours ago, he asked Lord Clare for Joan's hand in marriage and was accepted. It solves everyone's problems as to what to do with her."

Rhys looked past Simon to Hugh. "From what I understand, she would hardly be impoverished. Wasn't Rollo quite wealthy? After this tournament, he was going to retire."

"That is true, but he was going to be retiring from tournaments, not from Clare's service. He wasn't even forty, you know."

Rhys did know. As he himself was not quite forty either, he could understand why Rollo would want this to be his last tournament. Rhys was truly hoping it would be his one and only. "Why would Clare approve the match?"

Hugh looked puzzled. "Why wouldn't he?"

Simon spoke next, patience in his voice. "Joan's wealth, which was once Rollo's wealth, goes to Vincent."

"As it should."

Rhys narrowed his eyes at Hugh's obtuseness and spoke very carefully, "I would have thought that Clare would have preferred her to marry someone from within his own retinue, to keep things close to home, so to speak."

"I don't know anything about that. It isn't as if Rollo held any land." Hugh gave them a little bow and moved forward into the churchyard with the other mourners, following the casket to its designated resting place, which was clearly visible in the graveyard by the light of the setting sun.

Simon stayed where he was, frowning. "This worries me."

"In what way?"

"Could—" He stopped and shook his head. "No. It isn't possible."

"What isn't?" Rhys was feeling some real alarm at his friend's uncertainty.

Simon took in a breath. "Could Earl Clare have agreed to the marriage in exchange for keeping you as the investigator?" He shook his head again. "It seems absurd that Clare would care that much."

"But he does care very much. When we were in Rollo's tent, Earl Clare asked if Rollo had been tortured before he died."

Simon's head swung around. "You didn't mention that. What secrets was he worried Rollo could tell?"

Rhys laughed. "He wouldn't tell me."

"No. But it's something to think on. That and the fact that Clare would rather you discovered any secret truths about him than one of his own men or one of Valence's. Why?"

"I don't know."

"Because you're the king's spymaster? How would he even know that? We put out that I had taken over the job."

Rhys simply shook his head again. And truly, the job *was* being done by Simon as much as by Rhys himself, since most everything he learned he told to Simon.

Most everything.

Rhys still hadn't mentioned the meeting with Humphrey de Bohun. Simon was Rhys's superior within the king's guard, but Rhys had more autonomy in his role as spymaster, and this meeting with Humphrey was a secret he guessed the Bohuns were counting on him to keep. Similarly, perhaps, to Clare, and it had occurred to Rhys that Humphrey wanted or needed something significant from Rhys, maybe also similarly to Clare, to have made such an effort to speak to him alone.

Simon harrumphed and then gestured forward. "Shall we?"

"I think I will stay here. Better to watch the goings-on."

"Let me know what you see." Simon went after Hugh, catching him in a few strides.

Rhys was left behind with a host of questions, chief among them how Joan's engagement to Vincent had come about. Maybe it had nothing to do with the murder, but for Vincent to have murdered Rollo in order to marry his sister was well in keeping with his character. In which case, why Vincent might want to be the one to investigate Rollo's death was suddenly starkly clear.

22

Day Two

Catrin

Through her service to the Queen of England, Catrin was familiar with many of the noblemen who'd passed through Edward's court over the last two years. While she didn't feel confident walking up to John de Warenne, the Earl of Surrey, nor to his son William, who was now sitting at Bernard's table, to ask about the woman Justin thought might be the earl's niece, she did feel it was within her purview to speak to Bernard fitz Courcy.

"Might I ask you to introduce me?" she said to Justin.

He blinked. "Why?"

She tipped her head without answering, and he was perceptive enough that his eyes widened. "Are we investigating again, Mam?"

"We are."

A pleased expression crossed his face, and together they meandered through the crowd, trying not to look purposeful, until they arrived at the head of the table where the man in question was in discussion with his fellows.

With all the skill of a professional mummer, Justin passed Bernard by and then turned back, as if he'd just noticed him rather than having been directing his steps towards him all along. "Courcy! How goes it with you?"

"I am very well!" Bernard got to his feet, as did several other men along the table, being polite in the presence of one of the queen's ladies.

"May I introduce you to my mother, Lady Catrin." Justin made an elegant gesture in Catrin's direction. "She was just admiring my new boots."

"I hear you procured them for him." Catrin smiled graciously. "That was well done."

"It is my pleasure always to be of service." Bernard bowed over her hand. As he came up, she looked fully into his face for the first time and realized he was older than she'd thought, past forty, or at least he had more wrinkles on his forehead and around his mouth and eyes than appeared from a distance. She'd been confused into thinking he was younger by the darkness of his hair and its thickness. It was the opposite problem from Rollo, who'd appeared far older than his years.

"Please sit." He gestured for his companions to make room at the table. John, the heir to the Richmond earldom, remained at the far end, deep in conversation with William.

As Bernard's friends went back to their meal, Bernard looked at her expectantly. With a bit of shock, she realized she might have given him the wrong impression by coming over with her son and quickly hastened to divert him. "Justin and I are investigating the death of Rollo. It occurred to me that, with your contacts, perhaps you have heard something about who might have been involved."

She had opted to speak to him of the murder because of its distance from this issue of the girls, which was what she really wanted to know about. Instead of relaxing him, however, his lips pinched and his shoulders tensed briefly, before he rolled them and was back to smiling.

"Rollo? You mean Earl Clare's captain? I'm afraid I don't know anything about his death." Then he frowned. "How is it that *you* are charged with its investigation?"

Justin lifted a hand. "My mother is a close companion to the king's quaestor, Sir Rhys."

"Oh yes, of course." Bernard eased back on his bench. "I saw you together earlier. He served the king in the Holy Land, I understand, and in the same capacity."

"He did." Catrin didn't bother to correct him that Rhys had really worked for Prince Edmund.

Bernard made a little *huh* sound, but seemed satisfied with Rhys's credentials. "As I said, I don't know that I can be of service in any way. Rollo was not a close acquaintance of mine, and we were to have fought on opposite sides in the mêlée. With his death, our chances have improved." He put out a hand to Justin. "This is no slight on Hugh, but he is not Rollo."

"I am not offended, and you are not wrong," Justin said.

As they'd been talking, the young blonde woman from earlier had been approaching. She didn't see Catrin, or at least didn't acknowledge her. Though Bernard didn't acknowledge her either, for a moment they very clearly touched hands, to the point that Catrin could have sworn she saw the girl give him something small, before moving on.

While that was happening, Bernard said something more about the mêlée to Justin, who replied. But Justin had noticed the girl too and now asked outright. "Do you know that young lady who just passed, Courcy? I feel like I've seen her before."

Bernard turned his head to look, equally casually, though some of his initial tension was back. "That is Matilda, a relation of the Earl of Hereford, I believe. Would you like me to introduce you to her?" He spoke in a drawl that belied any of what Catrin was seeing in his body.

It wasn't until recently that Catrin had come to realize she had a knack for reading people's behaviors and emotions and had been sensitive to it at least since she was a girl. Perhaps it had to do with growing up at Prince Llywelyn's court, except she'd been petted and spoiled there and hadn't needed to worry about what other people thought of her. More likely, it had been a product of losing her mother young and having to mediate the complicated relationships between her brothers and father, who hadn't always gotten along.

The crucible had been her marriage to Robert. Though he had always been kind, if somewhat distant, establishing herself as a force to be reckoned with at his manor had required a singular focus at all times on what other people were thinking and feeling. The need to fit in, to not make people angry or upset, while at the same time asserting her own status as Robert's wife, had been pressing. At the time, she'd taken to the task with a will.

Now, at thirty-six, negotiating other people's feelings and emotions had become a way of life, though it was only since Caernarfon and working with Rhys in his investigations that she'd overtly acknowledged that's what she was doing.

In the case of Bernard, he was a bevy of contradictions, in that his words were always smooth and calm, but every now and again his body betrayed what he was saying as a lie, and his jovial attitude never quite reached his eyes.

Justin, who may or may not have been seeing all this too, lifted a hand again, though this time in a motion of dismissal. "It is not important. I was just curious. There are many beautiful women here tonight."

"One of the pleasures of a tournament of this magnificence is that it brings out the women." Bernard was back to expansive. "So much better than war for that!" He turned to Catrin. "We are lucky to have such a one at our table."

"You are too kind." Catrin had one more question to ask. "Have you heard anything about the failure of the viewing stand?"

Bernard had appeared ready to move on, but he straightened in his seat at her question. Where before he'd been tense, now he appeared interested, if not eager. "No. Have you?"

"We are investigating," was all she said.

"So sorry. I wish I could be of help." Bernard's expression briefly became one of disappointment, but then he stood, took her hand again, and kissed it. "I must leave you. Early start in the morning." He gestured down the table, which had thinned out while they'd been talking, to draw the attention of John, the Richmond heir, who was alone now except for one retainer. "My lord, might I introduce to you Lady Catrin and her son Justin, a knight in Earl Clare's retinue?"

"I say, how wonderful." John immediately made his way closer, bowing as Bernard had done over Catrin's hand. "Such a pleasure to meet you, my lady. And you, Sir Justin. Didn't I see you sparring with John Hastings this afternoon? That was well done."

"Thank you, my lord." Justin, in his turn, bowed, since John was of a much higher rank. "It is a pleasure to finally meet you. I am sorry not to have made your acquaintance earlier."

"I only just arrived from Brittany. Bernard mentioned the other day that you fought in the war our king brought to such a fine conclusion."

"I did," Justin said, and then added. "I lost my father at Llandeilo Fawr." He said the place name the Welsh way.

"My condolences." John didn't miss a beat and bent his head in acknowledgment of Justin's grief. "I was sorry to miss it, as my experience in battle is minimal. Though tournaments are no substitute, I am hoping to learn a great deal over the next few days."

John was remarkably open and innocent, talking so frankly about his inexperience that Catrin wanted to shush him. She didn't think he had even been drinking over much, but that this was just his way.

That he was the heir to the Earldom of Richmond was all that had protected him so far from the repercussions of too much honesty. Though she liked John on first acquaintance far more than Bernard, he perhaps could learn something from his father's steward about discretion.

Still, he was providing an opportunity she was willing to exploit. "You heard, I assume, about the death of Rollo, Earl Clare's captain?"

"Indeed. Such a tragedy." John appeared so accustomed to spouting platitudes that he did in this instance as well.

She put out a hand, almost touching him but not quite, since that wouldn't have been seemly. "He was murdered, my lord."

"So Bernard said. A thieving gone wrong, was it?"

"We don't know," she said. "We fear someone had a personal grievance."

John nodded sagely back. "Or wanted him out of the mêlée."

"Is that what you heard?" Justin eased back slightly from the table. "Someone murdered him so he couldn't fight in the tournament?"

"It seems logical," John said. "So Bernard said, and I concur."

So Bernard said. Catrin was suddenly concerned that the Richmond heir had learned too much from Bernard. He needed a minder, and quickly. Still, his innocence was endearing.

"Did Bernard say anything about these thefts?" she asked.

"Not to me."

"You haven't had any issues in your camp?"

"No. Not that I know, though, Bernard would be the one to take care of that sort of thing. I myself am not missing any items, however."

Justin drew John's attention to another of the beautiful girls, this one dark-haired and dark-eyed. She was laughing with William, the Surrey heir, to whom John had been speaking earlier and Justin had initially thought Matilda had been related. "Do you know that girl over there?"

John turned to look. "Aren't you married?"

"I am indeed." Justin smiled. "I wasn't asking for me."

"She's the niece of someone." He snapped his fingers. "Warwick, I think. Elizabeth is her name."

The Earl of Warwick had been a commander in the field for King Edward throughout the war with Llywelyn. In his forties, of an age with the king, his heir was twelve and not present at Nefyn. Unlike Clare, who was a few years younger, Warwick would be fighting in the mêlée at the king's side.

Catrin studied the way the girls, as well as their relations, had spread themselves around the room. If any of these girls actually were relatives of noblemen, then likely nothing was amiss, and she was reading far too much into what she was seeing. Bernard and the girl Matilda could be secretly in love, for example, but unable to speak openly because she was related to an earl and Bernard was merely a descendant of the bastard son of one, never mind that he was steward to the Earl of Richmond.

Alternatively, something odd was going on, and things weren't what they seemed. As Justin continued to converse jovially with John, Catrin sipped the cup of mead a serving girl had poured for her and considered what she'd learned so far. She didn't have anything like enough answers, and she didn't know if the situation with Bernard was in any way connected to her investigation with Rhys.

But her curiosity was piqued, and she would have been determined to find out what was going on even without her marching orders from the queen.

23

Day Two

Rhys

A s Rhys had discussed just that morning with the king, in a situation in which he was uncertain, either of his own wisdom or his companions' motives, it was sometimes best to brazen out his ignorance and act as if he knew what he was doing. He was not unaware that his success in that regard when he'd worked for Prince Edmund had led to an aura of omniscience and a reputation for always getting his man.

And while he had enough self-awareness to realize that he was more intelligent than the average fellow, he also knew that his success in resolving his investigations had more to do with the fact that he was also diligent and stubborn. But if people wanted to believe he knew more than he did, he had never seen the sense in dissuading them of their opinion. Often it resulted in them overthinking their own plots and plans.

He didn't know if that was what was happening now, but he couldn't be sorry that Catrin's words in the pavilion had proved to be prescient within moments of her speaking them. Over time, he *had* learned to trust the process. He'd merely lost his faith for a time.

Rhys finally spied Humphrey and Miles de Bohun standing next to William Mortimer. Normally the Mortimers and Bohuns hated each other. Rhys didn't know if the proximity and conversation, which was evident as Miles and William leaned in to speak to one another, nodding and straightening as one does when the conversation is amiable, was simply being conventionally polite or if it signaled some new *rapprochement*. King Edward had been insistent that his barons get along if he was to have a real Round Table in the spirit of Arthur.

Why William was bothering to attend this service, Rhys didn't know. It wasn't only the Bohuns who hated the Mortimers, but the Clares did too, in large part because the Mortimers had the distinction of being the one Marcher family that had always stayed true to the king. It made them superior in their own eyes too, which raised the hackles of everyone else. It had to be said, however, that King Edward didn't seem to feel the same allegiance, as it had taken him a disturbingly long time for him to approve Edmund to his father's earldom. That delay was one reason Edmund had lured Llywelyn into the ambush at Cilmeri, to curry favor with the king and prove his loyalty.

Those were sour thoughts, however, and none too useful at this late date. They also had nothing to do with William, who had not been involved in these machinations. He was from a cadet branch of the family, come to serve his wealthier, more endowed cousins in much the same way Miles served Humphrey. Since only Miles and William were interacting, perhaps these two lesser family members were serving as liaisons between their more powerful relations, just as Humphrey had sent Miles to speak to Rhys.

The churchyard had been laid out so the graves lay mostly to the south and west of the church itself, and a spot had been found for Rollo at the end of a row of more recent graves. Often it seemed people were put in the ground haphazardly, but at Nefyn the bulk of the graves were in ordered rows, either a quality of the Augustinians, having taken over the church a hundred and fifty years earlier, or the particular proclivities of the last few abbots.

Rhys found a spot from which to watch, some thirty feet from the gravesite and approximately ten feet behind and to the left of the Bohuns, who hadn't placed themselves towards the front of the crowd either. It would have been Humphrey's right as a high nobleman, but with so many earls present in one spot, some of the usual strictures about who had to stand where had been relaxed.

Neither of the Bohuns gave any indication they were waiting for someone (namely, Rhys), but then Miles looked casually around, and his eyes passed over Rhys as if he didn't see him. Then, as he turned back to face front, he nudged his nephew's elbow. Humphrey's only acknowledgment, if that's even what one could call it, was to lift his chin.

None of this was surprising, given the Bohuns' long and not-so-storied history of intrigue. Still, as Rhys studied the backs of the noblemen's heads, he could only admire the Bohuns' thoroughness and attention to detail for this meeting. He was, dare he say it, almost honored that they had chosen to include him in their little subterfuge and had assumed he would be able to play along. They might even have something to teach him.

From the churchyard, the land was essentially flat until it dropped off precipitously to the beach and the Irish Sea. Thus, it was possible to time the start of the interment to the exact moment the bottom edge of the sun started to fall below the horizon. The desire for a sunset burial could be the reason no houses or structures had been built directly to the west of the church. The view was spectacular, and Rhys allowed the rhythm of the Latin words, ones he'd heard a thousand times before (more's the pity), to wash over him.

Mass had already been said, so this was a matter of a few last words, and even though many noblemen were present and Rollo had been a staunch companion his entire life, nobody—not Clare, Hugh, or even Joan—said anything after the priest had finished. Then, as the sun descended further, the body was lowered into the ground with slow reverence, such that the ropes were loosened just as the last rays shot towards the church and reflected off the steeple.

Within a few moments the congregation began to disperse, and the gravediggers started throwing dirt over the body. As before, Clare and the priest went first, processing ahead of Joan, still on Vincent de Lusignan's arm, followed by many retainers. The majority had departed by the time Miles de Bohun fetched up at Rhys's elbow. "He'll be waiting in the church."

"And you?"

"I have other duties."

They were speaking in an undertone, standing casually near one another, and Rhys decided he would take advantage of the opportunity he'd been given. "You knew Rollo well?"

"Not so well, but I did know him."

"What can you tell me about his death?"

"Nothing." Miles chuckled low under his breath. "You are here to speak to my nephew, not me."

Rhys tsked through his teeth. "That may be, but I know Rollo only in death. You knew him in life even if *not so well*. Anything you can tell me would be helpful."

"I apologize for misleading you. We spoke to each other perhaps three or four times in my life."

Rhys decided he lost nothing by continuing his questions. "Have you any notion who might have sabotaged the viewing stand?"

Miles blinked a little at the change of subject and then spread his hands wide. "I am no carpenter." Then he gave Rhys a barely perceptible nod, indicating the conversation was over, and faded towards the stone wall that surrounded the church. Rhys was left alone under the protection of a spreading yew tree, set to the south of the church so it wouldn't block the view of the sea.

Although he'd struggled with patience when he'd been quaestor to Prince Edmund, the ability to watch and wait had practically been a way of life during Rhys's year of exile in Caernarfon. While these days Rhys was coming more and more out of his shell and starting to care very much about a great deal again, a fact almost entirely attributable to the return of Catrin to his life, ironically Rollo's death wasn't necessarily one of those things.

But even so, he was determined to discover who killed him and what relationship his death had to these thefts. Now that the tournament had started, if Rhys didn't wrap up this investigation in the next two days he never would. The participants and guests would leave Nefyn, returning to their far-flung manors and castles, and whoever was responsible would go with them.

The last of the townspeople passed through the churchyard gate, leaving in the graveyard only Rhys and a single gravedigger, who was more than halfway finished covering the body with dirt. Miles had disappeared, so it was left to Rhys to approach the gravedigger and toss him a small coin. The man ducked his head in thanks and began shoveling faster, understanding that the purpose of the coin was to pay him to depart. A dozen shovelfuls later, he hustled away, leaving Rhys alone in the growing darkness.

Only after the gravedigger disappeared through a side gate, heading for a shed where the tools were kept, did Rhys himself move, entering the church to find Humphrey entirely alone. By the freshly swept floor, the monks had already come in to clean. The next monastic service wouldn't occur for several hours.

Humphrey himself was kneeling on a padded stool before the altar, to all appearances deep in prayer. Since Rhys was here at Humphrey's request, he waited at the entrance to the nave for the Marcher lord to notice him, which he did a moment later when he stood, made the sign of the cross, and turned around. At that point, Miles opened the main door to the church, stuck his head inside, and made a twirling motion in the air with his finger. Rhys took him to mean that he would be doing a circuit of the building to make sure nobody else was watching or listening. Rhys thought, but didn't say, that in another quarter of an hour, it wouldn't matter who was milling about, since it would be too dark to make out anyone's identity.

Miles left again, and Humphrey strolled towards one of the alcoves on the northern side of the nave. He still hadn't spoken, which Rhys thought odd, but he settled himself on the bench next to Humphrey nonetheless, as the baron appeared to want.

And, once again, discovered Humphrey knew what he was doing.

Whether by accident or design, once seated in the alcove, all sound was dampened, to the point that the silence pressed on Rhys's ears.

Humphrey leaned back against the wall and stretched out his legs in front of him. Rhys himself didn't quite have the aplomb to relax so completely in an earl's presence. It was strange enough to be sitting beside him as if they were equals. He could have feigned confidence, but sensed that Humphrey would see right through it.

"I'm sure you're wondering why I asked you here."

"Yes, my lord." Rhys waited. He'd done everything Humphrey had asked, so it was up to Humphrey now to tell him why.

"If I can be of any assistance whatsoever in the pursuit of Rollo's killer, you need only to ask."

Rhys tried not to stare at the Marcher lord. That wasn't quite the impression he'd gained from Miles, who'd been reluctant to answer any question about Rollo. "What ... kind of assistance are you offering?"

Humphrey took in an easy breath and let it out. "It would be best if you asked your questions more specifically and in such a way that I could give you simple answers."

Suddenly, Rhys understood what was happening: while Humphrey wanted Rhys to know what he knew, he wanted to answer *yes* or *no* and little more. Rhys was to guess instead, which would allow Humphrey to keep his answers brief. And the only reason he would be concerned about this—and being seen with Rhys—was because he feared being questioned later by the king, other noblemen, or a member of the clergy. He wanted not to have to lie.

Interesting.

Perhaps it shouldn't have been, thinking back to their first meeting at Caernarfon Castle in April. Humphrey, of all the barons, had been the first to greet Rhys as if he was nearly an equal. Even now, Rhys didn't know why. Maybe, if this conversation went on long enough, he'd ask.

"Am I to understand that you know something about Rollo's death?"

"Yes."

Perhaps that answer should have been obvious, but it was worth asking the question, given the game they were playing.

"Did you know Rollo before the events of this week?"

The corners of Humphrey's mouth lifted. "Yes."

"Did you know that he was an inveterate gambler?"

Now Humphrey's eyes lit, and he actually gave Rhys a complete sentence. "You don't beat around the bush, do you? Yes, I did."

Maybe they were getting somewhere. "Do you see a connection between this fact and his death?"

That prompted a thoughtful look and a pause. "No."

"What about these thefts? Do you think you know something about that?"

"Yes."

"They are related to Rollo's death?"

Humphrey wet his lips. "Perhaps."

"How do you know this?"

"Ask me something else."

Rhys paused, thinking furiously about everything he'd uncovered so far. "I assume you noticed that Rollo's sister Joan left the church on Vincent de Lusignan's arm. If you don't mind me saying, you have no love for either the Clares or the Valences, but do you think their engagement has something to do with Rollo's death?"

"I had noticed." Humphrey sat up straighter. "But, no. It isn't her relationship with Vincent that concerns me."

That was a longer reply too. Fearing to push his luck but not wanting to stem the flow of information, Rhys put a fist to his lips and studied Humphrey over it. "Joan has a connection to someone whom you suspect of having a role in the thefts—and perhaps Rollo's death—but that someone is not Vincent."

"Correct."

"Who?"

But Humphrey refused to name him.

Rhys was tired of this game, even as he understood Humphrey's need for it. "Rollo was found suffocated underneath his cot, a deliberate attempt to delay the moment his death was discovered." He reached into his scrip to pull out the ring Catrin had found in the grass outside Rollo's tent. Hugh hadn't recognized it. Nor had Earl Clare when Rhys had shown it to him, but he was the man who handed out rings, not the one receiving them.

"Since we found it, I have made a study of the hands of the men here." Rhys pulled off his own ring, given to him by the king when he joined his service as an indication of royal trust. He'd worn it continually since April, and its removal revealed a pale band around the fourth finger of his left hand. "Nobody seems to be missing a ring." He put his own back on.

Brow furrowed, Humphrey took the ring Catrin had found and, after studying it a moment, tucked a fingernail underneath the garnet upon which the bird had been carved and flicked it. The stone flipped upwards on hidden hinges, revealing a compartment underneath.

Rhys coughed his surprise. "Have you seen this ring before?"

"No." But then as Rhys continued to look at him, he relented and said, "I don't recognize this particular ring, nor its crest, but my grandfather had one like it. He never wore it, but he showed it to me once, warning me to beware any vassal who wore one similar." Now he held the ring up to the light of a nearby candle. "As I thought." Eyes narrowing, he touched a pinky finger into the secret space, coming away with tiny light-colored grains that adhered to his fingertip.

Rhys hadn't entirely understood Humphrey's point until now. "Poison?" His insides turned cold.

"That was what my grandfather feared."

As soon as he could, Rhys resolved to show the ring to Cadell, the monastery's herbalist, and ask him about the powder. He might have asked Wena, but she didn't want to have anything to do with him or Catrin.

Then Humphrey changed the subject, reminiscent of the king and as if their conversation about Rollo had come to a satisfactory conclusion. "So you're back. How do you reconcile that decision?"

Rhys didn't owe even a high lord such as Humphrey an answer to that question and parried back, "How do you?"

Humphrey let out a snort of laughter and put up a hand. "Do not mistake me in thinking I was judging you. Quite the opposite. You are correct that we are apples in the same bin at market."

While true that they both were subject to the whims of the king and their loyalty was, in that sense, forced, it was another astounding admission and not one Rhys ever would have expected Humphrey to make. It made him wonder what new game the Marcher lord was playing. Suddenly, Rhys wondered if Rollo's death might actually be a minor issue to Humphrey, about which he knew nothing at all, and he'd used Rhys's interest in it as a lure in order to study him at close quarters.

Humphrey, for his part, looked blandly back. Although he'd been disloyal to the king at the age of sixteen and, once his lands had been returned to his family, had been fiercely protective of them from that moment on, he'd given no sign of rebellion in all the years since. Still, Llywelyn had been his father's ally—and thus Humphrey's own—in that long-ago war.

Rhys genuinely couldn't read Humphrey well enough to know why he'd brought him here—and why he had an interest in resolving this investigation, if he in fact did. And if all he wanted was to extend, as he had at Caernarfon, the hand of friendship, Rhys couldn't begin to say why. Long ago in another life, they'd both been at those meetings with Prince Llywelyn—as squires to their fathers—and on the periphery of great decisions. But Humphrey had risen to become one of the most powerful men in England and Wales, while Rhys remained merely a knight. He was a kingsman and the king's quaestor, but they were not equals and never would be.

Which meant it was Rhys's third position, that of spymaster, in which Humphrey was truly interested.

More than a little disconcerted, and with a cold feeling in his stomach returning tenfold, Rhys shot off the bench and said, probably unwisely, "My lord, you are the Earl of Hereford. You control great estates in England and Wales. I am a Welsh knight, who, only a few months ago, didn't even own a horse. If you're implying—"

Humphrey made a slashing motion with one hand, cutting off Rhys's protest. Then he tipped his head towards the vacated seat beside him. Rhys was still in no position to gainsay an earl and reluctantly sat again, irritated to the point of being angry, though more at himself for being lulled, even for a moment, into thinking Humphrey had something useful to say.

"You are smarter than that."

"Am I?"

"Don't pretend to be something other than what you are."

"Which is what?" Rhys wasn't going to help him anymore. If Humphrey wanted something more from Rhys, he was going to have to speak plainly.

"You are out of the ordinary, and someday I might have need of a man who has ceased to care what anyone thinks of him."

Amazingly enough, after a quarter of an hour of hedging, Humphrey had spoken his mind. But he was also wrong about Rhys, now that Catrin was in his life.

Rhys wasn't going to tell him that and went back to wrapping himself in a cloak of confidence he didn't feel, though the cloak itself felt secure and comfortable on his shoulders. "Did you have anything to do with Rollo's death?"

"No." Humphrey met his eyes, and Rhys saw no deceit in them. Then again, he was Humphrey de Bohun, the most accomplished liar Rhys would ever meet—and a man who could override his instinct to look away while he equivocated.

"You're worried about being able to speak the truth if questioned about speaking to me about Rollo's death, but not about the part of our conversation where we were apples in a bin together?"

"Nobody would believe this part of our conversation could ever happen."

"Fair enough." Rhys looked away, thinking hard again. "This means you think you know who is responsible for Rollo's death and fear the consequences of naming him."

"At the next meal, truly watch the guests, those you know and those you don't. And then tell me if you see what I think I'm seeing."

That still seemed unnecessarily cryptic.

"You are concerned about accusing someone powerful?" Rhys canted his head. "More powerful than you?" That description could include a truly limited number of people, but it was essentially what Simon had concluded yesterday after talking to Alard.

"This conversation never happened." Humphrey rose to his feet, not having answered the question, which by this point came as no surprise. "Miles can walk you back. He might never tell you, but he was pleased to renew your friendship."

Rhys was actually pleased about that too, though he didn't say so either. Humphrey had elicited far too much from him already, and he was supposed to be the clever spymaster.

Not clever enough by half, it seemed.

"What about you?"

A grin suddenly lit Humphrey's face, indicating the extent to which he reveled in the game he was playing. "I'm Humphrey de Bohun, Earl of Hereford and Constable of England. No need to worry about me."

24

28 July 1284

Day Three

Catrin

Suspicions were not proof, but between the two of them, they'd come a long way since standing over Rollo's body. Catrin didn't know, and wasn't in a position to ask, if the man Humphrey suspected of wrongdoing was Bernard fitz Courcy. What she knew of thieving wouldn't fill a thimble, but if Humphrey believed the steward of the king's brother-in-law was some kind of criminal, she could understand his reluctance to name him. John, the heir to the earldom, was a sweet boy—too sweet, in truth—but he was also the king's nephew.

"You're certain that the girl Matilda passed something to Bernard?" Rhys asked her.

"No, I'm not certain about that. They did touch hands, however, after which Bernard was far too casual about their acquaintance."

"So she passed him something," Simon said. "The question now is *what?*

Catrin shrugged. "I don't know."

"I'll take the bait," Rhys said, "and extend our suspicions to actual wrongdoing: Matilda stole something small from one of the men to whom she'd been speaking in the tent, and gave it to Bernard as she passed him."

Catrin, Rhys, and Simon were sitting in the palace guardroom yet again, breakfast dishes in front of them but somewhat forgotten. The general merriment outside was audible through the open window, but none of them were in a hurry to join the festivities. Catrin's husband had been of the mind that jousts, and tournaments in general, were terrible wastes of men, even as they were avenues to wealth and prestige. At one point he'd declared, "Haven't we all seen enough fighting by now?"

The answer remained, *apparently not.*

Simon and Rhys were taking in stride the idea of the existence of a thieving ring led by Bernard, using beautiful girls as the actual thieves. She didn't see how that was possible and said so.

Simon's eyes went to Rhys's and they both sighed before Simon chose to answer. "We've seen something like this before."

"In the Holy Land?" It was where pretty much anything that could have happened had happened, and this was hardly the first time they'd pulled out an incident there as an explanation for a more recent event.

"Yes, and in London. I have never encountered a ringleader as highly placed as Bernard, but London contains numerous street gangs working in different sectors of the city that use children and young women as thieves."

"You yourself noted that most of the victims are men," Rhys said. "Sadly, the young women often progress, or perhaps you would say regress, to prostitution. In most cases, it is a man who coordinates them and takes most of what they earn."

"You mean like in a brothel?" she said.

"Yes, as in a brothel, but women walk the streets soliciting as well." Simon's lips twisted in his distaste for the topic.

Catrin could agree that this was a longer conversation about prostitution than she had ever had before. Perhaps her own revulsion showed on her face because Rhys put his hand on the back of hers where it rested in her lap. "I regret exposing you to the dark underbelly of our society."

"I am not so innocent as that." Catrin said, even as she turned her hand palm up to grasp his. "We both lived through the war and saw what one man can do to another and what men can do to women."

"The question now is what to do about Bernard," Simon said, bringing their conversation back to the matter at hand. "We can discover the true identity of these women easily enough, simply by inquiring of the men who are their supposed relations."

"My guess is that at least one will be legitimate to hide the rest," Catrin said.

"That can be determined too." Simon looked at Rhys. "I'll speak to the Earls of Surrey and Warwick."

"I'll tackle the Bohuns. Probably Miles will be my best bet." Rhys had not told Simon the full extent of his conversation with either Miles or Humphrey. Catrin knew it was hard for him to keep secrets from his friend, but to speak fully would betray Humphrey's confidence, and so far what they'd learned from him had augmented what they already knew but not fundamentally changed it.

"What about that old friend of yours, Alard?" Catrin said. "He was a master thief in London once. Perhaps if we point him in the right direction, he will be able to confirm what I thought I saw."

To Catrin's surprise, the men actually thought that was a good idea, which was how, less than an hour later, she found herself in the company of the old thief turned valet, who seemed quite pleased to be of use on the proper side of the law.

Given their difference in station, Catrin wasn't going so far as to hook her arm through his, but he kept shooting her pleased glances as they strolled with a casual air through the crowds that had gathered on the tournament grounds, Alard occasionally whistling somewhat tunelessly. To make himself a target, he wore five different rings, most of them cheap. With the king's permission, however, Simon had cadged one ring from the king's chest that had real value, along with a brooch and a deceptively full purse that swung from his belt.

She glanced at Alard again. "You're having fun?"

"Oh yes, my lady!" His eyes were bright underneath his bushy white brows. "I had intended to spend the day at the encampment rather than at the tournament itself. Sir Eustace is a stickler for order, and he insists on an extreme degree of tidiness that preoccupies me for much of every day. I was grateful that you sought me out."

"This isn't going to get you in trouble, though, is it?" He'd made her a little worried now. "I have no intention of exposing your past to him."

"I did not fear you would. You handled your request for my services very nicely."

That had required some discussion with Rhys and Simon regarding the best way to approach Eustace. Since he was missing a silver cup, and Alard was his servant, they decided to come at it from that direction, with the idea that Alard might recognize someone who'd been around Eustace's tent. Given the hundreds of people at the tournament, the possibility of finding the thief this way was more than a little far-fetched in Catrin's opinion, though Eustace accepted the explanation easily enough. He *was* jousting today, so he had been more focused on his preparations than on what his valet was doing.

Simon was also drifting about somewhere, though at the moment she didn't see him. Rhys's intention to speak to Miles had so far been thwarted, since none of the Bohun men had made it to the second day of the tournament.

She and Alard reached an open spot on the rail on the far side of the jousting arena from the viewing stand. The joust was essentially a duel in which two opponents took up positions on opposite sides of the field, lance in hand, and charged, with the goal of unhorsing one another. Ideally, a knight would take the initial blow from the lance on his shield. If both combatants stayed on their horses for that first run, they were allowed two more attempts before dismounting to fight on foot. The duel would continue until one combatant ended up flat on his back on the ground with his opponent standing over him, or yielded in some other fashion.

Today, as decreed by the king even before he'd established the new rules for the mêlée, the lances were hollowed, blunted, and fitted with a crown or flower, rather than a point, to limit the damage done.

By the time Catrin and Alard arrived, the competition was halfway done. Nobody had died, which was an excellent outcome, and most had walked away unharmed. As they watched, however, Vincent de Lusignan, wearing a kerchief around his arm, which Catrin supposed to be Joan's, took the force of his opponent's lance on his shield. But while Vincent's initial blow also hit his opponent's shield, the momentum of the blow slid the tip of the lance upward and caught the side of the knight's neck. He fell backwards off his horse and lay unmoving in the dirt right in front of Catrin.

Vincent raised his arms in victory, which the judges conceded with a raised flag. Concerned about the fallen knight only a few feet away, Catrin ducked under the rail and fell to her knees beside the man.

It was Hugh. He was moaning in pain, but still conscious. She hadn't recognized his colors because he was jousting for himself, not Clare, as would be the case in the mêlée.

She pulled out her own kerchief and pressed down on his wound. At least his coif had diverted the blossoms on the lance's tip such that they'd scraped the length of his jaw instead of slicing through an artery in his neck.

Josef, the Jewish physician who'd attended to the wounded when the viewing stand had failed, had run onto the field by now, followed by two men with a stretcher, and bent towards him. "Can you speak?" For Hugh to be able to speak meant his jaw wasn't broken. "What is your name?"

"Hugh de Pevensey." Then Hugh moaned, tucked his left arm around his belly, rolled onto his side, and vomited into the grass.

"Concussion," Josef said succinctly.

Hugh lifted a hand, indicating disagreement. "I've been unwell since yesterday."

Catrin sat back on her heels, remembering Rhys mentioning it after his meeting with the Bohuns. "You should not have fought today."

Josef shot her a wry look. "These men don't withdraw unless they're on their deathbed. And maybe not even then."

Hugh had the strength to nod. "Honor was at stake."

Josef gestured that the men with the stretcher should lift Hugh onto it, but Hugh again waved a hand, this time in real dismissal, and demanded that they help him to his feet instead. As he stood, applause erupted from the viewing stand.

Catrin had been thinking there was little honor in dying in the joust when one was unwell. He'd participated and still lost, which she'd thought would tarnish his honor somewhat.

But from the cheers and the looks on the faces of the men hovering over him, nobody else agreed. They were nodding, as if satisfied.

Again, it was Josef who explained, his voice low as he stepped back and allowed the other men to assist Hugh's departure. "Now everyone knows he persevered despite his illness, and they honor him for it."

"He could have died!"

Josef shot her a quizzical look. "To men such as these, if that's the price they must pay, so be it. As the king declared, this is a *Round Table*. Honor is all." Then he followed after his patient to the hospital tent.

Catrin harrumphed, folding her arms across her chest as she watched them go. But then she too had to leave the field, since the next jousters were waiting to go on. Workers had already appeared with buckets of sand to sprinkle over the blood and vomit. It would be unfair if, in the next round, one of the combatants inadvertently slipped on what an earlier participant had left behind.

Sighing now, Catrin returned to Alard, who was waiting for her, and he grasped her hand to help her as she ducked between the rails. Straightening, she saw that he was grinning.

"What on earth are you so happy about? Hugh could have died!"

"Hugh's predicament was a fortuitous distraction. While you were tending to the brave lord, one of the young ladies you mentioned stole a neck chain from a spectator, and then I followed her to her master. My lady, you were right in every respect."

25

Day Three

Rhys

"You have to let me speak to her," Miles said. ""It was my family with whom she claimed alliance."

Rhys had finally tracked down Miles at one of the half-dozen stalls dedicated to drink. He'd been purchasing a cup for himself, and, at the sight of Rhys, ordered two. The one drink was going to be Rhys's limit. In the Holy Land, Miles had been able to drink any man under the table. Rhys had tried to outdo him once and learned his lesson.

They'd already determined, within the first moments of Rhys's arrival, that Miles had no knowledge of this relation Bernard had claimed for him. It was exactly as Rhys (and Catrin) had suspected, but he was pleased with the confirmation. He was also a bit shocked by the scope of Bernard's project—and the risks he was taking. Or maybe, if he'd done this sort of thing before, perhaps many times, he had become so accustomed to the danger he no longer saw what he was doing as much of a risk.

And really, if not for Rollo's death, Rhys would never have become involved in the first place, and everybody would have departed Nefyn after tomorrow's great feast none the wiser. Clasps broke all the time, and drunk wealthy men were not reliable witnesses to the misplacement of their own valuables. And even if they were, most would blame their servants at first. By the time someone realized how many men had lost items, the tournament-goers would be gone.

"Bernard claimed that for her. She may not even know he did so. Earlier, Catrin heard she was related to the Earl of Surrey." Rhys eyed his companion. He had opened up his investigative circle to Simon and Catrin, but Miles was a true lord. His aims and Rhys's were unlikely to be aligned on almost any issue, no matter what Humphrey had implied last night and for all that Rhys couldn't help liking him.

But he was directly asking to be included, and while Rhys could say *no,* he wanted to be clear within his own mind *why* he was saying no before he did. Was it because he didn't trust Miles (the obvious answer)? Or was it because he didn't want to share with anyone else what had become a responsibility, even a calling?

The thought brought him up short as he acknowledged that there was a grain of truth in that. Being a quaestor *had* become a calling. It was an anchor in the storm that had overtaken him and his country. In Latin, *quaestor* meant *one who asks questions.* That was something he knew how to do, and doing it for King Edward was better than not doing it at all.

So much for his own moral superiority.

Then again, to not do it would mean living the rest of his days in the village outside Caernarfon Castle. If he'd stayed there and refused the honor Edward had offered him, at times he could have pretended things were the way they used to be and he had some autonomy. But it would have been a lie, and he had pledged never to lie—to himself or anyone else.

Nobody was ever going to be able to hide away in the mountains as the Welsh once had. The king's fingers—and his taxes—reached into every household from the tip of Holyhead to St. David's. Rhys (and Catrin) had decided it was better to participate on their own terms, even if that meant a closer relationship with the king and queen.

"What has this woman told you so far?" Miles asked.

"Nothing. She doesn't know we are on to her."

"What do you mean?" Miles sat up straighter. "You mean she's still free!"

His outrage warmed Rhys to him, because it meant he had a sense of rightness. "She stole a neck chain, and our man followed her to Bernard, but he couldn't burst in on them and accuse them of thieving. He has no standing. We want to catch Bernard with his ill-gotten gains, not force him to run before we are ready."

Miles was looking intently at Rhys now. He would know, since his nephew did, that Rhys was the king's spymaster. "Your man, eh?"

Rhys hadn't shared Alard's identity with Miles, because to do so would betray a confidence. But if Miles participated in this investigation, he would recognize Alard as *Ned* the moment he saw him.

Unlike the petty thief Finnian had been, Ned had achieved some renown among the crusaders.

"He isn't *my man*, per se. Do you remember the spy who had the ability to pass as a Saracen—"

Miles interjected before Rhys had to say more. "Ned Thacker. I remember."

Rhys just looked at him.

Miles' eyes lit. "Ned! You're telling me *Ned* is here and working for *you!*" He laughed out loud. "This is too rich! I knew I was right in suggesting to my nephew that he come to you—"

He cut himself off abruptly, likely having said too much. Rhys didn't punish him for it. "His name is Alard now, and I need you to be respectful of his new identity. He spoke to me in confidence, trusting that I wouldn't reveal his past."

"Who is he now?"

"A valet for one of Earl Clare's knights."

Miles gaped at Rhys, and then he laughed again. "My word, that is precious." He sobered and put a finger to his lips. "I will keep his secret. I promise. He is simply one of your spies, and that is all I will convey to my nephew."

If Rhys hadn't been looking closely at Miles, he would have missed the raised finger on his left hand, as it rested on the table beside his cup. Rhys had spent many years in an army, and was a spymaster himself, so he recognized a hand signal when he saw one. He allowed his eyes to drift to the right to find the man to whom Miles had directed his signal. He was standing near one of the food stalls, dressed in the elaborate costume of a Saracen.

Rhys's lips twitched.

Miles saw it, as Rhys had meant him too, and grinned. "That was Humphrey's idea. So many men are dressed in costume today, we thought we'd take advantage."

Humphrey hadn't been wrong about that. In keeping with the idea of a Round Table, in addition to the Saracen and the Green Man Rhys and Catrin had encountered a few days ago, participants were dressed as, on one hand, Roman soldiers, early Christians, and monks, and on the other hand as back-draped crones, flower-festooned girls, and foreigners of every stripe.

"I suppose he looks more like a Saracen than some."

"He ought to! It isn't as if I don't remember how they dressed."

"Who is he?"

"One of our men." That wasn't really an answer, but it was all Rhys was apparently going to get. Miles jerked his head to indicate that Rhys should drain his mead and come with him, and together they strolled through the fairgrounds.

Rhys's mind flashed to when Justin had come to find them as they left the market fair and bring them to the king, and he was therefore grateful that they managed to pace along and come out the other side without being confronted with some new disaster.

Miles' men continued to follow them. In the course of their journey, Rhys spotted at least three who were walking alone and a bit too casually. And, as they approached the healer's tent on the edge of the tournament field where Catrin had said she would meet him, a fourth man, wearing Humphrey's colors, came marching up the road in their direction. He passed them with a *my lord* and a bow. Clearly, Humphrey had a retinue that knew what it was doing and, like Miles, appeared to be entirely loyal to him.

Which made Humphrey's approach to Rhys the previous night all the more interesting. The implication was either that Humphrey's loyalty to the king was in question—which would be an astonishing admission, even for a Bohun—or he had a very specific concern regarding the goings on in the king's court.

It had to be the latter, which meant Humphrey had chosen Rhys not because he questioned his loyalty to the king but because he was the one person he believed totally loyal.

"How long has your nephew known about the attempts on the king's life?"

Miles stopped dead in the road and had enough respect for Rhys that he didn't equivocate. "Since April when we were at Caernarfon."

"Someone talked."

Miles lips pressed together for a moment before he said, "People do."

Rhys wanted to know who that was, but understood Miles wasn't going to tell him here. So he nodded and gestured Miles towards where Catrin and Alard were waiting in the shade under a tree.

Alard and Miles looked at each other, and then Miles put up a hand. "On my honor, I will say nothing."

Alard bent his head. "Thank you, my lord."

With that out of the way, Miles asked, "Now that Rhys and I are here, we should confront Bernard immediately."

Rhys endeavored not to laugh at how quickly this had become *we*. "No."

Catrin had a little more sympathy for Miles' confusion. "We have been here before, my lord, and the question of what to do now is not an easy one to answer. We know some of the whys and wherefores. We even know some of the people involved, but Bernard may have already hidden the chain and not in his tent."

"We could look!"

"And if we find nothing?" Rhys said. "How outraged do you think the Earl of Richmond would be to have his steward falsely accused of so heinous a crime?"

Miles gritted his teeth in his frustration.

"It also doesn't necessarily help us with Rollo's murder," Catrin said. "Are we to believe that one of these girls killed him? Or that Bernard did? I wouldn't be surprised if he made a point never to get his hands dirty."

"So then what?" Miles said.

"We go round about," Catrin said.

Rhys checked the sky. "I can do nothing for the next few hours, as I am called to the tournament field to shoot." He looked at Catrin. "Until I'm done, you're in charge. Do what you think is best."

26

Day Three

Catrin

That Rhys was willing to give up authority to her showed how far they'd come as a team. So she said what was in her mind: "As much as I want to watch you win, it would be the perfect moment to search Bernard's tent. It might even be a little ironic, in that Bernard has women steal from others when they are distracted, and we can now do the same to him."

"Surely you don't mean to do this yourself?" Miles was aghast. "Better it be me."

Catrin frowned. "It should definitely not be you. You're uncle to the Earl of Hereford!"

"Exactly. I'm unassailable."

"Just like Bernard," Rhys said softly.

Miles wasn't to be persuaded. "It's too dangerous."

She laughed. "*This* isn't dangerous. Bernard has women around him all the time. Nobody will think twice about me entering his tent when he's away." Catrin didn't actually know that, but she wasn't going to give way to Miles, not when this was a task for which she was far better suited than he.

Alard hadn't contributed anything so far, but he wasn't really a servant, even if he'd lived as one for many years, and said, "I will go with Lady Catrin and keep watch."

"No," Rhys said. "We need you in the crowd, paying attention to the girls, who they steal from and what they take. If you can."

Alard looked affronted that Rhys would question his ability.

Miles looked as if he didn't want to back down either, but he grunted. "Then I suppose I should keep an eye on Bernard."

"While the Saracen keeps an eye on you?"

"The more men to watch our backs, the better. If I follow him into the Richmond encampment, however, none of my men can come with me without drawing questions."

In the end, Rhys decided that if he couldn't trust one of his fellow members of the king's guard, he shouldn't be doing this job and so opted to enlist into their conspiracy young Ralph, who'd fetched the king's physicians when the viewing stand had failed and who'd been keeping an eye on Catrin on and off since the first day.

While Catrin waited for Rhys to return with Ralph, she saw an opportunity to tick another task off her list and fetched up on the rail near the targets, in nearly the same spot from which she'd watched Hugh almost lose his life. Beside her was Joan, Rollo's sister.

To keep the woman at her ease, at first Catrin pretended not to notice her, and it was only when Joan cleared her throat to gain Catrin's attention that she turned to her. "I'm so sorry. How rude of me not to greet you right away."

Joan made a pretty gesture of dismissal. "Thank you for your conversation the other day."

"I was only sorry you had such a hard time for so long. How are you today?"

"Better. Thanks to you."

"To me?"

"You made me think about Rollo for the first time without hatred. Because of you, I was able to follow my heart."

Catrin couldn't help but blink. "Are you referring to your betrothal to Vincent?"

"I have loved him for many years, and it seems he has loved me all this time too."

Catrin gave a shake of her head, trying to reconcile Joan's version of Vincent with Rhys's. "Am I correct in thinking that Vincent was the man your brother refused?"

"He was the first."

"The first?" Catrin found herself repeating Joan again.

"As I told you, Rollo didn't want me to marry anyone. He believed it was my duty to serve him ... and Earl Clare allowed it." The same bitterness crept into her voice for a moment. Likely, it would take more days to dissipate than the few that had passed since Rollo's death. "I was younger then and still believed my brother was wiser than I. Because of his objections, I told Vincent to find someone else."

"Did he?"

"No."

"Did you?"

"Yes, up until earlier this week."

Catrin tried not to let Joan see that she was more than politely interested. "You mean your former lover is *here*?"

"Oh yes. But none of that mattered as soon as I saw Vincent. Even with all our years apart, the moment we saw each other, we knew we had to be together." Joan laughed prettily.

Catrin herself was having enormous difficulty envisioning Vincent de Lusignan as lovestruck, but she supposed it could happen to anyone, particularly at a tournament dedicated to the ideals of King Arthur. While it was hard to see how even requited love could have truly transformed Vincent, the combination of Rollo's death and Vincent's love had made Joan a different person.

Now Joan sighed, continuing her story, "I confess Bernard was not pleased to hear he was being thrown over for Vincent. He became quite heated in his outrage. I had to emphasize very strongly that I never wanted to see him again." She looked at Catrin sadly. "I even threw his ring at him."

If Joan herself hadn't been so completely lovestruck she might have noticed Catrin's jaw was on the grass, and she cursed inwardly that the ring was in Rhys's purse instead of her own. "Are you saying that when you arrived at the tournament your lover was Bernard fitz Courcy?"

"Yes. Didn't I make that clear?" Joan smiled, still oblivious to Catrin's shock. "In retrospect, I was a fool to allow myself to love him, and Rollo was right to think that such a man would not be a wise choice for me."

"You're saying Rollo knew about Bernard and you?"

"Of course, he did. It would be hard to keep from him that I was seeing someone. He forbade me to continue, but I defied him." She shrugged. "It wasn't as if he could doubly refuse me the right to marry him. He'd already done that."

"And Bernard was willing to ... what? Wait?"

"He thought Rollo would come around, especially now that the Richmond heir is back in England. Bernard was going to ask him to talk to Rollo."

"But now you think Rollo was right about Bernard?"

"Vincent has made me see his wisdom. You may have noticed that Bernard has many women around him. He told me it was to deflect attention from the fact that his heart was with me, but I realize now that he simply loves women—and not necessarily me!"

His motives were far more sinister than that, but Catrin didn't correct Joan. "Have you met any of these women?""

"Some of them." She waved a hand dismissively. "He brought four with him to the tournament."

"Four!"

"It is nothing nefarious, I assure you! Various barons who couldn't make the journey didn't want to deprive their relations of the chance to find a wealthy husband in such auspicious surroundings. Of course Bernard, and thus Lord John, graciously acquiesced to their presence in their retinue."

Far too many people over the last few days had used the phrase *of course*, as if there could be no question about what they were saying. Even now, despite her protestations to the contrary, Joan couldn't see anything fundamentally wrong with Bernard.

Catrin decided it wasn't her place to persuade her. That would be Vincent's job, and good luck to him.

"You are very fortunate to have found such happiness."

"I am indeed blessed."

Catrin said goodbye, having spotted Ralph, who'd arrived during the latter half of the conversation. She made her way to where he'd been waiting near the fence line. "Thank you for coming."

"I don't pretend to understand much of what you and Sir Rhys get up to, but Joan has landed on her feet. Vincent is a great catch."

"He is." Catrin concluded then and there that Ralph was not one to be a full participant in their investigations, not yet. The tournament had infected him, much as it had her son, and he saw things in terms of honor, loyalty, and courage. "Are you unhappy with this assignment, Ralph? I can do it on my own if need be."

"Not in the least!" Even so, his eyes strayed to the archery targets in the distance and the many onlookers between him and them. "Bernard is a thief! If we are to prove it, as Sir Rhys said, better to make sure we have the right man."

"Then we should go." She placed a hand on Ralph's forearm so he could escort her, and they set off for the Richmond encampment.

They'd gone only fifty paces, however, when Bernard and Matilda appeared, strolling through the tournament grounds towards the viewing stand. Matilda was perfectly coiffed and dressed as befitted a lady, and her arm was hooked proprietarily in Bernard's, with a level of contact unseemly in a young woman who'd never been married. The brazenness of her show of affection stopped Ralph in his tracks, and Catrin had to tug on him to move them both out of Bernard's line of sight.

Even after they'd passed, Ralph's mouth remained open.

Catrin started walking again, and Ralph collected himself enough to keep up, though his jaw was still bulging in outrage. "And she the niece of a great lord!"

"Ralph," Catrin said gently, "I am quite certain she is no such thing."

"But—" At Catrin's steady look, he broke off. "I see. You think none of the women are who they say they are. How could he think to get away with it?"

"He is getting away with it. Or, he would have if we hadn't become involved," Catrin said. "It shows how easy it is to take a beautiful woman, dress her in finery, and call her noble."

In the early days of her marriage to Robert, Catrin had seen herself in much the same light—playing dress up like a little girl in her mother's clothing. She'd thought herself a fraud and wholly inadequate to the role in which she found herself. Matilda, on the other hand, appeared to have taken to it with aplomb. It seemed she might also be besotted with Bernard, though that could be a veneer for his sake.

"We all believed it!" Ralph's eyes narrowed. "He is a villain. A true villain!"

"Let's make sure, shall we?"

Once they arrived at the Richmond encampment, they had no choice but to inquire openly as to which tent was Bernard's. Catrin let

Ralph do it, and a very hospitable retainer directed them towards the end of a line of tents. Like Rollo, Bernard had set up his on the edge of the encampment rather than in the center near Lord John's pavilion.

In as casual a manner as she could manage when her heart was beating out of her chest, Catrin walked towards the entrance to Bernard's tent. Ralph came with her initially, and then turned on his heel, looking for watchers. It looked suspicious because it was, though she still couldn't regret bringing him. The ease by which they'd arrived here unmolested revealed to her how simple it was for someone who appeared to belong to move in and out of any number of tents throughout every encampment.

Ralph halted while still outside. "I'll whistle if I see someone coming."

"I'll be as quick as I can." Catrin ducked through the flap.

The tent was approximately the size of Rollo's, ten feet by twelve, and she was able to stand in the center to her full height. Bernard was a few inches taller and would have been able to do so as well.

The bed sat against one wall, and Catrin went to it first, quickly patting down the wool-stuffed mattress and the goose down overlayer. Bernard lived well. She looked under the bed, which was raised up as Rollo's had been, likely having been brought whole in a cart from England. She could just hear Rhys saying, in that dry tone of his, that a man had to sleep on the road as well as at Nefyn, so he might as well be comfortable.

She had a moment of glee when she found a box under the bed, but she pulled it out to reveal folded linens and underclothing. Casting around for somewhere else to look, she went through the clothes hung on a stand and then to Bernard's trunk. It was locked, and she stared at the keyhole for a moment, on her knees and suspended by indecision.

Not ready to give up yet, she pulled the key to her own trunk from her purse, if for no reason than because the two trunks looked similar. At first the key didn't go into the lock, but after wiggling it back and forth, she got it to seat.

Though she was initially disappointed to find the trunk stuffed to the brim with more clothing, Catrin dug through everything anyway, which paid off when she reached the bottom and found a ledger, as might be used on an estate, and a clear glass vial. The vial in and of itself was uncommon, and her heart raced even more to see that it contained a white powder that bore a resemblance to the bits of powder in the ring she'd found in the grass outside Rollo's tent.

Given that Joan had just told her she'd thrown Bernard's ring back at him, Catrin liked to think the two rings were one and the same, and that it belonged to Bernard. The ledger, meanwhile, was revealed to contain lists of names and numbers, none of which she could make sense of in this moment. The latter half consisted of a great number of empty pages.

Then a whistling sound came from outside the tent, followed immediately by Ralph's voice. "I say, sir, have we met before? I'm

Ralph, and I serve in the king's guard. My uncle is Otto de Grandison."

Bernard's voice answered, followed by the low grumbling of another voice, which Catrin thought might actually belong to Miles.

Out of time, Catrin hastily shut the lid, turned the key, and then wrenched it out of the lock. Trembling, she next cast around for a place to hide. Short of crawling under the bed, which sent a chill down her spine, since that was how Rollo's body had been hidden, the tent was bare of options. Her heart was pounding so loudly she was afraid those outside could hear it, but she still had enough sense to remember another feature of Rollo's tent. As in Rollo's tent, a bit of breeze had separated the two ends of fabric along the bottom of one of the tent's rear seams. Her mouth so dry with fear she couldn't swallow, she pushed through the opening and sealed it back up as best she could.

Then she skittered away, anxious to put as much distance as she could between herself and her improvised exit, and came to rest some twenty yards from Bernard's tent. Once her heart stopped pounding quite so hard, she positioned herself so she could see Ralph, who'd remained where he was, and was just in time to see him looking helplessly on as Bernard brushed passed him to enter the tent. Miles followed. Only then, as she waved to catch Ralph's attention, did she realize she still held in her hand not only her own key, but the vial and ledger too.

27

Day Three

Rhys

All things being equal, Rhys would have just as soon dropped out of the tournament at this point, but he had to admit that the competition had started his blood racing. Today he was facing a reduced field of twenty archers competing in two heats of ten, and the winner of each heat would advance to the final round tomorrow.

Though the Saxon archer had been the favorite of the English onlookers, he wasn't in Rhys's cohort—and by this point had clearly lost to the man who was fast becoming Rhys's chief rival. As the onlookers held their collective breath, that man stepped to the line and made yet another perfect shot.

He was Mathonwy ap Rhys Fychan, Math to his friends, among whom Rhys had once been numbered, a lifetime ago when they'd both served Prince Llywelyn. His was an appropriate name for this tournament since Math ap Mathonwy was another king from Welsh legend. The Math currently winning his heat had been born in the south, the younger son of a nobleman and a relation of Prince Llywelyn to boot. He was also a decade younger than Rhys, so if Rhys had to face him tomorrow, Math might prove the stronger in the end. From the display he was putting on this afternoon, he'd done nothing since that cold December day but practice and now could shoot the wings off a fly. He was going to be hard to beat.

Shaking himself out of these perilous thoughts, Rhys glanced to his left to see Catrin standing in the shade of the viewing stand. She raised clasped hands and shook them, while smiling encouragingly. He chose to interpret her gesture to mean all was well. Leastwise, she hadn't been caught in Bernard's tent. Although loving someone was turning out to be far more stressful than he'd ever realized it could be, the sight of her settled Rhys's breathing a little more.

For some, having an audience made them more nervous, but for Rhys, knowing Catrin was well and watching was going to make him shoot better.

Whoever had set up the order of shooting had put Rhys last in his heat. Oddly, Rhys didn't know who that was and had actively avoided finding out, though from Simon's proprietary stance near the judges' station, his friend may have played some role. Shaking off that thought too, he nodded at Math, who'd just sunk his final arrow into the center of the target, to the applause of all and sundry. Having won his heat, he would be going to the finals tomorrow.

Now it was up to Rhys to join him.

Over the course of the afternoon, Rhys had hit all of his targets, placing the points of his arrows in the center white circle every time, but he hadn't been as crisp as he was going to need to be tomorrow. Even so, after two more shots, he won his round too, and, like Math, accepted the pats and accolades of his fellow archers.

Some of the crowd's enthusiasm had waned with Math's final shot (and thus the defeat of the Saxon archer), but with Rhys's victory, the cheers reached a crescendo. It was odd to have status again, much as he'd had when he'd served in Llywelyn's *teulu*. While he still couldn't be happy about how the world had changed, he could be appreciative of the respect his station gave him. To do otherwise would return him to the sour state he'd resolved to leave behind.

With the day's shooting over, Math and Rhys approached the king side-by-side and bowed before him. "Sire," they said together.

"Well done." The king was in a jovial mood, and who could blame him? The sun was shining, he had his nobles around him, and everything (barring the death of Rollo, which hadn't affected him so far) was going according to his plans. "Your face is new to me. Mathonwy, is it?"

"Yes, sire." Math accompanied his answer with another bow. "From Ystrad Tywi."

Understanding entered the king's eyes, which on another day might not have been a good thing for Math. "Your uncle Rhys holds Dryslyn for me."

"Excuse me, sire, but he is my cousin. My father was Rhys Fychan, who died fifteen years ago. My elder brother inherited Dinefwr, though he, of course, is also dead."

"Indeed."

The king studied Math's face, though Math himself kept his eyes downcast rather than look directly at the king, which would have been unseemly. "What is your condition, son?"

"Excuse me, sire, but I have none."

In that instant, Rhys became aware for the first time that he'd been so focused on himself and his own troubles that he'd failed to realize that someone more noble than he could be worse off than he. As that understanding dawned, he must have made some movement, which the king noticed, because he motioned for Rhys to come closer so they could speak privately.

Rhys obeyed, moving right up to the edge of the viewing stand, while the king actually got up from his chair in order to crouch almost in the exact spot Rhys had climbed up two nights ago after the collapse of the ceiling. None of his nobles commented or really even noticed. The king did what he wanted when he wanted.

"You know this man?" King Edward spoke in French, which everyone around him understood, but he kept his voice low so it wouldn't travel beyond the two of them.

"Yes, sire."

"He is from a rebellious lineage."

Rhys hesitated for a heartbeat. "As am I, sire."

That prompted Edward to let out a grunt of recognition. "Always the truth from you."

"Yes, sire."

The king returned to his seat, and Rhys stepped back to his place beside Math. Edward then lifted a hand, waiting for quiet to descend on the onlookers, at which point he raised his voice so all could hear. "The final jousts will take place in the morning tomorrow, with the archery competition in the afternoon." He paused, and his demeanor reverberated with satisfaction. "And then the mêlée."

Then he dropped his head to look hard at Rhys. "I trust even with the completion of the archery competition, you will not be too exhausted to fight at my side."

"I will be ready, my lord. The jousters will be in need of respite far more than I."

"Good." The king nodded his dismissal, and Rhys and Math bowed one more time.

By the time they raised themselves up, the king was making his way out of the viewing stand, and the rest of the royal court was following, talking amongst themselves. Rhys's impulse was to go straight to Catrin, but he stopped Math first with an outstretched hand. "I didn't know until yesterday that you were alive. How did you survive?"

Math gripped Rhys's forearm. "That morning, Prince Llywelyn sent me to Gwynedd, carrying a message for his brother. I did not even know about his murder and the destruction of our forces until three days had passed." He shook his head, remembering equally with Rhys the way their world had ended. They were speaking in Welsh, but even so, Math lowered his voice as the king had done so it was almost indiscernible. "Thank you for burying him with the honor he deserved."

And just like that, between one breath and the next, it was as if a weight had lifted off Rhys, one he hadn't known he was carrying.

He couldn't say how Math had learned what Rhys had done, but today he couldn't help but be grateful.

Then Rhys's mouth went dry to think of King Edward's wrath if he learned that Rhys had seen to the burial of Llywelyn's body. He might even raze the abbey to the ground, as he'd done with the Cistercian Abbey at Aberconwy.

But no, he knew by now that the king's vindictiveness was measured. Even if Rhys's actions did come to his attention, they would incite no censure. At this late date, with the victory complete, Edward would not begrudge the burial of his royal cousin in holy ground. And the abbey was remote enough, as most Cistercian abbeys were, that it would never become a place of general pilgrimage.

Besides, all around him, Math's reverence aside, Rhys could see the respect for Prince Llywelyn waning in the eyes of his own people. They still resented King Edward and their defeat, but some were beginning to accept the Norman explanations for it, that it was Llywelyn's failings and greed that had cost him the war, and *if only* he had bent the knee to Edward as he'd commanded, Wales could have been saved as a country. The prince himself had written to the king that such were the predations and depravities of Edward's men that the Welsh preferred death to submission to their rule. But such noble sentiments were cold comfort when those who'd made a stand were buried in the ground, and those who remained were left crawling in the dirt that covered their graves.

So he had to speak, because it was a hard truth Math needed to understand. "And now I serve the king." He kept his tone entirely level.

Math didn't misunderstand and replied in the same soft voice, "Don't we all, *combrogi*." The corner of his mouth quirked. "I passed through Caernarfon on my way here and had words with Father Medwyn."

Rhys studied Math's face for a long moment and then took a chance to ask, "If I were to suggest to the king that he could use another Welsh kingsman, what would you say?"

Math's eyes went wide. Though, now that Rhys thought about it, some sort of chance like this had to have been the reason Math had come to Nefyn. In the same way, this was what had been in the king's mind when he'd inquired to Rhys about him.

"You are suggesting that kingsman be … me?"

"Yes."

"The king would trust me with his life, knowing who my father was?"

"He trusts me knowing mine."

Math gave a grunt reminiscent of the king's.

Rhys tried again. "Do you love your people?"

"Of course."

"Then the king would view you as one of the most reliable of all his guards, knowing if you did anything less than your duty, your people would suffer."

Math drew in a harsh breath. "They are hostage to your good behavior."

Rhys raised his eyebrows. "Now you see the iron fist within the glove."

"And yet—" Math broke off.

"And yet you see the good you could do to be so highly placed."

Math's lip curled. "And if I win tomorrow?"

"All the more reason for me to speak to the king on your behalf." Rhys laughed outright. "It will mean the king has employed *two* of the best archers in Wales."

Math had been born the son of a prince of Deheubarth, but even so, he bowed to Rhys, and as he walked away, Rhys noted a slight spring in his step, which had been marred by desperation before.

At last, Rhys made his way to Catrin. She saw him coming, hesitated, and then seemed to win whatever war she was fighting with herself because she threw herself at him. "You did it!"

He swung her around, buoyed by her exuberance not wanting to let her go.

But then she added in a low voice, "I did it too—maybe too much."

28

Day Three

Rhys

"Bernard didn't see me, thanks to Miles and Ralph, who were able to delay him entering long enough for me to get away. The tent had a back entrance just like Rollo's and was located on the edge of the encampment like Rollo's."

Her initial words had given Rhys a fearful foreboding, but she'd done what she'd said she was going to, and survived to tell him about it. For the moment, that was all that mattered. "He wanted an escape route."

"Or simply a way to leave his tent without anyone seeing."

"Where are these items now?"

"The vial is with Wena." Catrin put a finger to his lips before he could protest. "We need to know what's in it, and she is the best person to ask in that regard. I feel like we are running out of time, and I didn't want to waste a moment that I didn't need to. You could certainly do nothing more until you finished your shooting for the day."

She wasn't wrong, but that didn't mean he had to like it. "I thought Wena didn't trust us anymore."

"I don't know that she does. She agreed to help once I told her we weren't pursuing a Welshman."

"And the ledger?"

Catrin patted her belly, which now that Rhys looked more closely was unnaturally flat under her dress, though her belt disguised this fact somewhat. "I didn't dare part with it."

"It seems you thought of everything."

"That's why you put me in charge, isn't it?" She hooked her arm through his and began walking with some speed away from the tournament grounds. For once, he had to take longer strides to keep up. "Ralph and Miles are still there. Hopefully, between the two of them, they have the watching well in hand. Even so, things might start happening now, which may or may not have been what you intended." This last bit was said all in a rush.

Rhys hadn't seen Wena since she decided he and Catrin were the enemy, but she didn't balk when they ducked around the back of her stall, nor resist coming over to speak to them. Wena had a helper, a girl of less than fifteen, with a braid of dark hair down her back. The two nodded at each other in silent conversation as Wena pulled the curtain across to screen the back half of her stall from public view.

Wena spoke first. "I apologize, my lord, for not trusting you earlier. I did not know who you were and what you've done." She was gazing at him with real respect.

As her apology came hard on the heels of his conversation with Math, he supposed the details of the last two years of his life were somehow common knowledge now. He couldn't regret it, if it meant cooperation, and he wasn't one to say *I told you so* anyway. So he said, "Thank you" instead and drew from his purse the ring Joan had thrown (and Catrin had found).

"Admirable work. The best I've seen." Wena held up the ring to see it better. "My *nain*, who taught me healing, had one similar, though a simple river rock took the place of the gem." *Nain* was one of the Welsh words for grandmother, the other being *mamgu*. Right then and there, Wena drew it from her pocket and set it beside the other.

Then she gestured down her work table, which was covered in various bottles and dishes, and messier than he would have expected for a person as contained as she. At the end sat a foot-high wicker basket. "Have a look."

"Do I want to?" But Rhys did anyway, moving a few steps and tentatively lifting the lid of the basket to find a rat lying at the bottom. It was moving sporadically but obviously wasn't well.

"Arsenic," Wena said flatly.

Rhys drew back. He had heard of the poison, but unlike hemlock or foxglove, arsenic was a metal. It didn't grow just anywhere but had to be mined. There had been rumors of men using it to topple kingdoms from Tallinn to Jerusalem. Some wondered if King Henry I of England had died from arsenic poisoning rather than eating too many lampreys, since his death had been preceded by nausea and vomiting. The consequences of his death had been dire indeed.

That Bernard had brought such a terrible poison to the tournament was a hanging offense in and of itself. "How long does it take to work?"

"It must be nearly an hour since I left you to watch Rhys shoot," Catrin said to Wena.

"I didn't give the rat the poison right away, since I needed to make some preparations first." Wena grimaced. "I gave him a goodly dose too, hoping it was something less harmful. Arsenic kills quickly in large amounts, but it is also known to kill slowly if given to the victim over time."

"How can we know at this late date if arsenic was used on Rollo?" Catrin said. "He's buried in the ground."

"When a man has been given a large amount of arsenic—and by large I mean more than a few grains—it resembles first and foremost what happens after eating foul food, with nausea and vomiting, followed by coma and death. But if he has been poisoned with smaller doses over a longer period of time, his skin can turn dark, mottled, and rough, and he will have rashes."

Catrin took in a breath. "That describes Rollo's skin exactly."

"Does arsenic have any medicinal uses, Wena?" Rhys asked. "Could Rollo have been taking it on purpose?"

"It has a hundred uses, though wisely most are applied topically, for severe rashes, for example, or to aid the course of a wasting disease." Her expression turned rueful. "Arsenic is not so common here in Wales and, even if I could get it, I would not use it. I have never known any treatment to work beyond a few weeks. Usually the patient dies anyway, usually with skin like you say Rollo's had become, or faster, like with the rat."

"But Rollo *could* have been taking the arsenic deliberately?" Rhys said.

"He would have been crazed to do so, but yes, he could have, especially a man such as he, with wealth and connections." Wena frowned. "Why does it matter if he could have administered it to himself?"

"If we want to accuse someone of murder, we have to consider that person's defense. Rollo is not here to say yay or nay, so we have to plan our own prosecution accordingly." Catrin bit her bottom lip. "I have to wonder now if Hugh's illness wasn't also caused by this selfsame arsenic, Rhys. Though in his case, he would not have taken it deliberately."

"I don't know that it matters, Catrin. Rollo didn't die of poison. He was suffocated."

"That doesn't mean Bernard wasn't slowly poisoning him. We have the ring and the powder. They connect Bernard to Joan to Rollo." Catrin looked inquiringly at Wena. "That is, if what is in the ring is the same as in the vial."

"It is the same."

"Would you swear to it before the king?" Catrin asked.

Wena gave her a long look before nodding. "I would."

"I don't know that it makes sense for Bernard to have been poisoning Rollo, Catrin," Rhys said.

"Rollo wouldn't let him marry Joan. He was willing to bide his time, but maybe he wanted some surety he'd have her in the end."

"Maybe." But Rhys felt they were missing some important pieces. "Even if Bernard was slowly murdering Rollo because of Joan, Joan threw Bernard over before his death, so what good did killing him outright do? I'll say it again: Rollo didn't die of arsenic poisoning."

Catrin's head came up. "Rollo *was* investigating the thefts."

"If Bernard feared he was on to him about his thieving, it's a completely sensible motive for murder. But does that mean he poisoned Rollo for months and then decided to suffocate him in the night at the end?"

"How ironic would that be!" Catrin said. "We started delving into the thefts only because of the murder."

"It still doesn't explain Hugh's illness," Wena pointed out. She'd been looking from Rhys to Catrin like someone watching a game of catch. They probably shouldn't have been discussing all this in front of her in the first place, but since she was the one who identified the arsenic, it was a little late to be concerned about discretion. "If he was, in fact, poisoned too."

"Unless Bernard thought Rollo had shared his suspicions with Hugh," Catrin said. "Which he didn't."

"Bernard wouldn't know that," Rhys said.

"I need to show this ring to Joan right now." Catrin dropped the ring into her purse. "We have to know if it's the one she threw at Bernard, and if she knew about the powder inside."

"And it's probably time," Rhys said heavily, "that I lay what we know before the king."

29

Day Three

Catrin

But it was not to be, or at least not immediately. They stepped out of Wena's stall to find Vincent de Lusignan and Hugh squaring off in the middle of the road that led to the tournament grounds. After the wound he'd received, that Hugh was on his feet at all was something of a miracle. He was definitely listing to one side.

He also wasn't wearing his armor, though he wore a sword at his waist, on the hilt of which he rested his left hand, looking as if he was prepared to draw it.

He stabbed a finger in Vincent's direction. "You are a coward and a knave!"

Vincent would have been within his rights to draw his own sword at this besmirching of his honor. He didn't, however. Instead, his expression was one of bemusement. "You are delusional and should return to your bed."

Hugh, for his part, was so unsteady he almost fell on one knee as he tried to pull his sword from its sheath. Thankfully, at that point, a dozen people intervened, including Joan, who got in front of Vincent and pressed a hand to his chest. Catrin could hear her saying, "Come away, my love. He doesn't know what he's doing."

Vincent put both hands on Joan's shoulders, as if to move her aside, but then he glanced around, his expression reluctant, and in the end did as she bid. Turning away, he was soon surrounded by various members of the Valence faction.

Catrin needed to speak to Joan, but first she went with Rhys to Hugh, who was being supported by several of Clare's men, including Eustace. Rhys took the place of another man, throwing one of Hugh's arms over his shoulder. "What is this about, Hugh?"

"Vincent murdered Rollo."

"Why do you think so, Hugh?" Rhys asked very reasonably. "We have nothing to tie him to the murder."

"We have Joan! He wanted what Rollo had, and when he wouldn't give it to him, he killed him!"

It hadn't been too hard to guess that's what Hugh had been thinking. It had certainly occurred to Catrin too. Rhys had suspected him from the moment he'd seen him with Joan. And yet, Rollo had been poisoned with arsenic, which was found in Bernard's possession. And while Vincent was another man who loved Joan, Catrin didn't think it would be his way to sneak into a man's tent in the middle of the night and suffocate him. From what she'd learned from Rhys and seen so far, in the jousts and otherwise, calling out Rollo in the middle of the road, much as Hugh had just done to him, was more his style. Or killing him in the joust.

At the same time, there was real irony in the possibility that Bernard was poisoning Rollo so he could marry Joan, only to have Vincent swoop in and murder him instead. It was really too bad that Rollo was no longer alive to question, because he could have cleared up many issues.

Such was the way of murder.

For Catrin's part, she could barely look at Vincent, knowing what he'd done to Rhys.

Regardless, Hugh was in no position to pursue his vengeance and, in short order, Rhys and Eustace got him headed back to the hospital tent. Once Hugh was moving, Rhys waved a hand at Catrin, sending her the other way after Joan and Vincent.

Fortunately, the pair had been walking slowly and had stopped in the road a short distance ahead, waylaid by enthusiastic supporters intent on congratulating Vincent— both on making the third day of the joust and on his upcoming nuptials. Now that the jousters and the archers had been reduced to a handful (eight jousters; two archers) and only the mêlée remained for the rest of the combatants, many people were expansive and relaxed. With no more tournament events for the day, two more makeshift taverns had sprung up, bringing the total along the road between the fair and the palace to eight.

Since Vincent had become embroiled in an animated conversation about jousting tactics, Catrin edged up beside Joan. "May I speak to you for a moment?"

Joan swung around, surprise on her face but no unhappiness, even when she almost spilled the cup of mead she held in her hand. "Of course." She eyed her fiancé. "He will be busy a while. What can I do for you?"

"I have something to show you." Catrin canted her head to indicate they should move off the road slightly, and they came to rest near a low wall that surrounded one of the village homes. "Do you recognize this ring?" She held it out.

Joan's recoil would have told Catrin she was on the right track even if the other woman hadn't agreed immediately that this was, in fact, Bernard's ring. "I don't want it, if that's why you brought it to me. Vincent has forbidden me ever to see him again!" Where before she'd been indulgent of Bernard, now she was angry. "Where did you get it?"

Catrin didn't see the harm in telling her. "I found it in the grass near the edge of Earl Clare's encampment."

"That's where I threw it." She sighed. "I suppose I should tell Bernard that it's been found. He was quite upset when it disappeared into the darkness."

"No! Please don't!" Catrin put out a hand. "I will speak to him myself. Vincent doesn't want you involved with Bernard again, and I would hate to cause you to disobey your future husband."

"That is very kind of you." Joan's expression softened. "Thank you."

It wasn't kind at all, and Catrin felt a twinge of guilt at deceiving her, but she carried on anyway. "You weren't this upset about

Bernard when I spoke to you earlier today. What has changed since then?"

"After I talked to you, Bernard approached me with that—" she made a disgusted face, "—slut, Matilda. Can you believe he wanted me to introduce him to Vincent? I told him to go away."

This must have occurred in the short window of time between when Catrin had seen Bernard with Matilda at the tournament grounds and when he returned to his tent with Miles. At the very least, that meant he had spoken to Joan *before* Catrin herself had found the ledger and vial. Even now, he might not realize they were missing. "How did Bernard take your refusal?"

"He was furious." Joan's nose went in the air, implying she could not care less how Bernard felt, though clearly she still cared a little or she wouldn't have been so irate.

It was clear to Catrin by now that Joan couldn't possibly know the ring contained arsenic, but that didn't mean she was entirely ignorant. "Did you know there is a secret compartment under the gemstone?"

"A secret compartment? You mean other than the one that appears when you flip open the gem?"

Catrin swallowed. "No, I mean that one."

"It isn't so secret really, then, is it? Bernard showed it to me when he gave me the ring. It was where he stored the herbs intended for Rollo's health."

"The ... herbs?" Catrin was having a hard time breathing evenly.

"Yes. Rollo has had terrible aches in his joints for years and years. Didn't I tell you?" She continued without waiting for Catrin to reply. "He didn't want anyone to know how much pain he was in all the time. To aid him in sleeping, he would take a glass of wine before bed, to which most nights I added a dollop of a different, strong wine Bernard gave me, along with the powder. Those nights Rollo always slept so much better."

"Did Rollo know you were doing that?"

"My heavens, no. He wouldn't have wanted me to help him, you see. He thought asking for help was tantamount to admitting weakness, which he hated to do."

"Do you still have the wine you gave him?"

"It's in my tent. You can have the rest if you want, though there's only a drop or two left."

When Catrin indicated she would appreciate Joan's assistance, the pair started walking towards the Clare encampment. As they were already halfway along the road to the palace, it wasn't far to go.

Then a curious expression crossed Joan's face. "As I think on it, the herb would have run out the day after Rollo died and, of course, I wouldn't have been able to ask Bernard for more." She paused. "Funny that Rollo fell asleep just fine the last two nights he was alive, even after I'd thrown away the ring, so I was unable to administer the powder." Then she brightened. "Maybe it had worked, and he no longer needed it!"

Catrin just managed to refrain from rolling her eyes at Joan's optimism. The man had been murdered, after all. The cure was irrelevant. "Did Bernard tell you what the powder was made of?"

"Willow bark." She smiled gently as she gestured Catrin inside her tent. "I hated my brother, but even I am glad that his last nights weren't spent in pain."

30

Day Three

Rhys

After getting Hugh to the hospital tent, Rhys had stood outside dithering long enough for Catrin to find him again and tell him of her conversation with Joan and her acquisition of the dregs of the *strong wine* she'd given Rollo. Another beautiful day was coming to an end, with the sun casting long shadows across the grass, and the furious pace of their discoveries had resulted in an urgency Rhys felt deep in his belly. Things were starting to happen, and he didn't have enough help to deal with them.

Although he'd told Catrin earlier that he needed to speak to the king, he couldn't approach him willy nilly without approval first from Simon, to whom he also owed an explanation. And Rhys didn't feel like he could take the time to track his friend down—nor study the ledger Catrin had found at the length it appeared to require. A quick perusal produced little beyond a headache, in that the ledger gave the initial appearance of being an account book, but closer inspection revealed it to have been written in a kind of shorthand, or even a code that made sense only to Bernard.

Since Rhys's next task was to find Ralph and Miles in the Richmond encampment, he left the ledger with Catrin. The last thing he wanted was to bring it back to, or anywhere in the vicinity of, Bernard.

"And then what? Are you going to follow Bernard around until he betrays himself?" At Rhys's steady look, Catrin laughed, just a little mockingly. He could hardly blame her, since he was mocking himself. "We did that before, and look how it turned out. Unless you catch him in the act of thievery, the evidence against him is hardly more than hearsay, even with Alard's and Wena's testimony."

"I have an idea about that," Rhys said. "This won't be like last time."

Catrin didn't necessarily look convinced, but she let Rhys go, the ledger stowed once more against her belly. Its contents had a high probability of being inflammatory, if only they could decipher what the words said. At least he'd persuaded Catrin to take the wine to Wena rather than entering the Richmond encampment again. Even if Catrin wanted to be included, she recognized the folly of her returning to the scene of her own crime so soon after committing it.

And while Rhys was anxious to find Ralph and Miles, he needed to acquire more help first. Specifically, he needed the help of someone he could trust.

These days, such persons were few and far between, especially since Rhys had already tapped Ralph. But he thought he knew who might fit the description, and to that end, he ducked under the hospital tent flap, avoiding the crowd around Hugh, and made his way to Dafi, the boy who'd been injured in the accident at the viewing stand. That he was still here was testament to the care the physicians were taking with every patient, regardless of his or her origins. When Rhys came upon him, Dafi was propped up on pillows, talking to a girl about his age. At Rhys's approach, she touched Dafi's hand and departed.

Rhys raised his eyebrows, recognizing her as the same girl he'd seen in Wena's stall earlier. Here might be another reason for Wena's softened attitude towards Rhys.

"I see you're making friends." Rhys grinned. "Are you bored of lying here yet?"

Dafi's legs were already swinging out of bed before Rhys had finished his sentence.

"Hold on, young man, can you even walk?"

Dafi's eyes were bright as he lifted his shirt to show off his bandages. "The wound was bloody and painful at first, but I can hardly feel it now. What can I do for you?"

"Nothing strenuous or dangerous, I assure you." Rhys didn't believe him, but he had to admire the boy's enthusiasm. "Just a little watching and maybe some message carrying."

Dafi was game, as Rhys had assumed he would be. No fifteen-year-old boy of his acquaintance had ever found lying in a sick bed a desirable way to spend the day unless he was very sick. Dafi had progressed from ill to healing.

Still, Rhys knew he shouldn't take him without approval from his minders. Casting around for someone to talk to, he spied Josef moving towards the collection of medicines. At Rhys's wave, he diverted towards their corner of the tent, and Rhys met him halfway. "Can I borrow Dafi for a time?"

Josef laughed. "You can keep him!" He looked past Rhys and spoke a little louder so his voice would carry, as before in French, "I never want to see him again!"

Grinning, Dafi came off the bed. Rhys had forgotten the boy spoke French. Including Dafi was becoming a better and better idea the more he thought about it. While Dafi seemed to sway initially, he righted himself and walked towards them.

"You are in pain?" Josef asked.

"No, sir."

Josef shook his head. "Do not call me *sir*."

Dafi grinned. "Yes, sir."

"Off you go." Josef laughed and jerked his head towards the doorway.

Once outside, Dafi heaved a great sigh. "A few times, they allowed me out to walk around the tent, but otherwise I had to stay in bed. They wouldn't even let me go to the latrine by myself! I had to pee in a pot like an old man."

Rhys was enjoying Dafi more by the moment. "Let me know if you start to feel unwell."

Then he led Dafi through the pavilion where food and drink were being served to those in the king's household, like Rhys, and the noble tournament-goers. Dafi had no rank, not in the slightest, but nobody questioned his presence beside Rhys, and they each picked up a small loaf, a skewer of mutton, and stopped long enough for several long drinks of water each. Wine was all very well and good at meals, but Rhys wanted to keep a clear head for what was to come, whatever that might be.

What with his performance at the archery contest, Rhys suspected he was enough of a notable figure that he couldn't go about unrecognized. Nonetheless, he walked purposefully past the guard at the entrance to the Richmond encampment with a wave of his hand, and then kept on, deciding again that if he looked like he knew what he was doing, nobody would question exactly *what* he was doing. Catrin had told him approximately where Bernard's tent lay, but in the end he didn't have to guess which one it was, since a hand reached out from within a tent as he passed and grabbed his sleeve.

"You've stepped in a hornet's nest this time, my friend." It was Miles de Bohun, whispering, since they were a few yards from Bernard's tent. His face was alight with good humor as he looked at Rhys.

"I think that was the idea."

Miles glanced at Dafi, who'd come inside as well. "Who's this? Another one of your recruits?" He smiled wryly. "I suppose I might count myself among them."

Dafi's eyes were bright too. "Yes, my lord."

"He's here to run messages." Rhys inspected the tidy space that included a pallet and trunk but nothing else. "Whose tent did you commandeer?"

"Someone who owes me a favor."

Rhys looked darkly at him, but then decided he himself was the one who'd brought Miles into this, and he couldn't complain after the fact about his methods.

"Where's Ralph?"

"Watching Bernard's secret rear door from the tree line."

"Good man." Rhys eased out a breath.

Miles scoffed. "I realize I haven't done quite this sort of thing before, but I'm not a complete idiot."

Rhys put up both hands. "Not everyone takes to investigating. It requires a certain kind of twisted mind and a willingness to expand one's ideas of what is possible."

By way of a reply, Miles looked steadily at Rhys, prompting Rhys to laugh. "I grant that it was likely you had those qualities, but if I don't ask, I don't know what you know. Better to err on the side of caution."

Miles waggled his head. "I can grant you that."

"And Bernard?"

"He's been in there a while. Alone. Do you think—"

Miles cut himself off as a single curse split the air from beyond the tent entrance, followed by, "Son of a—

It was Bernard, cursing in his own tent a few yards away.

Even if the other tents around him were occupied, Rhys wasn't sure anyone would think anything of what Bernard had called out. This might be a Round Table, but soldiers cursed as a matter of course. At least he hadn't taken the name of the Lord in vain.

If Rhys himself hadn't been waiting for the moment Bernard discovered the ledger was missing, he wouldn't have noticed either.

But if that discovery really was the source of Bernard's anger, the time had come for action. He turned to Dafi. "This is what I need you for. You told me you knew all the king's guardsmen."

"I do." Dafi rattled off their names.

"Do you know Ralph by sight?"

"He was at the viewing stand. He's the one who brought Lord Simon."

"I need you to find him within the tree line, outside the encampment. If Bernard leaves by the back entrance, Ralph is to follow, and you are to come here to tell me he's gone."

As Dafi set off, Miles asked, "You think Bernard is going to run?"

"I can't assume he won't."

"How can he? Where would he go? He's steward to the Earl of Richmond!"

"He *was* steward to the Earl of Richmond. The moment we bring any of what we've discovered to John of Brittany the position will be his no longer. The question now is at what point Bernard realizes it too."

31

Day Three

Catrin

"W illow bark?" Wena gave a low laugh. "I don't think so."

With the market fair over for the day, Wena had retired to her house, bringing the rat with her. Her house was just like her market stall except it was much larger, with enough jars and vials of herbs, unguents, lotions, powders, and tinctures to supply a castle. It occurred to Catrin only now that Wena had been the healer for the palace when Llywelyn had come to visit and no longer supplied the palace with advice and healing because the king had his own physicians.

"So Joan is wrong? You still believe the poison to be arsenic?" Catrin asked.

"From the way the rat died? Yes." Then Wena looked past Catrin to the door. "Come in, Cadell. Thank you for coming."

Catrin swung around to see the herbalist from the monastery ducking under the lintel. "A pleasure to see you again, my lady."

Catrin canted her head, less than happy that Wena had invited him, but not willing to be ungracious now that he was here. "The pleasure's all mine."

Wena frowned. "You know each other already?"

"Cadell consulted with us on the absence of Adam the carpenter." Catrin's eyes went to Cadell's.

He nodded, without her having to articulate her question. "I can be as discreet in this as I have been with that."

"We may need that quality from you more in this instance." Catrin directed his attention to the flask of wine by which Joan had modified her brother's drink. It sat next to the vial and the basket containing the poisoned rat, now dead. "Any thoughts on what we have here would be most welcome." She then stepped aside to give the two healers room to work.

Cadell poured the remainder of what was in the flask into a shallow dish, and then followed it up with some sniffing and low conversation with Wena. Then Cadell dipped his pinky finger into wine and touched it lightly to his tongue, prompting Catrin to flinch. Finally, as one, the pair turned to her.

"Cadell agrees the vial contains arsenic, not willow bark, and it is no wonder Rollo found relief from what was in the flask since it isn't wine but *dwale*." Wena pronounced the word as if it were Welsh, but Catrin, having lived for twenty years in England, knew it to be English. Or maybe, given the need among all peoples for *dwale* and the frequency of its use, it was both.

Dwale, however one pronounced it, was used the world over as a sleeping potion and to lessen pain in injured men. If a man was wounded in battle, the healer could give him *dwale* before amputating a limb or sewing up a gaping wound. Though one of its most important ingredients, poppy, was rare and didn't grow well in Britain, any healer worth her salt would move heaven and earth to ensure she maintained a good supply.

"Wouldn't Rollo have noticed the bitter taste in his wine?" Catrin asked.

"This *dwale* isn't bitter, as no vinegar was added," Cadell said. "Regardless, we believe it has a high concentration of poppy that would have served the intended purpose of easing pain and encouraging sleep."

Catrin had never had need of *dwale* herself, but then, she'd never been badly wounded either. According to Rhys, the monks who tended him after Cilmeri had been judicious in its use, since a man could grow so used to ingesting it that he couldn't live without it. Rhys suspected this fact was the reason vinegar was part of the recipe, to make it bitter and unpalatable, rather than because the vinegar itself served any healing purpose. If the *dwale* was being used for a procedure, afterwards a wash of vinegar and salt could be used to wake the patient, lest he fall into too deep a sleep.

"What could be the purpose of giving Rollo this combination of *dwale* and arsenic?" Catrin asked.

The two healers looked at one another, and then Wena turned a hand face up. "If the intent was to poison him in the guise of healing him, whatever he was given would need to be seen as doing something, else it could not continue. At the same time, arsenic in small doses *is* a prescribed treatment for swollen joints, from which your description tells me Rollo suffered."

Catrin harrumphed to herself. Joan had been altogether too gullible for too long. But that wasn't the healers' fault, so she thanked them, yet again begged for their discretion, and left in search of Simon.

Instead she found Matilda wending her way through the crowds of people, talking with some and laughing with others, making for the road out of the village. Though hands went out to her as she passed, she smiled and waved them off, and then hurried away with her head down, looking purposeful.

Catrin didn't think twice about following.

Perhaps she should have. Perhaps if Rhys had been with her, he would have cautioned against impulse. But if she hesitated at all, she would lose Matilda, who had picked up her pace and was now walking faster than ever. After another ten yards, she passed the church and kept going.

Catrin glanced back to see if anyone was following *her*, but by now she had come some distance away from the festivities. Fearing detection from the other direction, Catrin allowed the distance to grow between herself and Matilda, putting herself right on the edge of the road, so she was ready to hide in the bushes or a ditch if Matilda looked around and spied her. At one point, she allowed the other woman to get far enough ahead that she disappeared around a bend, forcing Catrin to hurry to catch up. But as she rounded the curve and arrived at another straight stretch, she pulled up short because Matilda had disappeared.

A bit befuddled, Catrin stood in the middle of the road, just staring. Then she began to look more carefully around, turning slowly on one heel. There were no houses here, no stone walls or fences, just fields and forest rising to meet hills and mountains to the east and much flatter land ending in the Irish Sea to the west.

At first, she couldn't discern anything out of place or different from the usual.

But then she noted a shoe print in the dirt, distinct amongst all the other prints that marred it. This was the main road from Caernarfon, so traffic had been heavy this week, with many people and horses traveling both ways. And no rain since the night Rollo died.

This particular print caught her attention because it was on the small side, similar to her own, and pointing directly off the road to the east. Catrin bent closer to the ground, thankful the sun had not set so she could still see clearly. Tracking was really Rhys's strength, not hers, but nonetheless she plunged forward through the bracken into the field beyond. For a few paces, the footprints were quite clear, and she looked up to catch a glimpse of a figure two hundred feet ahead of her, moving swiftly towards the hills.

It seemed more likely than not that Matilda had spotted her, but if she had, she gave no sign. Catrin was even more curious than before as to what the other woman was doing out in the middle of nowhere at dusk. All of a sudden, she felt like she was getting somewhere with this mystery—and she wasn't sorry that Matilda might lead her to it. She was a thief and a fraud, and that fact put up Catrin's hackles.

While Catrin would readily admit she hadn't always been up front with her doings when it came to helping her people, she was quite sure the queen was not deceived in the slightest. If anything, Eleanor found Catrin useful, if not amusing, so turned a blind eye to her activities. That was fine by Catrin. She was perfectly willing to push her boundaries as far as the queen would let her.

Thieving, however, was an offense against God and man. Just because Matilda and Bernard were stealing from the wealthy, who could afford the losses, didn't excuse them. And that wasn't even to mention the murder.

These thoughts gave haste to Catrin's steps. At first the ground was flat, though she did have to pick her way across a stream, but then it rose sharply, towards some farther hills. All the while, Matilda kept on walking, so Catrin did too.

The sun had started its descent towards the horizon, creating long shadows of the occasional trees as well as Catrin's own figure. She clambered over a stone wall, passed through a field of sheep, and then climbed another wall. Up head, Matilda marched steadily on, stopping only once to turn around. Thankfully, when she did, the sun lay behind Catrin, putting it right in Matilda's eyes. Catrin had been watching carefully and managed to duck behind a low wall. After a hundred heartbeats, she carefully looked again to see Matilda continuing on.

The going turned more difficult as they ascended a hill and entered the thick woods that covered it, causing Catrin briefly to lose sight of Matilda entirely. If she turned off this set course, Catrin wouldn't know it. At least Matilda hadn't chosen to climb Garn

Boduan, a greater hill to the south, upon which an ancient hillfort stood, since it was twice as high.

In the end, though there'd been some rough going, they traveled less than a mile. Catrin arrived at the top to find Matilda on her knees in front of an ancient cairn, rooting around at its base with determined movements of her bare hands. Catrin stopped abruptly at the edge of the trees, uncertain at what point she should intervene. While she dithered, Bernard appeared from the southern side of the hill, leading a horse and wearing an outraged expression on his face.

Catrin took one step back and almost jumped out of her shoes in her surprise to find Rhys right behind her. Hugely relieved, she shook her finger at him, whispering, "Am I ever glad to see you!"

He gave a chuckle low in her ear. "And I, somehow, am not surprised at all to find you here, *cariad.*"

32

Day Three

Rhys

Bernard had departed his tent by the back entrance, but because Ralph had Dafi with him, he had been able to follow Bernard while Dafi had come to find Miles and Rhys. Rhys then sent the boy to tell Simon what was afoot, while he and Miles set off after Bernard and Ralph. Fortunately, neither were particularly difficult to follow, since Bernard had gone first to where the horses were picketed, chosen one, and set off into the dusk of late evening.

Miles, Ralph, and Rhys had deliberated for a few moments before commandeering horses from the Richmond stock too. As Rhys and Ralph were members of the king's guard and Miles was a nobleman, it hadn't been difficult to convince the boys who tended the horses that their need was legitimate. The horses were saddled quickly, while Ralph procured a few supplies of food, water, and wine, stuffing them into a satchel because they didn't know how long this journey would take.

And then they followed.

They'd given Bernard a good head start, but Rhys had learned to track on his father's heels and had traveled all over Wales in his time, including to Nefyn and this very hill. His tracking was aided by the fact that Bernard wasn't making more than a show of being discreet—or maybe, having spent his life in towns, he didn't realize how wide a swath he was cutting through the countryside.

On top of which, he wasn't hard to follow initially because he stuck to the road to Pwllheli, riding perhaps two-thirds of a mile, before, with somewhat more discretion—meaning that he looked around before doing it—he left the road for the pastureland to the north. Almost immediately, the path sloped upwards as he climbed towards the heights of Mynydd Nefyn, at the top of which long dead Welshmen had built a cairn to bury an ancient king.

If Bernard had wanted to lose himself within a mile of Nefyn, this journey put him well on his way to achieving his goal. After that single curse in the tent, he'd moved quickly and with obvious intent. And, as far as they knew, had no notion they were on to him. His flight was a gift, and Rhys kept well back, determined not to waste it.

"What's he doing, do you think?" So far, Miles had maintained an amused detachment, but Rhys had known him since the Holy Land and had figured out by now that his attitude masked an intensity of interest that grew all the greater the more relaxed he appeared on the outside.

"I have no idea. He might not even be running."

"Why would you say that?"

"He took very little with him that I can see. If I were fleeing to France, I'd make sure my saddle bags were full before I started."

Once within the trees, Rhys picked up the pace, afraid they would lose Bernard, tracks or no tracks. Finally, when they were almost at the crest, he caught a glimpse of Bernard, who'd dismounted, and he put up a hand to indicate to the others that they should dismount too. Then, leaving Ralph with the horses (over his objections), Miles and Rhys crept forward, circling below the clearing which Bernard had entered.

Because they were coming at the cairn from slightly farther down the slope, Rhys saw Catrin before she saw him. Crouching together now, they were close enough to hear Bernard's opening salvo at Matilda: "So you mean to betray me."

Matilda jerked as if she'd been struck. "Betray *you*?" She rose to her feet. "I knew I had better take what we'd collected and go before you lost your nerve entirely."

Bernard was unmoved by her scorn and stood with his hands on his hips, glaring at her. "Where's the ledger?"

It was dark enough now that Rhys couldn't make out Matilda's expression, but her snort of derision was unmistakable. "I didn't take your damn ledger, as you well know. If you spent as much time on the plan instead of your stupid scribbling, we wouldn't be in this predicament."

"I don't know what you think I did—"

"*Think?* I didn't *think* I heard you pleading with Joan to take you back. You were embarrassing yourself." Matilda spat on the ground in front of Bernard. If Rhys hadn't already known she wasn't a lady, he would know it now. "You said you broke it off, and I might have believed you, if you hadn't agreed to do it so many times before." Her voice dripped with venom. "And they say women are too emotional."

"Joan's and my conversation had nothing to do with—"

"Liar!" Matilda stabbed a finger towards him. "If you hadn't been trying to help Rollo for Joan, he never would have known you existed! And you call yourself a man. You are weak, without even the guts to do what must be done. *I* took care of Rollo, not you. You couldn't even poison Hugh properly."

"Hugh is a child. It's that Welsh kingsman—"

"You won't touch him. You won't even speak to him." Matilda advanced on Bernard, who took several steps back to maintain a few feet of distance between them. "You'll muck that up too. It was one thing to get rid of the captain of Clare's guard. It's quite another to do away with a kingsman. You will leave him to me!"

And then, between one heartbeat and the next, a knife appeared in her hand, and she pounced on Bernard with a startling speed.

Bernard saw the knife at the last instant and leapt backwards, but not in time to entirely escape Matilda's downward stab, which connected along his right shoulder and arm, opening a foot long gash. Blood gushed from the wound.

Rhys had been waiting to intervene until Matilda had laid out the full story, but with her attempted murder of Bernard right in front of them, he charged forward from his hiding place, Miles hardly half a pace behind. Before Matilda's arm could come down again in what truly might be a killing blow, Rhys grabbed her about the waist, swung her around, and threw her to one side. Bernard, meanwhile, had fallen to the ground, moaning and writhing in pain.

"I'll see to her!" Miles shouted. "You tend him. You know more what to do than I. We need him alive."

Rhys was no expert healer, but Miles was right that likely he had done more of it in adverse circumstances than Miles—though never in a situation quite like this.

Catrin knew something about healing too, and she moved to Bernard's side in order to press down on his right arm. Blood continued to flow through her fingers. With the coat and shirt Bernard was wearing, not to mention the blood, it was hard to see the actual damage, but at this point, they just needed to stem the flow.

"Keep pressing," Rhys told her.

"I'm trying!"

Because he'd spent the afternoon shooting—and it was a hot summer day—Rhys was not dressed in mail anymore than Bernard was, though he still wore a tunic displaying the king's colors. He made to pull it over his head and use it to wrap the wound, but Catrin tossed her head at him.

"Use my headscarf."

Rhys tugged it free and wound the cloth tightly around Bernard's arm, starting right below the shoulder. If Matilda had cut through one of Bernard's life veins, he would have already bled out, so Rhys was hopeful that compressing the separated skin and muscle would allow Bernard to live long enough for Rhys to get him off this mountain.

While Rhys worked, Catrin moved to Bernard's other side and held his hand. "Did you know before Matilda killed Rollo that she was going to?"

Bernard lay on his back on the ground, his face white.

"Bernard!" Rhys spoke sharply, though he didn't shout. "I fear you won't survive your wound, so now is the time to tell us what happened. You want her punished for what she's done, don't you?"

It was a cheap trick. Bernard wasn't dying, but he didn't have to know that just yet. Rhys completely believed he felt like he was dying.

By now, Miles had subdued Matilda, producing out of nowhere a length of cord by which he tied her hands behind her back. He hadn't put a gag in her mouth, however, which turned out to be all to the good because she'd overheard their pleas to Bernard.

Now she surged forward, almost pulling herself from Miles's grip. "Don't tell them anything! Don't you dare say a word!"

Rhys raised his eyebrows. "It sounds like she thinks she's in charge. Does she really give you orders?"

Appealing to Bernard's male pride was another ploy, and this time Rhys had read his man right. Bernard's lips twisted in a sneer. "This was all her idea! I told her Rollo had talked to me about the thefts, and she took it upon herself to suffocate him in his sleep! She knew he would be insensible from the *dwale* and wouldn't fight back."

"That's a lie!" Matilda was straining forward again. If she hadn't been tied and held by Miles, Rhys believed with utter certainty that she would have closed Bernard's mouth for him permanently.

"You told me when and how! I even cut off that poor man's fingertip because you said to!"

"Why cut off the fingertip?" Miles hadn't known that detail before now, but he asked the question they were all thinking.

Matilda answered: "To make you think a madman had done it. Nobody sane would chop the fingertip off a dead person. We didn't want you to make any connection to the thefts." Her lip twisted. "You did anyway."

For Rhys's part, he was beginning to question Matilda's sanity, having already made an assessment of her moral core, of which she apparently had none.

"She's lying." Bernard opened his eyes to slits. "I didn't know about the murder."

"Not that it matters," Catrin said, "since you were already doing your best to kill Rollo with powdered arsenic."

"I wasn't trying to kill him!" Bernard's mouth dropped open. "I was trying to help him!"

Rhys wanted to believe the pain and fear Bernard was experiencing was enough to ensure he was telling the truth, but he couldn't be sure. "Help him how?"

"He had terrible aches in every joint. His knuckles were so swollen sometimes he couldn't grip his sword. I was trying to cure him!" Bernard's eyes narrowed. "How do you know this anyway?" Then he answered his own question. "Joan told you."

"Eventually, she did, though only after we found the ring outside Rollo's tent. She said you told her the powder was willow bark."

"I didn't want to worry her. I made sure she knew to put in only a few grains." Bernard was desperate now. "I did nothing wrong!"

Into this craziness, Ralph arrived, skidding to a halt on the edge of the clearing. He had lit a torch, so Rhys could see his wide, staring eyes. Rhys snapped his fingers in his direction. "Water and wine, as quick as you can. And any cloth you can find."

"Yes, sir!"

Rhys wasn't really Ralph's superior, but he was older, not to mention quaestor and spymaster for the king. He had apparently earned the boy's respect.

"Tell us about the thieving," Rhys ordered Bernard once Ralph was gone again.

"What thieving?"

Rhys couldn't believe he was actually going to deny it. "We knew about the girls and the thieving before Matilda talked about it. We have witnesses. Are you really going to tell me you know nothing about the stolen items buried beneath that cairn? Why else would you have come up here?"

"I knew about the thefts because Lady Catrin had mentioned them. I feared the ringleader was Matilda and felt it was my duty to confront her." It was remarkable that Bernard had enough strength, despite the blood loss and shock, to lie to Rhys's face. Alard had seen one of Bernard's girls take a man's neck chain and give it to Bernard. The thefts were real. At this point, they didn't need Bernard's confession to hang him for them.

Then Bernard's eyes rolled up in his head.

"He's a liar." Matilda wasn't shouting anymore, but her words were no less emphatic. "He was going to keep everything for himself."

Then Ralph returned. By holding the mouth of the wine flask under Bernard's nose, they got him awake enough to sit up and drink several gulps. Though Catrin's headscarf was holding his wounded arm together, in the end Rhys needed his tunic after all to bind the arm to Bernard's chest so it wouldn't flop around. While Rhys prepared Bernard for travel, Miles went to the hole under the cairn and dug around until he came up with a large sack containing many of the stolen items. Like Guy back in Caernarfon, Bernard had buried his treasure at a place sacred to the ancients. Rhys thought the impulse both odd and understandable.

Bernard watched these activities with a completely expressionless face while Catrin fed him wine, and then even a little water from the other flask. He had lost a great deal of blood and had every reason to be thirsty. He didn't speak again, however. They'd get no more answers from him on this mountain.

And maybe they didn't need to. With the sack, Matilda's confession, and what others had witnessed, they had enough evidence to lay at the feet of Earl Clare, John of Brittany, and the king.

To that end, Rhys leaned down to extend his left hand to Bernard. "Let's go." He levered the wounded man upright, holding him steady until he stopped swaying.

"I-I thought I was going to die." Bernard focused on Rhys. "You said I was going to die!"

"I implied it," Rhys said without apology. "You'll live only long enough for the king to hang you."

33

Day Three

Rhys

I t was nearing midnight by the time they brought Matilda and Bernard back to Nefyn and rounded up the three other girls who'd been part of the ring of thieves. With no prison to put them in, Simon arranged for the women to be locked up at the monastery, each in a separate cell designed for penitents, while Bernard was taken to the monastery infirmary.

Crime certainly existed in Wales in the past, especially in an internationally important trading port such as Nefyn, but every Welsh criminal had a family into whose custody the miscreant could be released. Provided he was later found guilty in court, by Welsh law (and as Rhys and Catrin had explained to Simon), the clan would then pay *galanas* to the victim's clan as compensation, never mind that a single person had committed the crime. This method of punishment put great pressure on every individual to conform—or at least to not get caught.

Bards' songs still told of one of the greatest crimes in Welsh history, committed in the previous century by a king's brother—the very prince, in fact, who'd established the monastery in Nefyn. He'd paid Danish mercenaries from Ireland to ambush and murder a rival king. Murder among royal families in Wales was at times more common than not, but usually it was brothers killing brothers. When caught, noblemen could be transported to a tower and imprisoned indefinitely, but even in this instance, fines were exacted, payments made, and the murderer restored to favor—for a time, anyway.

While English law applied now, the official buildings in Nefyn had yet to be adapted to this new reality.

Rhys also had the brilliant idea (if he did say so himself) of putting Dafi in the bed beside Bernard's. Running about hadn't necessarily done the boy lasting harm, but his wound had started bleeding again, and lodging him next to Bernard was an easy way to get someone Rhys trusted into the room. If Bernard talked in his sleep, or admitted to any wrongdoing, Dafi would be there to hear it. Besides, the boy really needed to spend at least another day in the presence of healers.

During the trip to Nefyn, Matilda had thought better of much of what she'd said on the hill, and was now insisting Bernard himself was not only the mastermind behind the thieving ring, but had murdered Rollo. Bernard himself was still refusing to speak. Fortunately, the other girls, Eliza in particular, had sung like larks in the morning. Since Rhys had recovered the stash of stolen items too, they were able to tie a fine bow on the investigation.

Simon went off as soon as the prisoners were secure to arrange for an audience with the king if at all possible. Since Rhys was the one with the full story, he would return to collect him if the king was willing to see them. Even though the request was fraught with peril at this hour of the night, Simon left whistling.

"When you tell the king about the events of the night, you shouldn't tell him of this ledger, Rhys." Catrin sat on a bench in the guardroom, flipping through the pages. Because it was so late, anyone else awake was on patrol, so they were alone. "Nor Simon." To emphasize her desire for secrecy, she spoke in Welsh.

"You want to keep it a secret?" He thought back to all their conversations and realized nobody had mentioned the ledger again since Bernard himself at the very beginning of his confrontation with Matilda. So much had been going on Rhys hadn't yet mentioned it to Simon either. The omission hadn't been intentional on Rhys's part; it just hadn't been relevant. "How can we? Miles heard him too."

"But will he remember and, even more, think it important?"

"What's really going on, Catrin?"

She raised the book, which was open in both hands. "Do you know what this is?"

"A record of some kind."

She laughed. "Well, yes."

Rhys laughed too. "Beyond that, I have no idea." He studied her downturned head, more impressed every day with who she was and how she thought. "But I see you do."

"You were never one to care much about politics, but as the wife of a lord, minor though he was, for twenty years I lived and breathed by documents such as this. It's more a *diarium* than an accounting book."

"A *diarium*?" It was a Latin word, but not one Rhys knew.

She waved a hand. "Like the one the queen's scribe keeps for her, a record of her days and business transactions. The king has one too—stacks of them, really, having ruled for as long as he has. They contain information about his days: who he is supposed to be seeing, and if he does see them, what he discussed. This way, when a petitioner comes back later and insists the king told him a certain thing, his clerk can return to that record and determine whether or not the man is truthful."

"The clerk records that for the king every day?"

"And the queen."

Rhys's hand hurt just thinking about writing that much, but he understood instantly why such meticulous detail would be important for the queen, king, or any lord, to record. King Edward could always deny a renewed petition if he didn't like what he heard, but he desired to be strict and just at the same time. If he told a man that something would be seen to, and it was not, then Edward would want to know the truth of it and could not possibly be expected to remember every detail of every day, weeks and months, if not years, later.

Come to think on it, that was why Rhys himself kept a journal of his investigations. He retained many details, but he found it helpful at times to review past investigations when they touched upon new ones. He also took notes about the condition of corpses he examined, to aid him in identifying causes of death in the future. To Rhys's mind, the ability to write things down, in fact, was what made him a cut above his peers, and he thanked his father every day for ensuring that his son learned. This added ability, when so many men were illiterate in both reading and writing, was part of what had prompted Prince Edmund to promote him all those years ago.

And, if he was being honest, which he tried to be at all times, he couldn't be sorry for it.

"What does Bernard's *diarium* tell us?"

"Well, it's coded, for one, and given that you've been away from England and the politics of the March for so long, I'm not surprised it didn't mean much to you." She opened the ledger to the first pages. "See this list of names?"

Rhys nodded. He could see the list, though he hadn't understood that it was a list of names until now. Next to each was a number, but the numbers didn't progress sequentially, and the *names* as Catrin called them, were merely strings of letters. It was also, naturally, in French.

She pointed to one halfway down the page. "This was the key to me. HDB/MDB 17." These particular letters and numbers were slotted between RLS 3, 32 and HDL 12.

"I see what you're pointing too. I have no idea what it means."

"Humphrey de Bohun, Miles de Bohun, page seventeen." To her credit, there was no impatience or condescension in her voice. "It isn't a difficult cipher, really, and likely wasn't intended to obscure or confuse anyone for very long. It was a shorthand way of writing for Bernard's own benefit."

"And what's on page seventeen?" Rhys found himself intensely curious.

Catrin turned to the page and read out one of the entries: "3MAI81 MDB. Probability low." She turned the book so he could read more scrawled words in the margin. "Too clever by half. Avoid."

Rhys looked up. "He underlines *avoid* three times." All of a sudden, he thought he knew what this was about. "Third of May, 1281, Miles de Bohun."

Catrin brightened. "I thought it had to be a date. But *probability low* refers to what?"

"With the additional comment of *avoid*, perhaps he was looking for allies and decided Miles couldn't be one?"

"Good decision, that." She closed the book again and held it out to Rhys.

He shook his head. "You keep it."

"You're the spymaster. The secrets in there might be well worth learning, if we can't get them out of Bernard directly."

Rhys still shook his head. "Better not. Taking a leaf from Humphrey's book, if we are keeping this from everyone but the two of us, I would rather not have an interview with the king tonight knowing exactly where it is. You found it; see what more you can learn from it. Then we can decide what to do with what you discover."

Catrin slipped the ledger underneath her overdress once again and belted it securely at the waist. "What will happen to Matilda and Bernard?"

"Matilda is a murderer, so likely she will hang. The other girls might get away with a slap on the wrist, because nobody likes to punish, incarcerate, or hang beautiful women. Bernard, however, is a nobleman. It won't be easy to decide what to do with him, much like it wasn't with Guy."

"Both were illegitimate sons, grasping for anything they could hang on to." Her expression turned a bit sour. "If Welsh law applied here, they would have inherited equally with their legitimate brothers."

"But this is England now, though we still call it Wales, and they were both granted positions of authority they proceeded to squander."

"And I suppose it was Bernard's father who was illegitimate, not Bernard himself." She sighed.

Rhys didn't see how that made a difference when it meant Bernard had no land or wealth. Rhys himself was well-practiced at living as an impoverished nobleman. But as he'd said to Catrin, both Guy and Bernard had been given a chance. Instead of taking it for what it was and building a life, they'd been consumed by greed and jealousy for what they didn't have. They could have been given a hundred trusted positions, each more lucrative than the one before, and still would have grasped for more.

He looked down at Catrin as she sat with her hands folded in her lap, her posture straighter than normal on account of the ledger at her belly. He wanted to speak to her about his feelings, and while now didn't feel like a good time, in three months, no time had ever been good. He'd loved her for thirty years and could not stand even one more hour of uncertainty.

As he came down on one knee before her, she looked up, saw his face, and straightened further. "Rhys?"

"Catrin." He breathed her name, filled to the brim with everything he wanted to say.

No words came out.

She was looking at him expectantly, and he knew he had to say something. It would be just his luck if Simon returned before he opened his mouth to speak. He loved her too much to ruin this moment.

So he squared his shoulders and took both of her hands in his. "I love you, Catrin. I have loved you my whole life, and I would like to marry you if you will have me."

Catrin's eyes had teared up before he finished speaking. Now, one tear trailing down her cheek, she leaned closer and kissed him on the lips for the first time since she was eleven and he thirteen, and they were experimenting with what it might feel like.

"I love you, Rhys ap Iorwerth, you wonderful man. Yes, I'll marry you."

A stab of joy went through him that was almost painful, and he pulled her closer so he could kiss her properly. Their arms were still wrapped around each other when Simon came through the door a quarter of an hour later, too late to interrupt the most important conversation of Rhys's life.

34

29 July 1284

Day Four

Rhys

The king looked up from the document in front of him. "Rhys."

As it turned out, he hadn't been asleep and claimed to welcome the interruption. As king, he always had documents in front of him, and Rhys had learned to ignore the irritated looks his clerks and scribes gave him whenever he approached the king. For his part, the king waved away the pen his servant tried to hand him. It was very late, past midnight by now, and the king had a big day tomorrow that would include watching the jousts and the archery finals, participating in the mêlée, and then, finally, enjoying the revelry of a grand banquet in the outdoor pavilion.

"Sire." Rhys stepped closer, Simon a pace behind, as was his wont.

"You have news?"

Rhys bent his head. "News, yes. And answers too, though not all of them. Not quite." It was essentially what Catrin had said earlier to Rhys, and no less the truth now than before.

"Normally you don't come to me until you have all the pieces fitted into little boxes and tied with a ribbon."

"Sire, that isn't to say we don't know something. We have learned who murdered Rollo."

Edward relaxed into his chair, a pleased expression on his face, and motioned that Rhys should continue.

"I'm afraid this affects both Earl Clare and John of Brittany."

"Are we going to need another diplomatic solution?" The king's mouth spasmed for a moment. "I can tell from your reticence that I am not going to like what you have to say."

"It isn't quite as bad as Caernarfon, sire," Simon put in, taking a step forward to bring him level with Rhys, "if that helps."

King Edward laughed. "From your tone, I imagine it won't."

"I apologize, my lord, for the roundabout way we sometimes approach you with bad news." Rhys then laid out for the king what they knew, beginning with Rollo's death and the condition of the body, and continuing with the thieving ring run by Bernard and the revelations on the hilltop that evening. He left out the ledger, as Catrin wanted, and emphasized how helpful Miles, and particularly Ralph, had been.

Edward had been leaning slightly forward in his chair throughout this recitation, focused and intent. "Bernard insists the arsenic was to aid Rollo's failing health?"

"Yes, as he would."

"But definitely Matilda murdered Rollo?"

"She admitted to it in front of all of us," Rhys said. "She claims she killed him because Rollo had discovered their thieving, but also that it was done at Bernard's behest. He told her what to do, even to the point of cutting off Rollo's fingertip. The poisoning with arsenic, meanwhile, was long-term and ongoing, administered as a treatment for Rollo's aching joints by Rollo's sister, Joan."

"How much of this do you believe?"

"I believe Joan thought she was helping her brother, and I believe Matilda," Rhys said. "She confessed to the actual murder and more besides, before she knew we were there. We found their considerable stash of stolen items buried on the hilltop, and from what I've learned about Bernard from his other women, it's only the beginning. This is not the first tournament he has attended, my lord."

"Right under our noses." King Edward sat with a finger to his lip. "I will have to lay this before Brittany and Clare myself." His eyes narrowed. "My chevaliers will breakfast here just after dawn. You will both make yourselves available if they have any questions."

By *chevaliers*, he meant his *Knights of the Round Table*, the earls and greater barons who were present for the tournament. The meeting was being held in the morning in case some of the men were wounded during the day. That night, rather than a private banquet in Llywelyn's hall, the king himself would be joining a much larger celebration, one he'd been planning for two months, in the pavilion outside. King Edward had always intended the physical round table, as in the legends he'd read, to be a private meeting place for his knights.

Rhys and Simon bowed, and Simon said, "Of course, my lord."

Edward had been tapping his lip with one finger and now dropped his hand. "What about the failure of the viewing stand?"

Rhys left Simon to answer that. "We know something, my lord, but not enough. Harlech's master carpenter, who oversaw the work here, swears it was intact when he left. On the whole, I'm inclined to believe him, especially since one of the carpenters is missing, and he left some of his tools behind. We are concerned he is the saboteur, but where he has gone we cannot say."

"Your safety remains a concern, my lord." Rhys felt compelled to speak. "I wish you had not chosen to fight in the mêlée."

King Edward turned his gaze on Rhys. "Why do you think none of King Arthur's *chevaliers* were named Rhys?"

"I couldn't say, sire." Rhys shouldn't have been startled by the change of subject. As always, the king's mind skipped around, though often in ways that proved later to be related.

"I will be bestowing a name on each of my guards who are fighting with me. As the only Welshman among them, it is fitting you fight as Caradoc."

Rhys swallowed. In some of the legends—these more French than Welsh but likely those upon which the king was drawing—Caradoc had served Arthur's father, Uther Pendragon, but had rebelled against Arthur when he'd taken the throne. Eventually, the two men had reconciled.

King Edward, as always, knew what he was doing.

Then the king added. "That means Catrin can be Tegau."

Rhys managed to stop his jaw from dropping. Not only was the king using the Welsh names instead of the French, but the love between Caradoc and Tegau was one of the three great romances of King Arthur's court.

"Sire—"

"It is well past time you formalized your relationship. Simon says you love her and want to marry her. Is that true?"

"Yes, my lord, but—"

"No *buts* about it. I can't imagine I need to speak to her for you."

"No, sire. It's just that—"

"You're afraid she will lose her place beside the queen." The king was looking at Rhys with a smile of utter and complete satisfaction. "My Eleanor has grown fond of your Catrin, who has a deft hand with young Edward." Here the king was referring to his infant son. "Rest assured, neither of you are going anywhere."

35

Day Four

Catrin

Catrin had not been invited to the Round Table meeting, but Rhys had told her about it afterwards. Even now, Bernard was being loaded onto a ship in Nefyn's port. The tide would turn at noon, at which point the captain would set sail for Brittany. Bernard might hang for what he'd done, but that was between the Duke of Brittany and Bernard. As far as Rhys knew, there was no plan to throw him overboard on the way.

A unique solution had been found for the girls, petty thieves as they were. They were to be sent to Ireland, under the auspices of the Earl of Ulster, and effectively sold as servants. Slavery had been abolished in Ireland two centuries before, but it was an island where, like Wales, everyone knew everyone else. There would be no escaping their fate.

As was perhaps inevitable, given the nature of her crimes, Matilda would face the king's justice and pay for the murder of Rollo with her life, but at a later date so as not to mar the festivities.

As the king had told Rhys last night, the breakfast meeting had occurred early enough that none of the nobles missed a single moment of the jousting, which resulted in Vincent de Lusignan being crowned as champion. That victory tasted bitter in Rhys's mouth, Catrin knew, but the fact that Joan was aglow with joy went a long way to salving that wound.

Besides, Rhys had his own troubles. It wasn't so much that Rhys hoped to actually defeat Math. He just didn't want to embarrass himself by losing badly. He had also hoped that fewer people would come to watch the archery final than had watched the jousts, but the king had adjourned for an hour only, and then returned himself, which meant that everybody else was there too.

Somewhat alarmingly for those who'd witnessed the failure of the viewing stand and the aftermath, it was packed again, top and bottom. Catrin eyed the upper story, willing it to stay in place. It pricked at her still that they didn't know for certain who had rigged it to fail. While they'd been mostly consumed with the murder of Rollo, they had expended nearly an equal effort to find someone—anyone—who'd seen or heard anything in the days and nights before it broke, but nobody had come forward other than Cadell recalling seeing Adam in the churchyard.

The beam *had* been sawed through though. That was an inescapable fact. Why Adam had done it, if he'd done it, remained an unsolved mystery.

She honestly didn't have any hope of discovering real truths today, but she nonetheless drifted through the crowd, listening to conversations and watching faces, until she fetched up beside her son. He had comported himself well in the jousts, making it to the second day before losing to Henry de Lacy, whom everyone considered a more than worthy opponent. Henry himself had lost in the semi-finals to one of Richard de Burgh's men, who'd then lost to Vincent.

Though great lords sometimes jousted, as Henry had done, it was viewed as a young man's game and a way to gain attention and honor, neither of which were necessary for someone who'd inherited an earldom. It wasn't necessary for Justin either, but he was not yet twenty and was in love with his life. He couldn't *not* joust.

She had told him the news of Rhys's proposal of marriage—and the king's approval—earlier that morning. She'd also sought out her brothers, Hywel and Tudur, and asked for their blessing. Rather than objecting, each in turn had picked her up and swung her around in congratulations.

"Will he win, Mother?" Justin kept his eyes on Math, who'd just shot his first arrow.

Each man had his own target for this contest, so their arrows wouldn't interfere with one another's. After each round, the judges—three Normans with (apparently) some knowledge of targets and archery—ran out to inspect the targets and declare the winner. Math and Rhys would be taking turns over the next half-hour, which was all the time this contest was going to take. Truthfully, moving the targets back so the archers could shoot a greater distance took more time than either man would actually spend in shooting.

Catrin didn't know if Justin was referring to Math or Rhys, so she answered with what Rhys had told her: "Mathonwy is younger and stronger. He might, in the end, be better. Or so Rhys said."

"Honest as always."

Catrin looked up at her son. "I agree, but I have not heard you express that opinion before."

"I don't know that I would have thought to—and please don't see it as a criticism—but it's what Earl Clare said to me not an hour ago."

"By your tone, it sounds as if Earl Clare did say it as a criticism."

"Never, Mother. He was delighted to have uncovered the murderer and the ring of thieves in one go. He is less happy that he himself is going to have to fight in the mêlée, since he has no adequate substitute for Rollo or Hugh. Not Rhys's fault, of course, and he acknowledges things might have been much worse without him."

Catrin could see why Clare would be less than thrilled with this turn of events. Though, with the king participating, it made sense that Clare would join in as well. Possibly, by this point, he saw it as his duty, since he was one of the pre-eminent barons in England and Wales.

Now Justin shook his head. "It's just—" He stopped talking as Rhys stepped to the line and shot with hardly a pause for breath. The arrow sank into the target, and a sigh at the perfection of it swept around the arena.

Math went next, this time to shoot three arrows in rapid succession, which he did with an expertise that told Catrin, even more than she'd seen in the two previous days, that he had a mastery of himself, and his bow acted as an extension of his own being. The Welsh onlookers knew it too, and she could see them nodding and talking amongst themselves across the field in the section reserved for them.

She and Justin were so nervous for Rhys that every now and then they clasped hands, unclenching them only when Rhys matched Math's feat. Catrin felt herself losing years off her life every time Rhys loosed an arrow.

Then, during a break in the action as the judges rushed in again to inspect the targets, she remembered Justin's cut off question. "It's just ... what?"

"I had thought the conversation over, because Earl Clare was walking away from me." Justin gave a little shake of his head. "Maybe he was speaking over his shoulder, or perhaps he hadn't meant anyone to hear."

"What did he say?" Catrin waited with bated breath, nearly as tense about this as about Rhys's shooting.

"*I just wish I knew what Bernard had done with that damned ledger.* Do you have any idea what he was talking about?"

36

Day Four

Rhys

*M*ath had missed.

Rhys stared at the target, unable to believe what he was seeing. He wiped at his eyes to clear them from sweat so he could look again.

The non-Welsh present weren't as aware of what had just happened, since they knew so little of archery, but a shocked silence had descended on the Welsh spectators to his right. Then, after a pause, their palpable disbelief transferred to those in the viewing stand and on the ground around it, who quieted too.

Math stood a few paces away from Rhys, his head high, looking at the targets in the distance, in this case a full sixty yards away.

Up until this instant, they'd shot exactly in tandem, tied together in their perfection. Rhys himself had never shot as well as he'd done today. Seeing Math's arrow miss the mark, however, made him feel as if a bucket of cold water had been dumped over his head. Up until this moment, exhilaration had coursed through his veins, but now it was draining out, leaving him empty and sick.

And as nervous as he'd ever been in his life.

Which was maddening, because he hadn't intended to care about winning this tournament at all. He hadn't even wanted to participate. With the investigation over, he would have been just as happy to watch from the sideline as Math defeated some other poor ninny for the trophy.

At this point, unfortunately, his pride was involved and at stake. He glanced again at Math, who'd turned to face him, his expression like carved wood, giving nothing away. There was something in his eyes, though, that caught Rhys's attention. It was there for a single heartbeat, before disappearing, but he could have sworn he saw ... guilt? Or was it pleading?

Rhys turned back to the target, finding that single look of Math's to be enough to settle him. He knew what had happened, and it made him angry, which was far better than being afraid.

In a smooth movement, like he'd done a thousand times before—ten thousand times before—he nocked the arrow and loosed it at Math's target. Technically, he should have shot at his own, so as not to interfere with Math's arrow, but Rhys was proving a point, which he thought was credibly made a moment later when his arrow thunked into the white mark at the dead center of the target, a fingertip from Math's own arrow, which had missed by only that amount.

The silence on the field lasted for a count of three, and then great cheers went up from the Welsh ranks, followed by louder *huzzahs* from the king's party. The king himself was on his feet, applauding. Some men were waving their hats while others stamped their feet, though fortunately not so much that Rhys feared the viewing stand would break again.

The judges, for their part, were not so sure what had happened. These men were all Norman, so had a Norman sensibility for order and *the right way* of doing things. They went out to the targets, first to look at Rhys's obviously empty one and then over to Math's, where both arrows stuck out like quills on a hedgehog. They took so long in their deliberations that the crowd started to get restless. Then they genuinely *ran* to the king, who was waiting for their decision to declare a victor.

It was obvious to Rhys who that should be, and his shot had been a fine bit of diplomacy, if he did say so himself, giving the victory to Math, as he deserved, without besmirching Rhys's own honor. The longer the judges conferred, however, the less likely Rhys's easy solution appeared to be the one they were settling on.

Math's face, meanwhile, had turned ashen. "What did you do?"

"What you should have done." They were speaking in Welsh, with no other Welshmen around them, so Rhys let loose with all the intensity he was feeling inside. "If you *ever* shank your shot again because you think it will please me or anyone else, I will see you begging in the streets, do you understand?"

Math swallowed hard, and his expression remained stricken. "Yes."

"Good." Rhys eyed where the judges were still talking to the king. "One more each?"

Another swallow. "It would be my pleasure, sir."

In unison, as if they'd shot together a thousand times before, Rhys and Math stood side-by-side on the line, nocked an arrow each, and loosed them at Rhys's target. The arrows hit with a satisfying *thunk* that was a little too close to what an arrow sounded like when it drove into a man's torso. But their mutual aim was perfect, and their arrows nestled together in the center of the target.

Then, also together, they walked to where the judges, who'd stopped talking at the cheer that had gone up, gaped first at the target and then at them.

"Sire." Rhys bowed.

"Reese." The king's eyes were full of restrained laughter.

Rhys turned to the judges. "Is there a problem in determining the winner?"

The chief judge, a tall, thin man with a overlarge chin drew himself up to his full height and said, "On your last *official* shot, you missed your target."

Rhys nodded gravely back. "By a wide margin, it seems."

"Thus, Lord Mathonwy is the winner."

"I do not disagree."

"But my lord! Sire!" One of the other judges intervened. He was younger, and likely had been outvoted, but the unfairness of the older judge's decision didn't sit well with him. Rhys's heart warmed to his freckled face, which was red under his orange hair. "Sir Rhys shot more cleanly than Lord Mathonwy!"

"At the wrong target!" The first judge was not about to give way.

"What if I resigned?" Math said, stepping in as the debate renewed. "Sir Rhys was making a point."

"And what point was that?" The third judge was shorter and a bit dumpy, but he had been trying to mediate between the other two and had a thoughtful look on his face.

Math didn't look at him, but at the king, still seated on his throne. "That if I am to serve you, sire, I must always do my best and never pretend to be other than I am."

King Edward's expression turned very grave as well. "I will expect it." Then he stood and raised both hands above his head. "The silver arrow goes to ... Sir Reese!"

A great cheer went up from every corner of the arena. The decision had been the popular one, not just because it was Rhys himself who'd won, but because it felt fitting.

The irony was that Rhys had actually intended to lose, which he said to Simon later, having been presented with the arrow and bag of coins. "The lead judge was correct. I honestly had no expectation the king would decide the matter the way he did."

Simon stood with his arms folded across his chest and a look of satisfaction on his face. "Mathonwy may well be the better archer, but he shanked his shot—if hitting the target less than an inch from the center counts as shanking. You of all people, Reese, should appreciate the king's message: it does little good to obey the letter of the law, when to do so violates the spirit."

37

Day Four

Catrin

The ledger sat open on her knees, and like Paul on the road to Damascus, the scales had fallen from her eyes, if that wasn't too sacrilegious a comparison. She could read what Bernard had written, and if her hair hadn't turned gray at the temples watching the archery competition, it surely would now at the implications.

Clare had wanted to find that *damned ledger*, as he'd said, before Rhys (and she) did, and now she knew why. It wasn't that Earl Clare had somehow colluded with Bernard. The idea of the Red Earl stooping that low was laughable.

But somehow he'd known enough of Bernard's doings to have ferreted out some of his secrets. And Bernard had known enough of Clare to do the same. While Bernard had written extensively of Clare's various liaisons with the women or daughters of powerful men, and these dalliances might disturb the king and pope, they were not as shocking as the rest of what Bernard had written.

She'd discovered it by accident. After reading through the first third of the book, with its pages of cryptic names, dates, and comments, she'd turned to the latter half. At first glance, the pages were blank, but closer inspection revealed the paper had a strange sheen to it. She couldn't make heads or tails of it at first, but then she'd folded back the binding (knowing her father would have been appalled at doing such damage to a bound book) and held a page up to a candle, trying to decipher what Bernard had done to it. She'd looked long enough, in fact, that she'd half-burned the page. But in so doing, she revealed writing inscribed in a brownish ink, words that up until that moment had been invisible.

Bernard had learned the secrets of men, high and low, and the ledger told a harrowing tale of deception, betrayal, and treason at the highest levels of the English court. Of those just at Nefyn, Bernard had stated flatly that members of the Clare, Mortimer, Valence, Bohun, and Burgh families were participants in a cabal set on wresting power and land for themselves at the expense of the king. That these families were in league with one another was incredible, given the grudges and hatred they'd held for one another for decades, if not centuries.

And yet, all these families ruled on the fringes of England. The desire for more territory and authority for themselves had been instilled in them from the cradle.

What's more, Bernard had written plain as day (once the writing was legible), that Miles himself might be responsible for the sabotage of the viewing stand. Bernard provided no evidence for it. He'd merely written that, earlier in the week, late at night near the church, one of his minions had seen Miles de Bohun speaking to one of the carpenters who built the structure. This minion, identified in the ledger as *Robbie,* had then spotted that selfsame carpenter coming out of the viewing stand in the early hours of the morning, during the rainstorm that had almost blown away half the tents in the fields surrounding Nefyn. That had also been the morning Rollo had died.

Fifteen hours later, the viewing stand had collapsed.

Bernard didn't name the carpenter, Robbie apparently being no Dafi, but as Adam had been discovered missing shortly thereafter, it wasn't a stretch to think the two men were one and the same. And maybe Miles had killed him.

As Catrin sat with the ledger in her lap, staring into the distance, she acknowledged that she'd been right to urge Rhys to keep the ledger a secret. Even having lived herself through wars, betrayal, and conquest, Bernard's accusations were so inflammatory, her impulse was to burn the ledger rather than let anyone else read it.

She wouldn't though and, in truth, shouldn't. She cast around for a good hiding place, kicking herself for not putting it under her pallet last night, in case one of the other ladies-in-waiting had seen it and been curious. She ended up wrapping it in her stack of menstrual rags. Nobody, man or woman, would ever touch them.

Then she stuffed the bundle back under the rest of her possessions in the bottom of her trunk and went to tell Rhys what she'd discovered. Such unwelcome—and dangerous—information was the last thing he needed to hear before he fought in the mêlée. But he needed to know what he might be getting into, as well as from whom—and from what—he really might be protecting the king.

38

Day Four

Rhys

Rhys hadn't fought beside Simon since the Holy Land, but they moved together as they had all those years ago when their lives depended upon every swing of their swords, and those swords were sharp instead of blunted. The mêlée was destined to last a single hour, which made their every foray all the more urgent.

He and Simon had not been part of the initial cavalry charge. That remained the purview of the hundred knights originally designated—plus the king and Prince Edmund. After the initial three passes, however, and once all the knights had dismounted, the rest of the participants had rushed in.

As was becoming clearer with each moment that passed, Simon and the rest of the king's guard were hardly needed, as from the start Earl Clare had set himself and his men to defend the king. The earl engaged all-comers with a ferocity that belied his forty-one years and his protestations that he was too old to fight. To be seen as loyal to the king, even at his own expense, would be in keeping with what Catrin had told Rhys, in a few hasty moments before the fight, about what she'd learned from Bernard's ledger. At this point, Rhys was wondering if Clare's position at the fore of the battle, even more so than Henry de Lacy's, their side's ostensible leader, had been agreed upon in advance by the other treacherous barons.

For his part, the king fought well, up to the moment his foot slipped on the grass, and he went down on one knee before Humphrey de Bohun. Before Humphrey could advance for a final blow—and the king's surrender—Clare intervened, beating Humphrey off again with a few judicious thrusts of his sword.

Then the rest of the king's guard moved in, and the Bohun forces retreated. While Rhys feared, as did Catrin, that one of these barons might want to do the king harm, the more he fought amongst them and against them, the less that appeared to be true. Besides, Bernard hadn't said they wanted to murder the king. They just wanted more power at the king's expense, to weaken him and raise their own standing, which was not the same thing. It looked to Rhys as if both Clare and Humphrey were well on their way to achieving that goal today.

If Catrin hadn't told him about what she'd read in the ledger, he might have taken the whole scene at face value. Truthfully, he couldn't help feeling that, up until now, he'd missed the vast majority of what had been going on in the English court.

Rhys's arm was starting to weigh twice what it normally did. Even though it had been all of half an hour at most that he'd been fighting, the constant swinging of his sword, countering and attacking against one knight and then another, revealed to him more than anything else could have that he really was thirty-eight years old.

Then he swung around, having lost Simon for a moment amidst the crowd of men, and came face-to-face with Vincent de Lusignan.

The two men stared at each other—gaped even—and then it was as if a red mist descended over Rhys's eyes. In that moment, all the humiliations and defeats of the last two years, all his grief at the destruction of his country, the death of his prince, and the loss of his friends, welled up in him until it spilled out of every limb. He attacked in a flurry of blows that caused Vincent to stumble backwards, and it was all he could do to throw up his shield as Rhys hammered blow after blow. Rhys couldn't care about the king's prohibition. He couldn't care about anything but driving his sword through the middle of Vincent's belly as Vincent himself had done to Rhys.

"What's that?" Gruffydd, Rhys's closest friend within Llywelyn's teulu, turned at the sound of hoofbeats.

The snow that had fallen throughout the night and most of the day muffled the noise somewhat, but the sheer number of horsemen coming towards them was enough to send Rhys's heart racing. Llywelyn had dismounted, along with a dozen of his personal guard, to wait for the arrival of Roger and Edmund Mortimer, who'd asked to meet him on the hill of Cilmeri, having suggested in a letter they were ready to change sides.

"Not the sound of friends!" Rhys was already running towards his own horse, which was picketed a few yards away with the others.

But there wasn't time. There was never enough time.

With a whistle, Iolo, their captain, called the men to him. Where the half-dozen of their countrymen who were supposed to be standing sentry had gone—or what had happened to them—no longer mattered. Swords out, they crouched low, forming a circle around their prince to face the Mortimer forces, which came crashing through the forest on every side.

Rhys sidestepped the first horseman who tried to run him down, in that first instance giving as good as he got, but then the fight was engaged with a fury that had his companions falling to the left and right like wheat from a sickle. When Iolo himself went down, Rhys ran to take his place, standing beside Gruffydd and three others to protect their prince.

Vincent de Lusignan planted himself in front of Rhys, and his blade moved in a flurry of stroke and counterstroke. Rhys didn't even know at first that it was he, and it was only after Vincent threw off his helmet so he could see past the sweat trickling into his eyes that Rhys recognized the beaky nose and fierce eyes.

Rhys fought ferociously, hopeful he might even be able to win and single-handedly turn the tide. But then a blow at the back of his head sent him to his knees. Hardly a heartbeat later, Vincent plunged his sword into Rhys's side ...

"No, Rhys!" The full weight of Simon's body rammed into Rhys and sent him sprawling.

Having landed on top of him, Simon pressed on the side of Rhys's head with his hand, keeping his face in the dirt, while the length of his body kept the rest of Rhys on the ground.

Rhys struggled at first, seeing Vincent's face in Simon's, even as he knew it was his friend.

Simon cursed. "You have to stop! By all that is holy, Rhys, you have to stop!"

And then, between one breath and the next, the earth shifted, the veil before Rhys's eyes lifted, and he could clearly see where Vincent lay on the ground too, in much the same position as Rhys, though he did not have a friend on top of him.

Rhys turned a hand palm up and said in a totally calm voice. "You can get up, Simon."

Simon hesitated, wary of trusting him, but Rhys added softly, "I am well," at which point Simon eased off him. Once he was free, Rhys pushed up on one elbow, his eyes never leaving Vincent's face. "Are you badly injured?"

Vincent looked at him for such a long moment, Rhys almost thought he wasn't going to reply. But then he said, "Only my pride."

It was so completely not the response Rhys had expected that he found himself unable to answer.

Simon, for his part, laughed. "Can I leave you two to it?" Even having asked, he didn't wait for Rhys's reply before moving away to engage one of Burgh's knights.

Rhys's attack had moved him and Vincent to the margins of the battlefield. Even had they been in the middle of it, he had the sense that everyone else would have given them a wide berth.

Carefully, feeling every muscle and sinew in his aged body, Rhys got himself to his knees and was preparing to lever himself to his feet with the help of his sword when Vincent's hand appeared in his line of sight. Rhys looked at it, hardly believing what he was seeing, and then glanced into Vincent's face. The other man was looking grim, but still kept his hand out for Rhys to take.

Rhys did.

Once he was upright, the two of them stood together three feet apart, both weaving slightly in their exhaustion. Rhys could find nothing to say. His mind was swept clean of any coherent thought.

So it was Vincent who spoke first. "I'm sorry. For everything."

Rhys shook his head, trying to clear it, and it was only after he'd done so that he realized Vincent might misinterpret the motion as a denial. "I—" He shook his head again. "When we saw each other in the great hall, you barely looked at me, but I see now you did know it was I at Cilmeri."

"Yes."

Another long pause, in which both again could find nothing to say.

Rhys decided it was his turn. "You—"

Vincent made a motion with one hand. "I did my duty, but that doesn't mean I wasn't sorry for it."

"Why are you saying this now?" Rhys shot back, suddenly finding his voice.

"Because for far too long I hated you." Vincent looked away, and Rhys had the feeling he wasn't seeing this battlefield. It was Acre, visions of which Rhys shared in equal measure. "I have recalled what you said to me, the last day we spoke, every day since. Nobody had ever confronted me like that before." Now it was Vincent's turn to shake his head. "My greatest regret is that you were gone before I allowed what you'd done to change my life."

Rhys swayed, finding Vincent's admission impossible to reconcile with his own experience. And then Vincent further stunned him with a sad smile and the words, "I counted you as a friend, once. I'm glad you didn't die at Cilmeri." With a final salute, he turned on his heel and disappeared into the throng of fighting men.

Rhys could do nothing but stare after him until the trumpet sounded, bringing an end to the mêlée.

Simon's helmet was askew, and rather than adjust it, he threw it off. "This could have been more fun, but it's hard to see how."

Rhys gaped at his friend, as he'd been gaping after Vincent, and then he laughed. And laughed some more, so hard all of a sudden that he had to hold his stomach because it hurt.

The king, who'd spent most of the last hour outside the sheltering circle of his men, refusing to be protected by them, threw his arms above his head in the same gesture of triumph he'd used when Rhys had won the archery competition. Rhys wasn't at all sure they'd won the mêlée, but the fact that he was still standing and was suddenly reconciled in some manner with Vincent was all the winning that was required. Even now he could hardly believe it.

"She's coming." Simon drew Rhys's attention to Catrin, who'd left the safety of the rail to run towards him.

What was even more remarkable was the sight of Queen Eleanor dashing across the grass in Catrin's wake, skirts held above her ankles so she wouldn't trip. Whatever invective Rhys might direct on a daily basis towards the king, he loved his wife, and she loved him. It didn't give Rhys hope, per se, but it did make it easier to serve him.

Rhys himself reeked of sweat and sun, but Catrin threw herself at him anyway, wrapping her arms around his neck. "Don't you ever do something like this again!"

Rhys laughed and swung her around twice, and he was so exhausted he almost lost his balance before managing to set her down without falling over.

"My love." He looked down at her.

"Everyone is watching."

"They are not," Rhys didn't bother to look around, "but even if they were, is that something we need to worry about? You kissed me the other day, saying it was about time everyone knew what we meant to each other. You've told your family you and I are to marry. Is that truly what you want?"

"It is."

King Edward himself roared his approval, his exuberance at surviving the mêlée uncontained.

"I think we need a wedding, sire," Simon said dryly from where he'd come to rest, now sitting on the helmet he'd discarded.

If possible, the king's eyes grew even brighter. "We will have it tonight at the feast, as in the days of Arthur!"

Catrin and Rhys had walked into that one unknowingly, and Rhys was none too happy about fulfilling the king's dreams about being the heir to the throne of Arthur. But he nonetheless pulled Catrin closer and asked in Welsh. "Yes?"

"Yes."

"Even I know what that means!" The king pointed to Gilbert de Clare. "Lord Bedivere! You must escort the bride to her wedding to Sir Caradoc."

Earl Clare bowed in agreement.

One of the king's stewards handed him a cloth to dry his brow and said, understandably a little tentatively, "Not to dampen your enthusiasm, my liege, but the banns have not been said—"

"What need we of banns?" The king clapped a hand on Rhys's shoulder and spoke in an outsized voice. "Catrin's son won't object to a hasty wedding. Nor will her brothers. And the only other person from whom we might need to ask permission is my queen." He swung around to look at Eleanor.

"Of course, my king," Eleanor said, in perhaps the sweetest voice Rhys had ever heard her use. "It is just as you say. A wedding tonight couldn't be a more perfect ending to your Round Table."

39

Day Four

Catrin

"Are you ready?" Earl Clare held out his elbow to Catrin. "More than ready," she said, prompting a rare smile from the earl.

"It is Reese whom you should have married instead of Robert, isn't it?" And at her quick glance at him, he gave a little snort. "I am not unaware that the alliance your father thought he was making in giving you to one of my vassals did not turn out as he intended."

"I was not unhappy as Robert's wife," Catrin said, "and I cannot regret my son."

"Nor can I." Clare *was* feeling expansive this evening, and maybe that was no surprise, since he'd comported himself well in the mêlée, despite being forced into it by the absence of both Rollo and Hugh.

With what she now knew about him—or had read that Bernard suspected—Catrin had feared she might be nervous taking his arm, but she felt only a rising excitement.

While Catrin had been given a matter of two hours to ready herself for her wedding, the royal household had been preparing for this final celebration of King Edward's Round Table for nearly two months, and no expense had been spared. The pavilion was festooned with branches and flowers, making it resemble in no small way a garden, the food was rich and bountiful, and the ornamentation of the participants—not to mention the entertainment—was as lavish as if they'd been in the king's hall at Westminster.

For the wedding ceremony itself, workmen had hastily constructed a lesser dais upon which Rhys and she were to stand so everyone could see them. The king and his court sat as usual at the high table, which was decorated with a white cloth, and every dish and candlestick was silver. King Edward's *chevaliers*, those pretending to be Gawain or Geraint or Bedivere, as Clare was, wore brightly colored tunics in jewel tones of red, blue, or green. The king sat below a banner with three gold crowns on a blue background, the significance and provenance of which Catrin herself was uncertain, but which had come to be associated with King Arthur.

She took in the pavilion with a sweeping glance, and then her eyes went to Rhys, who was looking at her as if she were the only person in the room. He was resplendent too, dressed in a white tunic emblazoned with a gold dragon, such as described in the Welsh annals. She didn't know if wearing such a crest had always been the plan for him for this feast, or if somehow his tunic had been created in the last few hours, specifically for him to wear to his wedding. Honestly, it wouldn't have been beyond the king to have ordered it in the moments after the mêlée, and his servants to have seen it done.

More likely, however, Edward had made it happen once he decided Rhys was to be Caradoc and she his Tegau.

And while Catrin could have done without the pageantry and the fact that she and Rhys were props in Edward's King Arthur play, she couldn't argue with the outcome. As she processed down the aisle that had been created between the tables, the winner of the bards' contest lifted his voice in song, in Welsh no less, and everyone in the pavilion rose to their feet.

Catrin had made few friends in the royal court, but she was touched to see Margaret's eyes shining, along with those of her son and brothers, who stood with Simon on either side of Rhys.

She took Rhys's hand and after that had no thought but him until the priest declared them man and wife. Then King Edward himself came down from his throne to congratulate them.

"Dw i'n dy garu di," Rhys said. *I love you.*

As Catrin said the words back to him, her heart lifted. Whatever tomorrow brought them, whatever challenge lay just around the corner, joy filled her to know the two of them would be facing it together.

Historical Note

A very exciting—and perhaps a little daunting—feature of writing a novel set in 1284 and the court of King Edward is how much is known about his activities. As any reader of *The Welsh Guard Mysteries* has realized by now, Edward destroyed many Welsh records, not to mention the palaces (*llys* in Welsh) inhabited by Prince Llywelyn.

Thus, for most of my other series, most of the time, little information about where a Welsh king or prince was on any given day or what they were doing has survived through the ages.

King Edward, on the other hand, was a meticulous record keeper. We know, for example, that his *Round Table* at Nefyn took place from July 27-29, 1284. We know that he called it a *Round Table* in deliberate homage to King Arthur, and that his purpose was to style himself as the inheritor of Arthur's throne.

Remarkably, we also know that, during the tournament, the second floor of a building collapsed in the midst of a dance! Special mention is made of the fact that nobody was killed in the incident.

Elsewhere, I have written extensively about King Arthur, not to mention written an entire book series about him. What I have to say about him is too much to put into an author's note, but you can find all the articles on my website here:

https://www.sarahwoodbury.com/all-about-king-arthur/

I'd also like to make special note of the various groups of people that make up the populations in this story, namely the Welsh, Saxons, and Normans. The Welsh, even to this day, are descended from the native Britons, who were conquered two thousand years ago by the Romans. They managed to hold off the Saxons for the next six hundred years, and then the Normans for two hundred years more, before finally being conquered in 1282 by King Edward's forces.

The Welsh are generally accepted as being of Celtic origin—or at least their language is—having moved into Britain starting in about 800 BC. *Saxon* is a catchall term for the Germanic peoples that began their incursions into England before the Romans left and continued their conquest until 800 AD, by which point the only kingdoms left within England proper were Saxon. The Normans are descended from Danes, who, having settled in Normandy in France in the 8th century, turned their attention to England in 1066 under the auspices of Duke William.

Much of this history can be found in my video series, Making Sense of Medieval Britain, the links to which can also be found on my web page (www.sarahwoodbury.com).

About the Author

With two historian parents, Sarah couldn't help but develop an interest in the past. She went on to get more than enough education herself (in anthropology) and began writing fiction when the stories in her head overflowed and demanded she let them out. While her ancestry is Welsh, she only visited Wales for the first time while in college. She has been in love with the country, language, and people ever since. She even convinced her husband to give all four of their children Welsh names.

She makes her home in Oregon.

www.sarahwoodbury.com

Printed in Great Britain
by Amazon

12790386R00202